JUNGLE SNIPER

A World War II Thriller

DAVID HEALEY

INTRACOASTAL

JUNGLE SNIPER

A World War II Thriller

By David Healey

Intracoastal Media digital edition published 2022.

Print edition ISBN 979-8-9872808-0-5

BISAC Subject Headings:

FIC014000 FICTION/Historical

FIC032000 FICTION/War & Military

"To the People of the Philippines, I have returned."

— GENERAL DOUGLAS MACARTHUR, SPEECH
AT RED BEACH, LEYTE, OCTOBER 20, 1944

CHAPTER ONE

TWO MONTHS BEFORE—GUAM Beachhead

LYING IN THE HOLE, staring out into the tropical night, Deacon Cole kept his eyes focused on the darkness and his finger on the trigger.

Anchored to the earth, he was like a creature of the forest. Each one of his senses felt alive. A rivulet of salty sweat ran down his face and stung his eye. He blinked it away. A breeze touched his cheek, carrying the smell of the jungle—decay mixed with the sickly sweet fragrance of a night-blooming vine that was almost like the honeysuckle back home. He heard singing insects and the distant snap of a twig.

The last sound served as a reminder that Deke and the rest of Patrol Easy weren't alone.

Somewhere out in that dark jungle were hidden Japanese soldiers—maybe hundreds of them. They wouldn't stay hidden for long. It was only a matter of time before they launched one of their nighttime sneak attacks. When they did, Deke and his rifle would be ready for them. He stroked the smooth metal of the Springfield 1903A sniper rifle's trigger, eager to shoot the first Japanese that he saw. Maybe it was his imagination, but the rifle felt alive in his hands, just as ready as he was to send a well-placed bullet drilling through the darkness.

He strained to see something, anything, but the jungle directly ahead of the US line remained as impenetrable as the darkness he'd see looking down a well. He stared until the blackness began to swirl, his brain imposing patterns on the void.

Only the sky showed lighter above the treetops, a few brooding hills beyond blotting out the stars. Not more than a quarter of a mile behind them was the beach that they had landed on this morning before fighting their way inland.

"Hold the line," had been Lieutenant Steele's command. "Whatever the Japs throw at us, we hold the line."

That had been the order, and that was what they were going to do.

Not that they had much choice.

If the Japs decided to push them back, the soldiers didn't have anywhere to go, other than to make a swim for it out to the US fleet. Maybe that was the generals' intention—it was either fight or drown.

He wasn't so sure that the squids would be all that eager to take back a bunch of grunts. Besides, the squids seemed to have their hands full with the Japanese Navy still on the prowl.

"I reckon we're caught between a rock and a hard place," Deke muttered to Philly, who shared the foxhole with him.

"Back where I'm from, it's called having your nuts in a vise," Philly replied. "As far as I'm concerned, the Japs can have this damn island if they want it so bad."

Deke had to admit that he'd never heard of Guam, which was just a flyspeck in the vast Pacific Ocean, until a few days before they had landed here. In terms of square mileage, the island was smaller than his native Hancock County back home.

Guam wasn't someplace famous, not like Hawaii or even Guadalcanal, well known after the godawful fight there, but Guam had been in American hands since the last century—until the Japanese had taken it over. Now the Americans were here to take it back.

"You see anything?" asked Philly, who was nothing more than a disembodied whisper coming from the blackness a few feet off to Deke's left. Deke was a loner by disposition, but out here in the night, he welcomed the sound of Philly's voice.

"Hell no, I don't see anything. It's darker than a banker's soul out there," Deke replied quietly.

"That's dark, all right," Philly agreed. Considering that America had just come out of the Great Depression, in most people's minds there wasn't much worse than a banker. It had been a greedy banker who had put Deke and his family off their land back home.

Although Deke couldn't see him, he could smell Philly's fresh sweat, with an added aroma of stale cigarettes. Deke was one of those rare GIs who didn't smoke, but he supposed that he smelled just as bad in his own way. His cotton fatigues had never completely dried out after getting soaked in the surf coming ashore, and he now felt soaked through all over again from sweat and dew.

It didn't help that this place was so damn hot and humid, like the worst August night back home. There was some breeze off the sea, but down here in their hastily dug foxholes, the movement of the night air didn't do them much good. The slight breeze wafted the fetid smell of the jungle toward them, close and dank. There was something unnatural and unhealthy about the smell, not at all clean and fresh like a mountain forest.

His eyes continued to play tricks on him, filling the black stew with swirls and shapes, any one of which might be a Japanese soldier sneaking up on them.

Deke felt a tickling sensation as something ran across his hand in the dark, some kind of many-legged beetle or maybe a spider. Lord knows he'd seen some big ones here at the edge of the jungle. The damn things could probably take down a rabbit. A few men had been sent back to the beach with bites that swelled up bigger than baseballs and hurt like they'd been smacked with a bat.

But spiders didn't much worry a country boy like Deke. He held still without letting go of his grip on the rifle, feeling the tickle of scurrying insect feet on his flesh. Thankfully, whatever the critter was, it moved on.

Philly cursed quietly: "Son-of-a-bitch Japs. I know they're gonna attack us. Why the hell don't they just get it over with?"

"Just keep your eyes open."

"Sure, I've got my eyes open, but what difference does it make? Might as well keep them closed. Can't see a thing."

"If there's anybody out there, you'll see them once they're on the move."

"I sure as hell hope so. Those sneaky Jap bastards blend right in."

In the dark, it was easy to think of the enemy as something inhuman, something right out of the heart of the jungle. Yet Deke had the passing thought that just maybe the Japanese were nervous themselves as they prepared to run at the American line. More than a few of them were going to meet their maker.

In addition to the fear factor of a night attack, the darkness helped the Japanese dodge American aircraft. Japanese planes had been in short supply, given the US dominion in the skies. However, the fighter planes did not fly at night, giving the Japanese a window of operation.

Deke glanced again at the dark where Philly lay shrouded in the foxhole. Philly might sound anxious, but Deke knew that he could count on him, even if he couldn't see him. They had been thrown together only recently, part of a sniper squad cobbled together under the command of Lieutenant Steele. The lieutenant lay hidden nearby in another foxhole, along with the rest of their sniper squad.

Having seen his buddy from basic training killed during the first few minutes of the landing on Guam, Deke had been reluctant to make any new friends. By his very nature, Deke tended to put a hard shell around himself and not let anyone in. But sometimes you did have to put your trust in the man on either side of you. Slowly Deke was realizing that he might be able to do that with the men of this patrol, starting with Philly.

The city boy was a loudmouth, all right, but from what he had seen so far of Philly, he would hold his ground if the Japs launched one of their dreaded banzai attacks. From the shooting test that Lieutenant Steele had given them earlier, it was clear that Philly wasn't the greatest shot. He certainly wasn't Deke's equal—not that many were when it came to a raw talent for hitting anything that he could put his rifle sights on.

Then again, marksmanship probably didn't matter as much as nerves when it came to fending off a nighttime banzai attack.

Deke reckoned that Philly could be forgiven for being more than a little nervous. As the green troops on Guam had quickly discovered, there was nothing more nerve-racking than waiting for a Japanese night attack.

Off to his other side was Yoshio, the baby-faced Nisei interpreter whom they had taken to calling "the Kid." Could he count on Yoshio? That remained to be seen. He glanced that way but saw only darkness.

"Kid?"

"Yeah?"

"Just checkin' to make sure the Japs didn't carry you off."

"Don't you think I'd ask them not to do that?" Yoshio was one of the few US soldiers who spoke Japanese.

"I ain't sure they'd listen."

"I'd ask them nicely—the first time, anyhow," Yoshio said.

Deke smirked into the darkness. At least the kid had a sense of humor.

In addition to carrying a rifle and fighting, the idea was that Yoshio, using his ability to speak the enemy's language, could help question prisoners. So far there hadn't been any prisoners. It was becoming apparent that the Japanese would just as soon shoot themselves or blow themselves up with a hand grenade than surrender. This fanaticism was something that the Americans had trouble understanding. It made the enemy seem all the more strange and frightening. As for the Japanese willingness to take any Americans prisoner, the general consensus was that you couldn't count on it.

Considering that no attack had taken place yet, Deke almost dared to hope that maybe the Japanese were clear on the other side of the island. It was just like the Japs to keep them guessing. The enemy soldiers were masters of the nighttime attack—in part, Deke supposed, because of the added element of fear that such attacks produced. The situation had been no different for his ancestors on the frontier, fending off the Chickamauga.

While Deke sided with his pioneer ancestors and was grateful to them, he could see how the Chickamauga had a point. If Deke had been an Indian, he wouldn't have much liked a bunch of palefaces taking over his land.

Unfortunately it was becoming clear that the Japanese had not slipped away into the night. Deke's ears told him everything that he needed to know, even if the jungle remained a dark blur. From time to time, opposite the American line, he heard a low, guttural voice issue what sounded like an order.

The occasional noise of metal on metal reached his ears, sounding like the buckle of a rifle sling clicking against a steel barrel. Every now and then he heard the sound of a branch breaking or a muffled footstep. The sounds provided all the evidence Deke needed that the darkness was crawling with the enemy.

Philly must have heard the noises, too, because he muttered, "Son of a bitch."

Deke gripped his rifle and waited.

Having grown up hunting, Deke had plenty of patience. If it came down to it, he could sit still as a stone for hours on end. He also had no problem with killing. He had grown up killing in order to put food on the table. Now he was killing for an equally fundamental purpose—to stay alive.

From his hunting days, he knew that the best strategy was simply to stare straight ahead, waiting for the target to show itself. If anything moved, he'd pick up on it. Still, the waiting was the hardest part. From time to time, Lieutenant Steele or another one of the officers spoke up to say, "Hold your fire, boys. And whatever you do, don't get out of your foxhole—not unless you want somebody to shoot you by accident."

Not long after Steele's warning, the silence from the dark tangle of vegetation before them deepened. All sounds of shuffling feet and rattling equipment stopped. The darkness seemed to inhale and didn't let out its breath.

It was the quiet before the storm.

"Here they come," Deke muttered, just loud enough so Philly and Yoshio would hear him.

An instant later, shouts and cries shattered the stillness. The Japanese assault had begun.

The attack was made all the more eerie by the fact that the Japanese did not fire a single shot. Instead, their plan seemed to be to cross the open ground and bayonet the Americans. They could all hear the pounding of the enemy's boots as they raced closer. Screaming Japs were pouring at them out of the darkness.

They had all heard about the Japanese banzai attacks on Guadalcanal, the furious charges that had been terrifying to behold. So far the Japanese attack remained cloaked in darkness.

But not for long. Brilliant flashes of light blinded Deke as machine guns opened fire from the American side, the tracers stitching patterns of flame in the night.

A few tanks had been brought up from the beach. Their big guns, so useful against enemy gun emplacements, seemed only to go over the heads of the attacking infantry and explode in the jungle beyond, starting fires in the undergrowth. They changed tactics, and their machine guns opened up on the advancing enemy with more telling effect.

Star shells fired from the American lines arced up and then fell back to earth, illuminating the incredible scene spread before them. The Japanese charged en masse, their visible faces contorted in battle fury accentuated by the glow of the burning shells overhead. Each enemy soldier seemed to wear a mask of rage. Bayonets and even sword blades glinted in the light. It was as if hell's gates had unleashed masses of furious demons.

Deke felt his insides clench at the sight. A man could almost be forgiven for turning tail and running at the sight of the horde approaching them. But Deke wasn't the running kind.

Neither were Philly or Yoshio. In the glare from the star shells, he could see them on either side of him, bent over their rifles.

Deke settled the crosshairs of his telescopic sight on a Japanese soldier who had outrun all the others, apparently intent on being the first to reach the American lines. He seemed to want the glory of being the first to die, and Deke decided to oblige.

He put his crosshairs on the Japanese soldier and fired. The man spun around and went down. Seconds later, his comrades trampled over top of him.

Already the Japanese had covered so much ground, and so quickly, that Deke was able to pick out individual faces in the glare of the star shells. The enemy soldiers were no longer a uniform mass. He could see that some were taller, some shorter, some skinny, and some solid. Suddenly the war was getting up close and personal.

Deke picked out another target, this time settling his sights on an officer waving a sword. The fact that the officer wore round eyeglasses made him look somewhat like a demented schoolteacher.

Deke touched the trigger, and a round from the Springfield hammered into him. The officer crumpled.

Of course Deke wasn't the only one shooting. On either side of him, he heard Philly's and Yoshio's rifles banging away. The firing from the sniper squad was more methodical because they were armed with bolt-action Springfield rifles versus the semiautomatic M1 weapons with which most troops were equipped. No matter—the snipers made each shot count.

Up and down the line, soldiers poured fire into the oncoming enemy ranks. Added to the machine-gun fire, the small-arms fire was having a devastating effect on the enemy. Whole rows of troops were mowed down at once. Deke was reminded of how old-timers back home used a scythe to mow hay or cut fodder, each sweep of the blade laying out a neat row of cut grass in the field. It looked as if they had taken a scythe to the Japs.

Despite their losses, the Japanese attack showed no signs of faltering. No matter how many enemy soldiers fell, more seemed to surge in behind to take their place.

Shouted orders could now be heard in the Japanese ranks.

"Yoshio, what the hell are they saying?" Philly demanded.

"They are telling them to open fire!"

Startled, they realized that the Japanese had not been shooting back but had been intent on closing the distance to the US position. Just as Yoshio had warned, the Japanese started shooting for the first time. Bullets whistled overhead. Most of the shots were not very well aimed, with the oncoming Japanese simply firing their rifles from their hips. A few soldiers dropped to one knee so they could take better aim at the Americans in the foxholes. Like the snipers, the Japanese were equipped with bolt-action rifles, giving them a slower rate of fire. The American star shells overhead now worked to the enemy soldiers' advantage as they took aim and picked off targets of their own.

Bullets began to find their mark. Off to Deke's left, a man whose voice he didn't recognize screamed, "I'm hit! I'm hit!"

"Medic!" somebody else shouted. There seemed to be wounded all over the place.

A soldier wearing a white armband ran past, risking his life to save another.

More bullets zinged past. There was nothing quite like the sound of a passing bullet to make your spine turn to Jell-O. Even above all the shooting, they could hear the frenzied war cries of the Japanese. Were these humans or madmen?

It was anybody's guess as to whether the US position was about to be overwhelmed.

A fresh strategy on the part of the Japanese also became clear as several soldiers who had been scattered throughout the ranks suddenly pressed forward into view. These soldiers carried stick bombs—long poles with an explosive charge attached to one end. The Japanese called them *shitotsubakurai*.

Though primitive in appearance, there was no doubt that the stick bombs would be more than effective. All that one of the Japs had to do was jam the explosive tip against a tank or even a machine-gun emplacement, wiping them out. He'd blow himself up in the process, but that thought didn't seem to trouble the attackers.

One of the bombers separated himself from the horde and began to run right at one of the tanks that had been brought up in support of the US position. The light tanks were not as invincible as they looked. The Japanese had quickly learned this early in the fight for Guam and the tank now made an irresistible target for the bomber.

By some miracle, the Japanese soldier had managed to dodge the streams of machine-gun fire, intent on cutting him down. He juked and dodged as he ran, making him a difficult target for the infantrymen.

"Deke, get him!" shouted Lieutenant Steele. Armed only with a combat shotgun, the lieutenant must have realized that the Japanese was out of range.

The lieutenant knew that Deke was a crack shot. If anybody could bring down that bomber before he reached the tank, it was Deke.

Deke didn't waste energy responding but put his crosshairs on the racing soldier. It was a difficult shot in that the man was moving fast and was an athletic runner, leaping over obstacles that now included the bodies of his own fallen comrades. He seemed to run even faster as he got closer to the tank. In another few steps, the bomber would reach the tank and slam his explosive-laden pole against it. Deke would have to lead him, same as he would a running deer.

Before he could fire, a Japanese bullet whipped past Deke's ear, causing him to flinch. He resettled the sights and was swinging them out just ahead of the bomber—

A little voice in his head said, *Hurry, hurry*, but Deke forced himself to go slower. He knew that he'd have only one shot, and he couldn't allow himself to miss.

Overhead the star shells that had been illuminating the battlefield began to burn out all at once, plunging the battlefield into darkness.

Deke's target disappeared in the inky backdrop.

Where in hell—

He couldn't see the Japanese bomber anymore, but Deke knew that he was still out there, running at the tank. He kept the rifle moving, hoping that he had kept pace with the now-invisible runner.

He pulled the trigger.

An instant later, the darkness erupted with a tremendous explosion in that very spot. Deke had no way of knowing if he'd hit the runner and caused him to drop the explosive tip of the charge he was carrying into the ground, or if he'd somehow hit the charge itself, causing it to detonate.

He reckoned it didn't matter. The result was the same. The Japanese soldier hadn't reached the tank. As another star shell climbed into the sky and lit the battlefield again, it was clear that all that was left of the Japanese runner was a hole in the ground.

Philly whooped. "Got him!"

"Good shooting, Deke," the lieutenant shouted. "I knew you could do it."

Even in the midst of battle, Deke felt a warm glow from the lieutenant's praise. For the last few years, Deke had been indifferent to what anyone thought of him, with the exception of his sister, Sadie. With his pa gone, and then his ma, life had been too hard, and filled with too much loss, for him to seek anyone's approval, or to much care.

But he felt different around the lieutenant. This was a man whose opinion mattered. A few words from Steele felt about as good as a medal.

A nearby shout forced him to ignore his momentary elation at having shot the runner. *This fight ain't over yet.*

The Japanese had reached the line. Their numbers had been thinned out considerably, as attested to by the bodies that lay scattered in the kunai grass. But in the moment, however many got through still seemed like too many.

A screaming enemy soldier appeared out of nowhere, racing toward the foxhole. Deke swung the rifle up and shot him, simply pointing the muzzle rather than aiming. The scope was no damn use at point-blank range. Before he could even work the bolt, another soldier charged at them, shouting furiously, "Banzai! Banzai!"

Light flashed off the bayonet that was angled right at Deke. He started to raise his own rifle, hoping to use the barrel to parry the blade. The Springfield was not equipped with a bayonet.

Off to his right, Philly's rifle cracked. The Japanese soldier crumpled.

Deke looked over and nodded at Philly.

Like a wave against rock, the Japanese banzai attack broke in an angry froth. A few of the attackers launched themselves down into the foxholes, stabbing furiously with their bayonets.

The soldiers responded with their own bayonets, rifle butts, knives, or fists. The hand-to-hand combat did not last long, but it was brutal and savage.

Deke watched as a soldier in a neighboring foxhole used his entrenching tool like a club to bring down the Japanese infantryman who had decided to leap into the hole with him. There was a sickening crunch of metal against bone; then the GI struck a couple more times to make sure the job was done.

The dying screams of American soldiers were mixed with the battle cries of the Japanese. A few Japanese had loaded themselves with hand grenades and leaped into foxholes, turning themselves into human bombs that detonated savagely, blowing themselves up in the process.

The Japanese might be determined, but, ultimately, not enough of them had managed to cross the killing ground. The savage, swift skirmishes in the foxholes brought the attack to its bloody end.

"Cease fire, cease fire!" Lieutenant Steele shouted, finally getting the battle-crazed machine gunners and soldiers to stop shooting. A strange silence settled over the battlefield, punctuated by the groans of the wounded and dying. The Japanese attack had broken like a wave on shore, with only a few of the enemy ebbing back into the jungle. Incredibly, Deke and his companions in the foxhole had survived.

Philly began to laugh, softly at first, then harder and harder. Deke started to worry that Philly had completely cracked up. It had been known to happen to more than one man.

"Dammit, Philly. Pipe down, will you? If any Japs are still out there, they'll know right where to find us."

"Can you believe it?" Philly managed to say, barely able to talk. His laughter faded into a few chuckles, then weary silence. "I can't believe it. We're still alive."

"For now," Deke muttered.

* * *

JUST A FEW WEEKS LATER, Deke stared into a different darkness, the one in the cramped sleeping quarters of a troopship. Guam and even the raid on Hill 522 were now behind him. He was lying in his narrow bunk aboard the ship waiting to take them back to Leyte. He felt the ship rolling in the ocean swell. That wasn't something he'd ever get used to, and he'd be glad to get back on land.

Then again, more Japanese would be waiting for them when they returned to Leyte. There might be more nights like the one on Guam.

He couldn't help but wonder if they'd be as lucky when they faced the Japanese this time around. Deke tended to think of luck being a limited commodity, like moonshine in a mason jar. Sip by sip, sooner or later, that 'shine ran out.

Deke just hoped that his own jar stayed full for as long as possible.

CHAPTER TWO

ABOARD USS *ELMORE*, Deke wasn't the only one tossing and turning in his bunk. An air of anxious anticipation permeated the ship, so thick that you could cut it with a combat knife.

"How long do you think we'll be on this damn ship?" Philly asked for about the hundredth time.

"I ain't the captain—or the admiral, or whoever is in charge of this tub," Deke replied, for what *felt* like the hundredth time. "And I sure as hell ain't General MacArthur. Why don't you go ask him?"

It wasn't the answer Philly wanted. "Aw, stuff a sock in it, you ugly redneck."

Philly rolled over and stared at the bulkhead, where he had entertained himself by scratching profane words into the paint. He could shout them all he wanted, but etching the words into the side of the ship was so much more satisfying.

Deke wouldn't have let anyone else talk to him the way Philly did. Being called "ugly" had a bite to it, considering that Deke really *was* ugly, thanks to the scars raking one side of his face. He had gotten into fights over a lot less. But an insult from Philly ran off him like rain off a rock.

Besides, he had learned to listen to Philly in the same way that some folks listened to the radio. When you got tired of what you were hearing, you just tuned it out.

To be honest, Deke didn't blame Philly for being in a bad mood. Who wasn't? They all felt miserable aboard this ship. They had been extracted from Leyte just a few days ago and had welcomed being on the ship—for about five minutes, until the boredom set in.

They had been picked up by the ship after the patrol had been sent to Leyte ahead of the invasion to neutralize the massive Japanese battery on Hill 522. Those guns would have played hell with the US fleet that would soon arrive in Leyte Gulf. The successful mission had not given them any kind of free pass. Patrol Easy would be taking part in the invasion of the Philippines.

As bad as Patrol Easy's behind-the-lines mission had been on Leyte, they were just about ready to go back if it meant a chance for fresh air and activity. Maybe that was what the army was trying to do, Deke decided—drive them all up the wall until they were begging to fight the Japs again.

As if by unspoken agreement, nobody had talked much about what had happened on that Philippine island. In fact, they had been ordered *not* to talk about it. Maybe it hadn't quite been a secret mission, but the higher-ups didn't want word to get out about how well fortified the Japs had been on that island. They didn't want the troops to get discouraged before they even landed on the beach.

There had been a price to pay for their silence, however. Another squad of snipers had somehow managed to get the credit for the mission. You could thank the rumor mill for that. Maybe it was because those other guys looked the part. They had been adopted as a pet project by a colonel named Woodall who had managed to get them outfitted with the army's new camouflage uniforms, M1 rifles with scoped sights, and even their own special badge. They had even picked up a name—Woodall's Scouts. In comparison, Patrol Easy had the appearance of a motley crew of rejects from other units—which they basically were.

The scuttlebutt on the ship had it that Woodall's Scouts had done the dirty work on Leyte—at least, that was the story going around whenever men from different units found themselves trading rumors.

"I hate those idiots," Philly said, watching Woodall's Scouts doing target practice from the stern one day, using the seagulls that trailed in the ship's wake as targets.

The marksmanship practice had drawn a crowd of bored sailors and soldiers, who had quickly been impressed by the crack shooting with the semiautomatic sniper rifles. In comparison, Patrol Easy was equipped with battered Springfield rifles that Lieutenant Steele had managed to obtain by begging, borrowing, and at least a bit of threatening. Though accurate, the bolt-action rifles did not have the higher rate of fire of the M1 weapons.

All in all, US forces approached sniper warfare in a haphazard manner compared to the Japanese, who viewed the use of snipers as an important tactic against the enemy. Likewise, the Krauts gave special attention to training snipers.

"You'd think Lieutenant Steele would say something and set the record straight that it wasn't Woodall's Scouts who took out that battery," Philly griped. "It was us, dammit."

"If Steele doesn't care, why should we?" Deke pointed out. "Just so long as the job got done."

Philly scoffed. "You know what? You sound just like him. I know I shouldn't care about what the latrine mayors have to say, but dammit, I do."

Deke grinned. A *latrine mayor* was slang for the gossips who liked to stand around jawing and spreading rumors, often in the long lines to use the heads on the crowded ship.

"Don't you worry your pretty head," Deke said. "Woodall's Scouts will get their nice uniforms dirty soon enough. We both know that shooting Japs ain't the same as shooting seagulls from the back of a ship."

* * *

DEKE THOUGHT BACK AGAIN to the mission. Patrol Easy's job had been to make sure that the island stronghold was a lot less well fortified. Similar missions had been carried out by Army Rangers on several of the small islands ringing Leyte Gulf in an effort to knock out the outlying Japanese defenses.

The Rangers had their hands full elsewhere, so the snipers of Patrol Easy had been sent ashore to take out the enemy battery located on Hill 522. Named for the hill's height—exactly 522 feet tall—the hill had been turned into a heavily fortified position by the Japanese.

This hadn't been just any gun battery. The guns were twins to the massive batteries aboard the *Yamato*, Japan's most formidable battleship. It seemed that the Japanese had made a few spare versions of these guns and didn't want them to go to waste. They might have been short on massive battleships, but they had plenty of islands that needed defending. The range of the guns enabled them to reach far out to sea, and special shells made them highly effective antiaircraft weapons.

Fortunately Patrol Easy had knocked out those formidable guns. They couldn't take all the credit, having been joined by a couple of demolition experts on loan from the marines and a band of Filipino freedom fighters. If they hadn't been successful, USS *Elmore* and any other ship in the invasion fleet would have been sitting ducks for those big guns.

For Deke, it had put his skill with a rifle into perspective. Sure, he could hit just about anything he could see, but those Japanese artillery boys had apparently been able to hit even what they *couldn't* see. They had possessed the ability to sink targets out of sight beyond the horizon. One of the navy gunners had explained how such feats involved lots of mathematical calculations and figuring the azimuth. Deke could figure fast as lightning in his head what others needed a pencil and paper to do, but he'd never had any real formal schooling. He had decided right then and there to leave the azimuths to the navy boys.

The mission had been a success, but that success had come at a price. Deke had seen things that he wished he could unsee, such as the execution of the Filipino guerrillas who had helped them with the mission. Those poor bastards—the ones who hadn't been killed in the raid itself—had the bad luck to be captured by the Japanese and had literally been put to the sword.

That had been hard to watch. Deke shuddered at the mental picture of their headless corpses staining the dirt red.

Actions like that made the enemy hard to fathom. Who the hell were these Japanese, anyhow? Barbarians, plain and simple. To shoot a prisoner was bad enough in Deke's book, but to cut off his head with a sword went beyond understanding.

Then there had been that Japanese sniper. He'd been a crack shot, managing to pin down Deke and Philly on Hill 522. Deke had gone head-to-head against that sniper, who was every bit his match. If anyone thought that the Japs were bad shots, they were sadly mistaken.

They'd only just barely managed to slip away. The enemy sniper had then chased them relentlessly through the Leyte jungle as Deke and the rest of Patrol Easy made their way to the beach, where they had been picked up by a navy rescue boat.

Deke didn't like boats or water all that much, but he'd been damn glad to see that boat.

All in all, it had been a hellacious adventure they'd been lucky to return from.

Now they were on a ship headed right back to that godawful place.

* * *

THE SENSE of anxiety they all felt was compounded by the fact that the interior of the ship was hot and smelly from so many men in close quarters. The ventilation system, such as it was, might have been adequate for a ship in the chilly reaches of the Atlantic, where the emphasis was on staying warm. It wasn't hard to believe that the ship had been built in Bath, Maine, where the temperature rarely exceeded eighty degrees even on the hottest July day. However, the ship's systems were not designed for the tropical environment. In these cramped quarters, the constant heat and humidity became almost unbearable at times. The porthole was propped open, but it was at least ninety degrees and steamy.

It was hard to describe the particular hell that was being in limbo in these less-than-ideal conditions, all the while knowing that the only way out involved running toward more Japanese machine guns.

At first, despite the discomforts belowdecks, many of the GIs on the ship had reassured themselves that at least they didn't have to sleep with one eye open, as they'd had to on Guam. That notion soon proved false. Japanese aircraft did their best to target any ships that they came across. At night, the interior of the ship was often dark as the belly of a whale due to a strict policy against any lighting that might make the ship a target for enemy night fighters or bombers. The Japanese Navy also remained a threat—especially the submarines that lurked beneath the waves.

It was probably the thought of a submarine attack that caused the most fear, given that an attack might come without warning and without a chance to fight back. Soldiers didn't like to feel helpless.

"One minute you're sleeping in your bunk," Philly had philosophized. "The next minute you're shark bait."

"Don't you ever shut up?" Deke groused. He couldn't help but squirm at the thought of going down with the ship. As a mountain boy born and raised, he wasn't fond of the sea.

USS *Elmore* was no battleship, but she wasn't helpless, either, against the marauding Japanese Navy or aircraft that hunted for American ships. Every square inch of the designated attack transport ship was crowded with soldiers and equipment. The few spare inches of the ship's deck bristled with the equipment of naval warfare, including five-inch guns, antiaircraft batteries, and antisubmarine depth charges. Of course, there wasn't much that the ship's crew could do to defend against a surprise attack.

For the soldiers, as if the threat of Japanese attack and the conditions aboard ship weren't bad enough, they also had to contend with monotony. This may have been the greatest enemy of all. The boredom seemed to make everything worse. According to a few GIs who had experienced jail, life on the ship wasn't so different in this regard.

Soldiers who had defended one another to within an inch of their lives during the fight for Guam found themselves ready to rip out each other's throats at the slightest provocation.

It all served as a reminder that this was no pleasure cruise. They were required to stay belowdecks most of the time, in their cramped and airless living quarters, sweating in the heat. They were allowed up on deck for only a few precious hours each day for fresh air and exercise.

This policy wasn't deliberate cruelty on the part of the officers—there were simply too many soldiers and not enough space on deck to give them free range of the ship. It wasn't that the ship would become top-heavy and capsize—it was just that the crew needed elbow room to operate the vessel.

Even when on deck, the GIs couldn't help but feel a little like cattle crowded into the stockyards, anxiously scanning the skies for the first appearance of an enemy plane with the dreaded "meatball" symbols on the wings.

For far too many soldiers and sailors, the sight of the dreaded Rising Sun symbol had meant impending death. There was a reason the Rising Sun was the color of blood. If enemy planes suddenly appeared and raked the deck, there would be nowhere for the soldiers to go. They were sitting ducks, and they all knew it.

So the soldiers spent their time belowdecks as best they could. The atmosphere remained stifling, with not nearly enough air flowing in through the portholes. What breeze blew in was too warm and humid to be refreshing. Many men stripped down to their boxer shorts, but the sweat still streamed off them. Destroyers had the nickname "tin cans," but they weren't the only ship where the crew and human cargo felt like sardines.

For Deke, this went beyond simple boredom. Deke couldn't define it, but something in him faded when he was away from the outdoors for too long. The mountains energized him, as did the cool rush of wind in his face. Even the hushed jungle brought him to life. Being stuck in the belly of a troopship, not so much.

As a boy, he had spent nearly all his time outdoors, either working on the farm or roaming the valleys and forested peaks, often armed with a rifle or shotgun. He had known most of the country for miles around like the back of his hand. More than a few times, he had wrapped up a chunk of salt pork and maybe a couple of apples and walked deep into the mountains. Deke had welcomed losing himself among the high wooded peaks in all kinds of weather, from snow to the fall days when the clouds came right down to the peaks. There had been bear back in the deep mountains, bobcat, deer. Deke hadn't always been there to hunt, but just to explore. There hadn't been anyone else around, certainly no one to stare at his scars or ask questions, which suited him just fine.

"I'm afraid that one of these times you ain't gonna come back," Sadie had said. "You'll build yourself an itty-bitty cabin back in them woods and become a mountain man."

That had sounded all right to Deke back then. In the belly of the crowded troopship, it sounded even better.

If the men of Patrol Easy hadn't already been aware of their ultimate destination, it would have been hard to know that the ship was basically in position for the coming invasion of Leyte. This was because USS *Elmore* continued to steam across the surface of the ocean, zigzagging endlessly to make a difficult target for any Japanese on the prowl. There was no land in sight, and the officers had been vague on the details. Hell, maybe some of the officers didn't even know what awaited them.

"There's not much to do but wait," Philly said. "It's gonna drive me nuts. How much longer are we gonna be on this ship?"

"Get some sleep," Deke told him. "Let tomorrow take care of itself."

"Where did you get that nugget?" Philly wanted to know. "They must be handing out fortune cookies in the mess hall."

Deke grinned into the darkness. He couldn't take credit for that one. He remembered it being one of the phrases that Sadie had employed during their bleak days in the boarding house, after they had lost the farm. To Deke's surprise, the words had stuck with him.

"Just something my sister used to say."

"She sounds like a smart one."

"You have no idea," Deke said, and grinned.

CHAPTER THREE

PATROL EASY OCCUPIED a cramped corner of the ship's quarters. There they staked their turf. Even if they had somehow taken a back seat to Woodall's Scouts, with their newfangled camouflage uniforms and rifles, the snipers of Patrol Easy had enough of a reputation that the green beans on the ship showed them some deference as combat veterans. In other words, they were left alone.

Even during the relatively brief time that they were on the ship, they did what they could to make themselves at home. Somewhere Philly had found a torn poster of Veronica Lake and stuck it to the bulkhead with chewing gum, designating the popular pinup girl as their mascot. Outsiders were not welcome, especially those replacement soldiers or sailors looking for a few souvenirs from the veterans aboard.

Word had gotten around that Philly had a samurai sword, which, along with Japanese pistols, were considered to be the most prized combat souvenirs.

Hardly an hour went by without some eager bastard coming by their quarters, looking to make a trade.

"Hey, buddy, I've heard you've got a samurai sword?" asked one fresh-faced soldier, appearing in their doorway.

"Beat it, green bean," Philly said.

"C'mon. I hear you can just pick up swords left and right on the beaches. What do you want for it? Ten bucks?"

"Not for sale."

"I'll even throw in two packs of smokes. How 'bout it?"

The silent glares that he received from several sets of eyes accustomed to staring through rifle sights were enough for him to get the message that he wasn't welcome. If those looks had been daggers, he would have been bleeding by now.

"Last chance," Philly said. "You know where I'm going to put that sword if you don't get out of here?"

"All right, all right. Don't get sore."

The soldier moved on to the next doorway to try his luck. You couldn't blame these guys. Most of them did more than their share in rear-echelon support positions and just wanted to bring back a tangible piece of the war. But Deke, Philly, and Yoshio had seen what those swords could do. In the hands of the Japanese, they weren't just for decoration.

Across the ship, the soldiers bet their meager pay in endless card games. The winners always made sure the losers paid up—once they got to Leyte, there was a good chance they'd never see that money if their card-playing buddies bought it on the beach.

Some men filled the time with endless conversation, but their stories and jokes grew stale, especially when you had been around the same guys for weeks or months at a time. Even the most extroverted soldiers found themselves sinking into a sullen silence. They lay in their bunks, chain-smoking, adding a fog of tobacco smoke to the already thick, humid air.

Some, like Philly, seemed to get louder, as if they could talk themselves out of these doldrums. Others, like Deke, simply retreated deeper into themselves. He just dug himself a mental hole and crawled right into it.

He recognized that this was how he had survived that awful stretch after his family had lost their farm to the bank and they'd had to move into a boarding house in town. It was not a memory that he wanted to return to. Deke was built for action, not for wallowing in self-pity. To keep busy, he spent the time sharpening his custom-forged bowie knife and cleaning his rifle for what seemed like the umpteenth time.

Once again, Yoshio was reading a Western novel. This one was called *West of the Pecos.* Deke never had been much for books, but he was a little envious that Yoshio could be so easily drawn into the pages. With a book, the time seemed to pass more easily.

"I've said it before, and I'll say it again, although I can't believe I'm saying it," said Philly. "The truth is that I can't wait to get back to Leyte."

"You'll get your wish soon enough," Deke replied. "I can't say that I disagree. I've had just about enough of this ship. Sure am glad that I ain't in the navy."

As far as he was concerned, the sooner they had a crack at the Japs again, the better.

* * *

IT SEEMED MIRACULOUS, given the vast distances involved, but mail managed to arrive. There was almost nothing so welcome, because it helped to break the monotony of being trapped on the ship. It was also a reminder of home many thousands of miles away and the fact that someone gave a damn about them, whether it was a girl, a wife, or a father or a mother.

Some soldiers wrote letters home every day, sometimes more than once a day, using the thin paper provided to them for this purpose, but it was clear that the letters from home had predated these. No matter —each word from home was savored like the last bite of an apple pie.

To Deke's surprise, he received another letter from Sadie. His sister was working as a police officer, one of the few female law enforcement officers in Washington, DC. She'd been a wartime hire due to the shortage of men and the occasional need for a female officer to deal with the influx of young women to the nation's capital.

Deke was proud of his sister. She was right smack-dab in the heart of things. And here he was on a ship in the ocean more than half a world away.

He'd be the first to admit that her tough demeanor made her perfect for the job. Sadie never had been one to back down from a challenge. Also, Deke had to admit that his sister was at least as good with a rifle as he was. He didn't expect her to be any less of a shot with a police revolver.

The nation's capital had become so busy during the war that Sadie worked long hours. She even had a few funny stories to tell. One thing for sure, Deke thought, was that they were both a long way from home. How Deke missed waking up in the old farmhouse on winter mornings, so cold that he could see his breath hang in the air. He longed for some of that cool air as he lay in the hot, cramped metal bunk.

It was funny, in a sense—times had been hard, but in hindsight they might also have been some of the best times in his life—at least before Pa had died in an accident at the sawmill.

Pa had been a silent, hardworking man. He had fought in the trenches of Europe during the Great War but had never talked about it. Pa had brushed off Deke's occasional questions. Now that he had experienced combat for himself, Deke understood his father's silence. There were things in this world that a man kept to himself.

He settled down to read Sadie's letter. It was more of a short note, really—neither he nor Sadie were much for writing long letters.

* * *

Dear Deke,

I hope you are doing all right fighting the Japs. It sure seems sometimes like the war in Europe is what most folks care about. On the police force, they are always telling us to be on the lookout for German spies, but never a word about the Nips. I guess maybe Washington seems pretty far away from Japan.

My friend Peggy that you met during your visit here was asking about you. I gave her your address, so maybe she will write to you.

It is getting to be fall and I remember all the good times we had picking up apples for cider from the windfalls on Old Man McGlothlin's orchard, or even making sausage. You can't get sausage like that here in the city, not no way, no how. But I do like having hot running water. No more heating pots on the stove for a bath!

You be good and lick the Japs—I know you could do it with one hand tied behind your back if you had to.

Your sister,

Sadie

* * *

HE FOLDED the letter carefully and tucked it away to read again later. He supposed that he ought to write back to Sadie, but he never had been much for writing letters. He jotted a short note to let her know he was all right and that he appreciated hearing from her. On the page his handwriting was neat but blocky and almost childish from lack of practice.

As for Peggy, he remembered her as a quiet and serious young woman who had also grown up on a farm, somewhere in Maryland, so they'd had that much in common. The city was filled with young men and women fresh off the farm, stuffed into city clothes and trying to look like they knew what they were doing, when a few short months before they had been milking cows or hauling slop to feed the hogs— or even sharing a decent pair of shoes with a brother or sister. The Depression had been slow to let go in a lot of small towns and farms. For these young people, the war meant opportunity.

He hadn't gotten any letters from Peggy. No wonder—he was sure that his scars had scared her off. Like any young man, Deke was interested in women, but he had mostly put them out of his mind because of his looks. He had gotten to the point where he reckoned that no woman would have anything to do with him. He was damaged goods.

So far, women remained a mystery to Deke. Not that he didn't yearn for their company sometimes. If he wanted any loving, he supposed that he'd have to pay his two dollars for a few minutes of vigorous humping like all the other desperate GIs had back on Hawaii —and then feel ashamed about it later. It wasn't how Deke wanted to treat a woman—or himself, for that matter.

Sadie's letter didn't say much, but it prompted a flood of memories.

Deke also had to smile, thinking of all those times they'd had growing up on the mountain farm. The chores had seemed endless, and it was true that life wasn't always easy—far from it. But it hadn't been all bad either. Then again, he supposed that it had less to do with happy child-hood memories than it did with taking pride in surviving adversity. He and Sadie had come through a lot together.

If he managed to survive this war, he'd have to see what he could do about getting back the Cole family's land. The farm didn't seem to matter all that much to Sadie—she seemed to have moved on and embraced her new city life, with all its possibilities.

When he had visited Sadie in the city, she had caught him studying her with admiration when she had been about to head out the door in her uniform. The uniform had made her appear mature and official. She even wore a touch of makeup and lipstick, something their own mother had never worn a day in her life. Between the makeup and the uniform, she had not only looked older but appeared right at home.

"What are you lookin' at?" Sadie had snapped, suddenly sounding every bit like the Hancock County girl that she was. "Did I grow two heads overnight?"

Deke had shaken his head sheepishly. "No, you look different is all. Like you belong here in the city."

"I can't look like a rube, not if I want to be taken seriously," she'd retorted. Then her voice softened, and she touched the back of his hand to reassure him. "Don't you worry, Deke. You know me. I'm the same old Sadie under this lipstick. I'll always be a country girl at heart."

Knowing Sadie, he reckoned that was true. Still, he was proud of her for having the courage to move to the city and make a new life for herself.

Maybe the city life was fine with Sadie, but Deke had other plans. He wanted nothing more than to return to the mountains, to see the lush valley farms and the peaks covered in forests. To wake up on a crisp winter's night to the sound of a fox barking and see the full moon glowing on the snowy fields.

He felt a pang, though, thinking about those farms and fields. Deke swore that if there was one thing he was going to do in this life, it was get the family farm back and kill the son of a bitch who had robbed his family of it in the first place. Given time, they would have paid back the money that his father had borrowed, but that no-good banker hadn't given them more time.

It all came down to greed. Taking the land was bad enough. Worse yet, he blamed that banker for bringing about his mother's death. She'd already been frail, and the loss of the farm was a final blow from which she had never recovered.

As for him and Sadie, that banker had stolen their happiness when they'd been forced to move into a boarding house in town. He'd had to find what work he could. His time in a dusty, noisy sawmill had been sheer misery for a young man used to working the land, but it had been a matter of survival because they had needed his wages.

But revenge would have to wait. That snake of a banker was safe enough for the time being.

Right now there were a whole lot of Japanese and a vast ocean between Deke and that goal. If he ever wanted to get home again, the first thing he had to do was survive the war, and there were no guarantees about that.

CHAPTER FOUR

IN HIS BUNK NEARBY, Philly let out an indignant snort. He'd been reading a copy of the shipboard newspaper, a slim rag called the *Anchor Chain*, that he now threw down in disgust.

"What got into your craw?" Deke wondered.

The thin sheets of newsprint offered a roundup of news from home and tidbits about the men and officers in the unit, such as births of children back home. Aside from a few stale military announcements, there wasn't much actual news; it was all kind of innocuous, but it was a welcome slice of normalcy. The *Anchor Chain* was meant to boost morale. It was hard to see how something in it would have upset Philly.

Philly tossed the newspaper at Deke. "Look at what's on the front page."

There at the top of the fold was a photograph of Woodall's Scouts, wearing their fancy matching uniforms and brandishing their sniper rifles. Colonel Woodall stood beside them, looking like their prim-and-proper scoutmaster. The last sentence of the photo caption read, "The Japanese snipers are really going to fear these boys!"

"I'll be damned," Deke said.

"They haven't even fought the Japs yet," Philly fumed. "After all that we've done, you'd think that we'd be the ones to get their picture in the paper."

"Philly, it ain't the *New York Times*," Deke said, picking the name of the biggest newspaper he could think of. "It's just that little rag that goes around the ship."

"Yeah, but still. Credit where credit is due, you know."

Deke was more curious about their rifles. He looked more closely at the photograph, but the fuzzy newspaper photo did not offer much detail.

"I like my Springfield just fine, but I wouldn't mind trying one of those M1 sniper rifles," Deke said. He wondered if the semiautomatic sniper rifles really offered an advantage. "Then again, all you really need is one good shot."

"Our dignity is wounded, and you're worried about their rifles." Philly shook his head and reached out a hand as he got off his bunk. "Give that here a minute."

"I thought that picture made you mad. You gonna put that in your scrapbook?"

"Hell, no, you dumb redneck. I've got to hit the head, and you know what? Now I've got the perfect use for that newspaper. Woodall's Scouts are going to make a good asswipe."

As it turned out, the business with Woodall's Scouts wasn't over yet. Deke and Philly were exercising on deck later that day when they ran into a couple of the scouts, recognizable by their camouflage uniforms. The uniforms looked a little ridiculous on the deck of a ship at sea, but Deke had to admit that the pattern would help the soldiers blend right into a jungle setting.

Philly promptly bumped into one of the men with such force that he nearly knocked him over.

"Hey, watch it!"

"Sorry, buddy," Philly said, grinning like a Cheshire cat. "I guess I didn't see you with all that camouflage on."

"Very funny, pal." The soldier gave Philly a harder look and scowled. "Wait a minute. Aren't you guys those snipers that the Japs shot the hell out of on Guam?"

"What do you mean, 'shot the hell out of us'?"

"That's what I heard," the other man said. "That's why Colonel Woodall organized a sniper unit, so that we'd have some actual countermeasures against the Japanese."

Philly looked at Deke. "Do you hear that, country boy? That's awfully fancy talk. Countermeasures."

"You mean, like shooting Japanese snipers?" Deke asked Philly.

"That's sure what it sounds like." Philly turned back to the other man. "How many Japs have you shot?"

"None yet, but we'll shoot plenty once we get ashore."

"Uh-huh."

"You don't believe me?"

Philly considered. "I tell you what. Your best man against our best man. We'll see who's the better shot."

"You're on."

It didn't take long for word of the shooting contest to spread across the ship. Nothing broke up the boredom like a good fight—or a grudge shooting match, at least. When Patrol Easy reconvened on the stern with Woodall's Scouts, they were joined by at least a hundred spectators. Naval officers had come out to watch, and they didn't even have a dog in this fight. Colonel Woodall was there, looking smug even though the match hadn't begun, but Lieutenant Steele was nowhere to be seen. The lieutenant had made himself scarce as hen's teeth since coming aboard the ship.

"Let's make this interesting," Philly said. He held up a crisp new bill so that it fluttered in the wind. "Twenty bucks says you'll be the first one to miss."

Somebody whistled. That was serious money, close to what a working man earned in a week back home—or had earned. Wages had gone up since the start of the war.

The other man grinned. He introduced himself as Shaw. "It'll be like taking money from a baby," Shaw said.

"Oh, you're not shooting against me," Philly said. "I said best shot, remember? That'd be the Deacon here."

Deke stepped forward, holding his battered Springfield rifle, which showed the wear and tear of the Guam campaign and the mission on

Leyte. Shaw's confident grin faded somewhat, but Deke's appearance tended to do that to people. It was like encountering some back-woodsman here on the deck of USS *Elmore*.

"All right," Shaw said. "I wouldn't put that money back in your pocket just yet, if I were you. You're about to lose it."

They flipped a coin to see who went first. Deke called heads—and lost.

"Go on then," Deke said. "Let's see what you got."

Shaw stepped up to the stern rail. It had been determined that their targets would be the seagulls trailing the ship's wake. They were close enough to shore that the fleet had attracted flocks of sea birds eager for whatever scraps the ships jettisoned.

Hitting any target from the deck of the moving ship would have been difficult, but shooting a flying bird out of the sky was extra chal-lenging. The gulls swooped and swerved, riding the air currents. Then again, there was no shortage of targets.

Shaw didn't waste any time. He fired confidently, the shots almost equally spaced. Deke had to admire the new rifles, with their higher rate of fire. The Japanese didn't have anything that compared—neither did the Germans, for that matter. The Garand M1 would be giving US troops a definite combat edge.

But in the end, sniper warfare came down to one well-placed bullet at a time. The rate of fire didn't matter.

Looking on, Colonel Woodall held his fist high and pumped it in encouragement. "Attaboy, Shaw! Show 'em how it's done!"

Shaw fired again. Another white bird pinwheeled out of the sky.

Deke shook his head. "Wasted meat."

"You'd eat a pigeon?" Philly made a face.

"They're seagulls."

"What's the difference? Rats with wings. Don't take this the wrong way, but I sure hope you never invite me over for Thanksgiving dinner."

"That bird being a seagull ain't the point. Where I come from, you eat what you kill."

Philly could see that Deke was in one of his moods, but he couldn't resist. "Then see if you can shoot me a New York strip or maybe a porterhouse. Maybe even a good-size chicken. I sure would appreciate it."

Then again, the gulls were not completely wasted. Gulls weren't the only denizens of the sea following the ship, hoping for an easy meal. Sharks also cruised in the wake, snapping up the fallen birds. Like the birds, they welcomed whatever came their way from the ship, but it was also as if they knew that by biding their time, there might be even bigger rewards.

Here and there, the men on the stern could see the sudden swirl in the water where a bird was sucked down by a shark. The sight was more than a little disconcerting to men who might find themselves in that water if a Japanese sub got lucky with a torpedo.

Finally Shaw missed his sixth shot. The gull appeared to swoop just as he fired, unwittingly dodging the bullet. Nonetheless, a whoop rose as one from the throats of his fellow scouts. They seemed certain that Shaw's show of marksmanship would be hard to beat—and they were probably right. Some of the squids who had gathered to watch managed to let out a cheer.

Even Deke had to admit that it was impressive shooting.

"Ain't bad," he said in acknowledgment to Shaw as he passed him at the stern rail.

"Yeah? Let's see you beat that."

After witnessing the results of the initial shooting, bets were being placed by sailors and soldiers in the crowd, the odds suddenly favoring Shaw. To the spectators, it seemed doubtful that Deke could do any better.

Even Deke wondered what the hell he had gotten himself into.

Shooting birds on the wing was normally done with a shotgun because the spread of pellets gave the shooter a better chance of hitting the bird—a shooter didn't need to be exact. Hitting a flying bird with a rifle required precision—and no small amount of luck.

Deke settled in at the rail. He had to think of these birds as stationary targets, but he had to be quick about it. There could be none of the usual lingering over a target. These would be hunting shots, as he'd done as a boy back home. An animal didn't stay in the same position for long. Once your sights were lined up, you were best off to squeeze the trigger and be quick about it.

Through the scope, he could see several birds spring closer, flitting through the crosshairs. He let the sound of the shouting men behind him fade away. The wind seemed to be at his back as the ship forged ahead toward Leyte. He hoped that the wind wouldn't interfere too much with his bullet once it left the muzzle.

Sometimes when he was shooting, he realized that he benefited from switching off the thinking part of his mind and letting instinct take over. His eyes, the muscle memory part of his brain, even his finger on the trigger all seemed hardwired together like a light circuit.

He exhaled, picked out a bird, and waited for it to settle into riding one of the invisible air currents trailing the ship. As soon as his crosshairs hovered for an instant, he pulled the trigger.

To his relief, the bird tumbled from the sky.

Cheers arose behind him.

"One down!" someone shouted. "Four more to go!"

"Not gonna happen!" Shaw boasted.

Deke obliged by quickly shooting down those four birds in rapid succession. He needed to knock one more out of the sky to beat Shaw.

Easier said than done. After taking so many losses, the birds seemed to be wising up to what was going on. They hung back farther from the ship and grew more skittish. They weren't offering themselves up as easy targets.

Deke had no choice but to pick out a gull that was farther out than the others. He had lined up his sights when the bird suddenly dropped, disappearing from the scope's field of view. Dammit. Fortunately he hadn't fired yet, but he had to spend a moment acquiring the target again. The bird appeared to have dropped farther back.

Once again he let the crosshairs float across the bird. The instant they were lined up, he fired.

At first, nothing happened. The bird kept flying.

"He missed!" somebody shouted.

"That's it! Pay up!"

But Deke knew that his bullet had gone true. He could feel it. He kept the scope focused on the bird.

All at once, the gull's wings folded and the bird tumbled gracelessly from the sky and hit the sea with the smack of all its deadweight.

Deke considered that it hadn't been the first time that something he'd shot hadn't immediately known it was dead yet. It took a moment for the body to tell the brain, *All right, you're done.* Whatever conscious-ness that even a bird or animal possessed clawed and fought for life up until the final breath. Deke had seen that it was the same with humans in this war.

Something swirled up under the bird, and it vanished.

Six birds to Shaw's five. Deke had shown up the other shooter. He could have gone for seven birds but didn't want to push his luck.

Nobody came over to slap him on the back. One look at Deke was all it took to know that any such gesture would not be welcome.

Philly was the exception. He swatted Deke on the shoulder with a meaty hand.

Deke let it go.

"Ha! How about that!" Philly said. He had added a few bills to join his crisp twenty. "I guess we showed them!"

Deke gave him a look. "Who is this *we* you're going on about? Last time I checked, it was just me doing the shooting."

Shaw came over, trailed by the other men from Woodall's Scouts. Colonel Woodall stood to one side, scowling. The rest of Patrol Easy came to stand beside Deke.

"You got lucky on that sixth bird," Shaw said.

"Maybe," Deke agreed.

"Gee, we hate to show up Woodall's Scouts like that, them being so fancy and all," Philly said. "Woodall's Scouts. Sounds like Boy Scouts to me."

"Yeah, keep it up," Shaw said. "I still need to earn my merit badge for busting noses."

The men in both squads tensed up. It wouldn't have been the first time that a rivalry turned into a fistfight.

"Knock it off, boys," Woodall said. "Save it for the Japs."

Nobody could argue with that—but still. The tension eased and the two groups began to drift away.

But Shaw seemed intent on having the last word. "This isn't over," he said. "We'll have ourselves a proper match sometime on dry land. Actual targets, not seagulls. You'll see some real shooting then."

Deke nodded. "I reckon I'll look forward to it."

CHAPTER FIVE

IF THE MEN aboard ship felt that they were cogs in the wheel of the US war machine, then General Douglas MacArthur was the man cranking that wheel in the Pacific, at least where the army was concerned.

This October morning found him alone in his office, sucking on his pipe, studying maps and scanning reports. And yet he didn't allow himself to become too absorbed in the paperwork. That was what his staff was for. First and foremost, MacArthur had come to realize that his primary role was to think and plan. He did that best while in motion, pacing his office almost like a caged lion. Definitely a lion, because it was a more regal beast than a panther or a striped tiger.

There was something of the last century that clung to the general's persona and attitudes, including his ideas of battle. In part this was likely because his own father had fought in the Civil War. More than forty years into the twentieth century, the MacArthur clan still hadn't completely embraced it.

Studying the maps, the invasion of Leyte weighed heavily on his mind. A great deal was at stake, from the lives of thousands of men to the future of the Pacific War to his own reputation. It might even be hard to say which one of these things MacArthur valued the most.

To be sure, MacArthur was an old soldier in more ways than one. A graduate of West Point, he had been first in his class in 1903, which would have been a foregone conclusion to anyone who'd known him in those days. He had led troops in combat during the First World War as a young officer. Even then he'd had a flair for the flamboyant, wearing a custom-made nonregulation uniform. He'd gotten away with it because he was MacArthur—and even those who didn't like him had to admit that he was a bold son of a bitch.

The so-called Great War was supposed to end all future wars. It went without saying that the peace promised by that Great War had not been lasting, and had actually set the stage for conflict due to the punitive stance taken toward Germany. It was a lesson in management that MacArthur would later bring with him to the occupation of Japan.

After all, the general was not just a soldier and strategist but also a student of history. Back when he had been commandant of West Point, he had insisted that the students be trained in more than engineering and warfare. He understood that winning was only half the battle—the victors must also be occupiers. An officer with some grasp of history and civics made for a much better peacetime administrator, in MacArthur's view.

He'd made other changes at West Point, such as working to do away with the savage hazing that took place against cadets. One solution was to eliminate older cadets being in charge of drilling and discipline. Instead, he put veteran army sergeants in charge of training. They weren't any easier on the cadets, but at least they were professional.

His ideas for changing the curriculum at West Point had not been popular, but MacArthur had forged ahead, despite the naysayers. He never had been one to worry about what others thought as long as the ball was carried forward. Besides, once MacArthur had made up his mind to get something done, he was about as flexible as a steel beam.

While his exploits during the Great War had won him the command of West Point, many people were not as familiar with his more youthful adventures. As a young military surveyor in the Philippines, he had shot and killed two brigands who'd ambushed him in the jungle.

Then, in the US adventure into Veracruz, he had undertaken a daring solo mission and single-handedly held off several attacks by bands of Pancho Villa's cavalry during the course of a single desperate day, ultimately shooting and killing seven men in the process.

His personal bravery in battle was clear to all—even his detractors and rivals had to admit that MacArthur was a man who was willing to lead from the front.

Now MacArthur was no longer leading a single unit on the battle-field but commanding an invasion force. All in all, his daring gunplay decades before was hard to square with the regal general currently looking over the maps and pages of typewritten documents.

There was a knock on the door, and an aide entered.

"Here are the latest reports, sir," the aide said.

Inwardly MacArthur groaned. It sometimes seemed as if he would be buried in reports. Each day he seemed to face a blizzard of paper. "Anything I should take a look at right away?"

"I think it's just the usual chatter, sir. Troop movements, mostly. Whatever our codebreakers were able to pick up."

"Just put them there with the others."

"Yes, sir."

"Thank you, Jim."

The aide did as he was told and then quickly retreated from the office.

Thankfully, the aide shut the door behind him, drowning out the sounds of the busy outer office.

For his headquarters, MacArthur had chosen to establish opera-tions in the Australian Mutual Provident Society Building in Brisbane, in part because that city offered the best access to communication with MacArthur's widespread military operations in the Pacific.

The reports that the aide had delivered largely came from Ultra, which was the secret US system used to break Japanese military codes. The intelligence had proved invaluable for planning purposes. It was like putting an ear to some enemy general's door and listening in.

Of course, the Japanese had their own ears at the Americans' door.

MacArthur had thought a lot about the Japanese. He thought that the best way to defeat an enemy was to understand him. He sometimes dwelled on what his adversary might be thinking about *him*. Trying to anticipate his next move. Probing for weakness. Using his strength against him. MacArthur had no particular hatred for the Japanese. He didn't go around crowing about killing Japs as Admiral "Bull" Halsey did. For MacArthur, the Japanese were simply a problem to solve, and he loved the challenge of a smart adversary.

Later he would see the results of their heavy hand—even atrocities —in his beloved Philippines with distaste and sadness, but not with enmity toward all Japanese. MacArthur would eventually see to it that the bad apples were hanged for their war crimes.

He sat down, then stood up again, got out from behind the desk, and began to walk around the office, both hands clasped behind his back.

Although he was well into his sixties, he had a great deal of energy, a man very much in his prime. He was ambitious to the point that he'd even had his eye on the White House. Tall and imposing, he possessed the physical charisma of a Washington or a Lee. If he'd been a film star instead of a soldier, central casting would have picked him as a Hollywood version of a commanding officer.

But MacArthur was no empty uniform or Hollywood actor. He was, in fact, a military mastermind who usually managed to stay not just two steps ahead of the Japanese, but also at least one step ahead of the competing officers in other branches of the service.

After all, there were only so many resources to go around. This meant that each command-level officer had to be an advocate and even something of a robber baron at heart by promoting his own branch of the service and his own strategies, sometimes to the detriment of other forces. The role played by Australian and British forces added a whole new layer to the politics of it all. They were Allies—to a point.

At command level, these interservice rivalries could be bitter, akin to a blood sport. Fortunately the commanders did manage to set aside their differences when it came to defeating the Japanese. No one ever seemed to lose sight of the fact that the real enemy flew the Rising Sun banner. When push came to shove, rivalries fell aside in the name of victory.

It wasn't always a perfect arrangement, but it was far better than the piecemeal way that the Japanese Army and Navy interacted, resulting in a dysfunctional overall military strategy. Their lack of coordination sometimes made it seem as if they were fighting two different wars.

Not that MacArthur was going to complain about that. The thought of the Japanese Army and Navy working more cooperatively made him shudder.

Lost in these random thoughts, MacArthur paced his office and read over the reports on his desk, then paused to study the maps on the wall.

Each day presented a changing situation. It didn't help that the intelligence reports were continually mistaken. Just when the Japanese Navy seemed depleted, more ships would suddenly appear on the horizon. More submarines would make their presence known beneath the waves. There were times when so many enemy aircraft had been shot down, sometimes hundreds in a single day, that it seemed impossible that there could be more remaining. Yet more squadrons bearing the dreaded meatball symbol on their wings appeared in the sky.

On land, just when it seemed that the Japanese could not possibly fight their way out of the corner they were in, they proved everyone wrong and refused to be defeated. They would fight to the last man, exacting a terrible price and leaving the American troops to wonder, *Why in hell won't they just give up?*

It was a source of exasperation but also of grudging admiration for an enemy that believed in total war and simply did not know when to quit. Even when the deck was increasingly stacked against them.

It was frankly amazing that the island nation could produce so many ships, soldiers, and aircraft. Then again, what many Americans failed to realize was that Japan was roughly the size of California, a long broad island in the Pacific with a satellite of buffer islands. What Japan did lack was natural resources, being totally reliant on imported rubber and oil to keep its war machine going. In part this was why Japan had undertaken its path of conquest—to feed its growing demand for natural resources. But it had overreached when it had attacked the United States that awful December morning at Pearl

Harbor. MacArthur had been in Manila at the time, and it had soon been the Philippines's turn to come under Japanese attack.

It was hard for MacArthur to understand the madness that had come over the Japanese people. He had met more than a few Japanese officers in the years leading up to the war and had found them to be reasonable and capable.

Hitler he could understand—one man grabbing the authority all for himself, a charismatic leader who promised to lift up a battered nation. Japan's descent into madness had been a more collective effort. The general hoped that American democracy would always remain strong so that same totalitarian mindset did not seize the reins of power. Would America's system of checks and balances still hold up in fifty years, or a hundred? He sure as hell hoped so. Every man in uniform was fighting for that democratic future.

Since the string of Japanese victories in the wake of Pearl Harbor, the tide had turned, and Japan's island empire was now falling one by one to US forces: Guadalcanal, Guam, Peleliu, Saipan.

MacArthur hoped to add the Philippines to that list. He put his hands on his hips, unconsciously striking a pose as if there were a photographer in the room—which often there was. Although he was alone, the general was a man constantly aware of outward appearances.

The Philippines would not be an easy nut to crack, not if reports could be believed that several hundred thousand Japanese troops were stationed there, well equipped, with plenty of ammunition and ready to fight to the death. These were tough soldiers, some of them even elite units that had fought in China.

Surely the Philippines would suffer in the process, and this thought saddened MacArthur terribly. He had a deep affinity for the Philippines and its people. He loved the islands' rich history that mingled the culture of the Filipino people and the Europeans who had settled there, starting in the sixteenth century with the arrival of the Spanish. Since 1898, the Americans had added their own unique spice to the mix.

The result was that Manila had been a charming, almost old-world city that could have been placed in Spain or Portugal. But now, at the cruel hands of war and the Japanese who sought to leave destruction in their wake, he feared that Manila and all its lovely avenues and historic buildings would be reduced to rubble and ruin.

There was always a price in war, MacArthur thought. Lives would be lost. Farmland burned, cities ruined, towns and villages destroyed. He never forgot that reality.

Also, MacArthur never lost sight of the fact that a victory in the Philippines would make good on his promise to return to the islands.

After defeat had been handed to him by the Japanese in 1942, he had managed to slip away and avoid capture. He would have preferred to remain behind and go down fighting, but orders had come directly from FDR, who had ordered MacArthur to leave the Philippines. The president of the United States did not need the added complication of such a high-ranking general falling into the hands of the enemy as a prisoner of war. Losing the Philippines itself was bad enough. And so MacArthur had left like a dog with his tail between his legs, leaving thousands of US soldiers behind to suffer through the Bataan Death March and the cruel POW camps.

Leading up to the invasion of Leyte, MacArthur had ordered the location of any of these camps to be marked on the map. He was going to make liberating the soldiers a priority as his forces swept across the Philippines.

However, it would be a difficult battle. The Japanese were expecting them. They were still thought to have hundreds of aircraft with which to attack and harass the American invasion fleet.

MacArthur feared that the cost on the beaches of Leyte would be terrible. The marines had certainly paid dearly for Guadalcanal. Now it might just be the army's turn to pay a similar price. And yet MacArthur remained optimistic. He believed in his troops. He believed in his strategy. Most of all, General Douglas MacArthur believed in himself.

* * *

IN THE OUTER OFFICE, Captain Jim Oatmire could barely believe that the great MacArthur himself had actually remembered his name.

"I'll be damned," he muttered, just loud enough to be heard by

Andy Tatum, who occupied the desk next to his—when either man had time to sit.

"What is it?"

"The Old Man actually knew my name when I dropped off his reports this morning."

"Huh. You know, that could be a good thing, or a bad thing—a very bad thing. As in, 'Captain Oatmire, why the hell didn't you get those reports on my desk sooner? Captain Oatmire, you are personally going to lead the next beach landing.'"

"You know what? I wouldn't mind seeing some action."

"You must be a fool, Captain Oatmire," Tatum intoned, imitating the general's commanding voice. "Do you want to get shot at by the Japanese, Captain Oatmire?"

"Actually, he called me Jim."

Tatum shuddered. "Good God, that's even worse. Just don't slip up and call him Doug."

"No worries there. The Old Man isn't exactly all that familiar, now is he?"

"I don't know what you mean by that. Heck, the two of us were just chatting about baseball scores." Although the war had gutted the ranks of baseball leagues back home, the games still went on, and the scores and accounts of the games were a welcome relief that at least something normal was still happening back home. Tatum never missed a chance to crow when news trickled in that his beloved Yankees had won a string of games.

"I call bullshit on that, because I am pretty sure that the general has never been to a baseball game."

"What do you mean? I heard the Old Man was in charge of our Olympics teams back in 1928."

"Sure, that makes sense. The Olympics are all about classic sports like running, the javelin, that disc thing that they throw—"

"The discus."

"Exactly. Not bats and balls and peanuts in the stands."

"You can't get any more American than baseball."

"If you say so."

"Shh, don't look now, but here comes that ballbuster Major Lundholm."

Beside him, Tatum ducked his head and went back to work, studying several documents at once in an effort to look busy. Sometimes it seemed as if the war were being fought with paperwork, as if mountains of paper could somehow replace bullets and bombs, ships and planes.

Around them, the large office hummed with activity—shouts, ringing phones, hurrying men, and a few women. The place was semiaffectionately known as "the bullpen"—a term taken straight from Wall Street.

Captain Oatmire decided to go down to the street and get some fresh air. The brief interaction with the general, however small, had left him dazed.

Out on the street, he lit a cigarette and surveyed the traffic passing on Queen Street. Many of the vehicles were of British origin, with the exception of the US jeeps and trucks that went rushing past. Though the people in the street spoke English, their accents sounded jarring to his American ears.

It was hard to pinpoint what Australia was like—he had struggled to describe it in his letters home. It wasn't quite British, and it definitely wasn't American. *I guess Australia is Australian.* He hadn't had time to explore much of the country. He worked long hours at headquarters. There wasn't much sightseeing taking place, considering that there was a war on. Some of his fellow junior officers—and some not so junior—seemed determined to meet the local sheilas, but Oatmire had kept his head down in that regard, at least. There seemed to be ten eager men for every available woman, anyhow.

Even if there was tension over dating the local girls, the Australians were mostly welcoming of US forces—and for good reason. It had less to do with the money that the soldiers and officers spent at the bars throughout Brisbane than it did with the fact that there had been real fear that the Japanese might invade Australia. The Japs had bombed the city of Darwin and had even used midget submarines to raid Sydney Harbor—or *Harbour*, as the Brits and Australians spelled it.

Not far from Australia, savage battles had been fought against the Japanese on New Guinea.

Back when fears of invasion had been at their height, there had been good reason for Australia to be worried. Japanese Imperial forces would have overwhelmed their defenses. But with the influx of US forces and recent victories against the Japanese, those invasion fears had subsided. The Japanese were far from defeated, but they had been knocked back on their heels. They were fighting a defensive war now, although nobody was ready to say they were on the ropes.

He watched a squad of hollow-eyed soldiers pass by. Their uniforms looked dirty and ragged, stained in places with what might be blood. Judging by the battered stocks of their rifles, their weapons had seen hard use.

Clearly these men had experienced the horrors of combat. Oatmire felt a twinge of guilt. He came from a wealthy and well-connected family that had made its money, ironically enough, in manufacturing military supplies during the Great War. After graduating from college, he had soon found himself in uniform as a staff officer. His war was very different from the one being fought by the veteran troops who had just marched past. More than once, he had expressed his interest in seeing action rather than shining a chair seat throughout the war.

But staff duty was not without its perils, not when you were dealing with someone like MacArthur. If Oatmire wasn't careful, he might find himself leading the first wave going ashore in the Philippines. Sure, he had said more than once that he wouldn't mind seeing combat, but in his mind's eye, he saw himself observing from a safe distance. He'd always imagined himself strolling ashore once the heavy lifting had been done and the only gunfire was off in the hills.

He flicked away his cigarette stub and began to make his way back to the bullpen.

At the top of the stairs, he was surprised to see the unwelcome figure of Major Lundholm standing in the doorway. With a sinking feeling, he realized that Lundholm had been waiting for him. *Uh-oh.* That couldn't be good.

"Oatmire, where the hell have you been?" the major wondered, scowling. "Probably flirting with those damn sheilas. I hope you don't have any hot dates, because it's time to pack your gear."

"I don't understand, sir."

"This is the army, son. What's there to understand? Anyhow, it looks like you got your wish."

"My wish, sir?" Oatmire instantly felt his belly knot with worry.

"You're going to be part of the landing on Leyte, after all, you lucky son of a bitch."

CHAPTER SIX

THE TWO JAPANESE soldiers watched intently as workers toiled to complete the defenses on the beach and beyond.

"These lazy fools must work harder!" declared Major Hisako Noguchi, watching the defensive preparations that were continuing to take place on Guinhangdan Hill, what the Americans called Hill 522, one of the anchors of the Japanese defenses on Leyte. He used his walking stick to point at one of the soldiers deepening a trench. "You there, put your back into it!"

"Perhaps you should hit them with that stick instead of just pointing it at them, sir," said Akio Ikeda, who stood beside the major, watching the work take place. The major was something of a paper tiger. If the soldier that the major had just scolded began to dig faster, it was most likely because Sergeant Ikeda stood nearby.

But Ikeda was not satisfied. He shouted at the soldier, "Dig, damn you! You will wish that trench was even deeper once the Americans land on that beach, but it will be too late by then."

The chastened soldier redoubled his efforts. Dirt flew as the shovel bit into the rocky soil. Noguchi gave a *harumph* of annoyance and turned away.

Everywhere that it was feasible, the island was being converted to a fortress. Extra attention had been given to several hills, including Hill 522, in hopes that the high ground would provide the Japanese artillery an advantage over the invading Americans.

The Japanese strategy would not be to meet the Americans on the beaches. While the landing would not be entirely unopposed, the Japanese had always seen the advantage of inland defenses.

To that end, bunkers had been built under the hills, like a massive honeycomb, over the weeks leading up to the invasion. They had been dug deep into the hillsides and reinforced when the reports indicated that the Americans were coming. And now, with the Americans approaching the island, those bunkers were being filled with men, ammunition, and grenades.

With the major's permission, Ikeda had given special attention to the creation of rifle pits. Ikeda was a *gunsō*, or sergeant. He carried a rifle with a telescopic sight. He commanded the *sogekihei* squad—men with special ability as sharpshooters. These men would be on the front lines once the American attack came, as it surely would.

In many ways, Ikeda had become the major's right-hand man. The two were as different as tea and sake. Noguchi was more of an engineer than a soldier. In fact, he had built houses and roads in civilian life before the war. His uniform always managed to appear rumpled and dusty, attesting to the fact that he was an engineer first and a soldier second, happiest when he was elbow deep in a hole somewhere.

Short and near to plump, he spent his days shoring up the defenses wherever he could. He was a familiar figure, huffing and puffing as he made his way through the network of defensive trenches on his short legs. He waved his walking stick when he became agitated, but the troops and soldiers knew that his bark was worse than his bite.

Ikeda was the one to be feared. Ikeda was definitely the sake part of the equation. When he moved through the trenches or the nearby jungle, he moved with a supple and lithe energy that more closely resembled one of Japan's fabled Tsushima leopard cats.

Also, he was never without his Arisaka rifle with its telescopic sight. There were rumors that he sometimes drank too much and sat up here on the hill, shooting Filipino laborers in the distance. Looking into his dark eyes, the rumors were easy to believe. The major might complain and cajole, but it was Ikeda who would make sure that his orders were carried out.

The two men walked on, Ikeda trailing a respectful distance at Noguchi's elbow. Noguchi was an officer, after all, and several years older. Ikeda never lost sight of the fact that the major had transformed this hilltop into a formidable fortress—Ikeda's sense of strategy was limited to what he could put his rifle sights on and shoot. There would be time for shooting soon enough. Until then they could all be thankful for Noguchi's talents, Ikeda included.

"Sir, when do you think that the Americans will arrive?"

Noguchi chuckled. "You may as well ask when the next typhoon will hit."

Thinking about the vast force that was surely arrayed against them, Ikeda decided that a typhoon was an apt analogy. Both were unstoppable forces. "We know that a typhoon will arrive sooner or later, just as we know the enemy will."

Noguchi lowered his voice, even though there was no one in the vicinity to overhear him. "I have seen the reports from the spotter planes. They have detected that the American invasion fleet is only a short distance away. One or two days, at most."

"If the spotter planes have found them, then our fleet must destroy them!" Ikeda said hotly. "Our planes must send them to the bottom of the sea!"

Noguchi sighed. "If only it were that easy. The enemy is well prepared, Sergeant. They have vast numbers of planes, and we do not —at least, not anymore. The ships carrying their troops are well screened by their destroyers, battleships, and cruisers. We can hope that the navy will crush them or that our planes will bomb them, but in the end, it will be up to us to stop them from recapturing the Philippines."

Ikeda touched his rifle. "Hai!"

"There have also been rumors of attacks on outlying island outposts," Noguchi added. "There is no doubt that the Americans are closing in. Mark my words, Sergeant. They will bring the battle to us soon."

"I do not fear the Americans. Let them come."

They both looked out at the sparkling sea. For the moment, at least, the vast blue water remained empty. Even the Japanese vessels that had been in the area seemed to have been withdrawn. It was hard for Ikeda to register how he would feel if that sea suddenly filled with American ships.

Those ships would target and shell whatever Japanese fortifications they could find, including this hill. That was exactly why Noguchi had dug the defenses so deep. Most of the hilltop had been stripped of trees, although there were still vestiges of jungle in the lower reaches. The hill somewhat resembled a bald man with a fringe of hair.

Just a short time ago, the defenses had lost some of their teeth when American raiders, helped by Filipino guerrillas, had come ashore and managed to destroy the hill's battery of massive guns. These had been intended as a deterrent to the invasion, with the ability to sink enemy ships beyond the horizon. There had also been "beehive" shells, almost like a giant shotgun blast, with the ability to sweep enemy aircraft from the skies.

However, the small group of raiders had managed to destroy the battery. It went without saying that Ikeda felt bitter that the American raiders had escaped—although a handful of guerrillas had been captured and killed. Ikeda was intrigued by the fact that at least one of the men had been a sniper, judging by the rifle with its telescopic sight that the US soldier had carried. The man hadn't worn a helmet like the others but had donned a bush hat with one side pinned up, giving him a distinctive look. Ikeda would have liked to have shown him just who the better shot was, but there had been no opportunity to settle that score. Maybe Ikeda would have a chance to do just that once the Americans invaded.

Ikeda had felt the loss bitterly as a personal loss of face. After all, it had been Ikeda and his squad who were tasked with defending the hill. Major Noguchi had been more pragmatic in the wake of the raid. He had wasted no time in clearing the wreckage of the big guns and installing a smaller artillery battery in the bunker.

"Let them come," Noguchi said with satisfaction. "The enemy will pay dearly!"

Noguchi was making no idle boast. The hill was nearly a perfect natural fortress, with the muddy Bangon River running along the base and serving as a kind of moat. The river was too deep and swift to ford. At the base of the hillside that faced the sea, separated from the hill by the river, nestled the town of Palo.

This town had been a source of frustration, especially for Ikeda, who was tasked with controlling the local guerrillas, who constantly harassed the Japanese. They were the equivalent of the French Resistance. It was clear that the guerrillas were supported by the townspeople, with many of their husbands, fathers, and brothers in the ranks. These resistance fighters knew better than to launch an all-out assault on the Japanese, but their ambush attacks interfered with the supply chain and whittled away at Japanese morale. Many small groups of Japanese soldiers who had made the mistake of traveling the jungle roads alone had disappeared.

The town was provincial, with its key feature being its centuries-old Catholic cathedral. The church was woven through the fabric of the town, and Ikeda knew that its priest supported the rebels. When Ikeda had gone to arrest him, the man had slipped into the jungle and could not be found, warned by the townspeople. Now the priest was a thorn in Ikeda's side, because he was living in the jungle with the Filipino guerrillas, providing them leadership and faith. If Ikeda ever caught that priest, there would be no mercy for a man of the cloth.

Meanwhile, Sergeant Ikeda took out his frustration on the town. He took his *sogekihei* squad door to door. Some of his men had been chosen for their ability with a rifle—he wanted a team of crack snipers —but they tended to be men who were discipline problems and that other units were more than glad to be rid of. Thanks to Ikeda, they now had the perverse sense of pride that came from being in a unit of fellow outcasts. They were also loyal to a fault.

"Spread out. You know what to do," Ikeda told them.

His men seized extra food and even blankets that might go to help the guerrillas. If a young woman was dragged into a house or hut so that the soldiers could have their way with her, so be it. Anyone who opposed them faced a severe beating. The arrival of Ikeda and his squad had become a much-feared sight on the streets of Palo. To be sure, the Japanese would not find any friends among the local Filipino population.

Ikeda joined the men checking a house. A woman answered the door, fear etched on her face.

"The guerrillas," Ikeda demanded. "Where are they?"

The woman shook her head and stammered a response that Ikeda could not understand.

Frustrated, he repeated his question, louder this time. The woman just shook her head.

One of the difficulties they faced was the language barrier. The townspeople did not know any Japanese—or at least they pretended not to. Ikeda and his men did not speak any of the local language and couldn't be bothered to learn.

The only bridge across this language gap was English. The Americans had been a presence for so long in the Philippines that most of the townspeople knew at least a little English. Many Japanese also spoke some English.

Ikeda hated to use English, because it represented Japan's enemy, but in this case it could not be avoided.

"Your man?" Ikeda asked. "Where is he?"

The woman looked surprised to hear the question in English. Without thinking, she blurted a reply, "The forest."

Ikeda nodded curtly. In his mind, the woman had just confirmed that she collaborated with the guerrillas. In one smooth motion, he raised his rifle and struck the woman hard in the face. She cried out as she crumpled and then lay on the ground without a sound.

"Search the house," he ordered his men. "Take anything of value."

Stepping over the unconscious woman, Ikeda's men hurried to ransack the house. They would gladly relieve this woman of her meager possessions and food supplies.

When she finally came to, wouldn't she be surprised?

Ikeda had his reasons for such cruelty. After the raid that had destroyed the massive battery on the hill, Ikeda had wanted to take a large force of soldiers and punish the town—possibly even by putting it to the torch. Major Noguchi had a cooler head and would not allow it.

"Anyone who supports these guerrillas will be punished," Noguchi had said. "Continue to do that, Ikeda. But show some restraint. Do not destroy the entire town, or you won't just have me to answer to. General Yamashita himself would not be pleased. We must show restraint."

Ikeda had obeyed orders, although he felt as if he had one hand tied behind his back as far as the town of Palo was concerned.

But he managed to take his revenge in other ways.

First, he had to wait for Major Noguchi to be out of the way. Although Noguchi tended to see his own men, and certainly the local Filipino laborers, more as a means to an end than as human beings, he was not overtly cruel. Ikeda had no such compunctions.

After a while, Noguchi was called elsewhere, occupied with another one of the problems that arose endlessly. He finally disappeared into the hilltop bunker that had once held the massive battery—*before the American raiders had destroyed it*, he thought bitterly.

Ikeda waved over one of his *sogekihei*, a silent man named Kazuyuki Morosawa. Although Morosawa was a good shot, Ikeda mainly appreciated the fact that Morosawa never seemed compelled to fill any silence with idle conversation. For a sniper, that could be a life-and-death quality.

Ikeda climbed higher on the hill, Morosawa following closely. Ikeda was in good shape, but the effort of climbing the steep hillside still made his heart pound. He mopped sweat from his face using a rag, then tied the rag around his head under his noncommissioned officer's hat. For what he had planned, sweat running into his eyes would be an annoyance. Morosawa was sweating just as profusely, but he didn't complain.

From up here, he had an even better view of the sparkling blue sea beyond, still blessedly empty of enemy ships. He also had an uninterrupted view of the long slope of the hillside below, where groups of men labored. This perspective of looking down on others and the heft of the rifle in his hands made Ikeda feel a little of the power possessed by a god. This must be how the Emperor himself felt. Ikeda had a high opinion of himself, but even he felt a twinge of unworthiness in comparing himself to anyone so exalted as the Emperor. Still, it was an incredible view.

However, Ikeda had not climbed up here to admire the scenery, beautiful as it was.

"Come on," he said to Morosawa. "I want to reach the top before it gets any hotter."

"Hai," the man responded.

Ikeda moved on toward his destination. Hill 522 did not rise to a single peak but had a forked or Y shape toward the summit, with one branch of the Y slightly higher than the other. From the air, pilots said that the hill resembled the tip of a lizard's forked tongue.

It was this higher branch of the hill's summit on which the cave-like bunker was located. Ikeda felt reassured that Major Noguchi was still nowhere in sight. As much as he respected Noguchi, there were things that the major didn't understand or even approve of.

The sun had climbed overhead, blazing in the humid sky almost like a light bulb swathed in cotton gauze. Ikeda found some shade in a machine-gun pit that had been carved into the slope. Netting had been strung up to provide camouflage from the marauding enemy aircraft that had begun to appear with more frequency in the skies above.

Ikeda settled into the hole and took a drink from his canteen, enjoying the shelter from the sun that the netting offered. Morosawa settled in nearby. Like Ikeda, he also carried a sniper's rifle with a tele-scopic sight, but he kept it slung over one shoulder. He knew that Ikeda would tell him if and when he needed it. The other man sat quietly, not asking any questions. Ikeda was reminded of why he liked the man.

The shade from the netting was welcome. Below, the workers laboring across the hillside were not nearly so fortunate. The tropical sun beat down mercilessly upon them. Officers cajoled and berated the men to work harder, but the heat was taking its toll. Men who couldn't keep up were sometimes kicked or hit with the sticks that the officers carried as a badge of authority.

Ikeda had no idea that Americans with their democratic ideals would have been astonished by this treatment of soldiers, but the Japanese enlisted man expected it. Japanese society had a strong class system in place, going back centuries to the era of the samurai. As part of the ruling class, officers were not to be questioned. Ikeda and his band of *sogekihei* fell somewhere outside the accepted order. They were more like ronin—ancient warriors who had served as roving mercenaries. Ikeda gave a rare smile at the thought.

The constant weeks of labor had taken their toll on the workforce below, leaving the troops exhausted, their uniforms looking worn out and dirty. Soon enough, they would still be expected to put down their shovels, pick up their rifles, and fight. It was a hard life without much to look forward to except achieving the final glory of death.

Ikeda put the rifle to his shoulder. This was a high-quality version of the standard Type 97 Arisaka rifle. Lately the rifles arriving with replacement troops had been of poor quality, made in a rush to meet wartime quotas, often using inferior materials, showing where corners had been cut in their blocky wooden stocks and roughly finished barrels and actions. His own rifle was one of the beautifully made early models that showed pride in craftsmanship.

The bolt-action rifle had been developed by its namesake, Japanese Army colonel Nariakira Arisaka, and adopted by the military in 1897. The rifle was reliable, in many ways the epitome of fine Japanese craftsmanship, but it had become somewhat dated in the intervening decades compared to the semiautomatic M1 rifles developed by the Americans.

Essentially, the rifle had changed little since its introduction, other than the fact that millions had been made for the war effort beginning in 1939.

Ikeda's version had an effective range of fifteen hundred meters, which was farther than most of the sniping done in the jungle settings of the Pacific islands. He certainly wouldn't be shooting at those ranges today—no more than a few hundred feet.

His Arisaka compared favorably to the Springfield rifle often used by US snipers, although it fired a lighter cartridge. Was one rifle better than the other? In many ways, it came down to the talents of the marksman. In Ikeda's hands, the Arisaka was definitely a deadly weapon.

He studied the laboring men through the telescopic sight. He ignored the Japanese troops, focusing his attention elsewhere.

Mixed among the Japanese were groups of local Filipino laborers. It was these men whom Ikeda watched through the telescope. These men were little more than slave laborers, pressed into service without pay.

They were mostly a pathetic rabble, several of them too feeble for hard labor. These men shuffled back and forth under their burdens. Many of the more capable younger men had slipped into the jungle to fight with the guerrillas, meaning that the Filipino laborers were mostly men past their prime or barely more than boys. They might be locals, but they were not immune to the effects of the midday sun. The heat and humidity did no one any favors. Normally the local people knew better than to work during the heat of the day—the old Spanish tradition of the siesta wasn't unknown in the Philippines.

There was no rest for these men, however. They knew there would be dire consequences if they sagged to their knees or dared to sit down. Their actions tended to slow as the heat grew, but their Japanese overseers were having none of it. If Japanese soldiers were berated, with an occasional smack with a stick or a kick in the hindquarters to serve as motivation, the Filipino laborers received far worse. They were treated cruelly by the officers and sergeants overseeing them. It was hard to say what the average Japanese soldier thought about the Filipinos—he was probably just glad that they were taking the worst of the punishment.

Nearby, Morosawa grunted with approval as they watched one of the laborers being struck with a stick. "Serves him right," Morosawa said. "Those people are useless."

"I am glad you agree," Ikeda said. "Why stop at a stick?"

"Sergeant?"

Seeing Ikeda's cold smile, Morosawa had figured out what Ikeda intended to do. For all his composure, Morosawa seemed shocked. "Are you going to shoot that man?" he asked, a little anxiously.

"Be quiet, Morosawa."

In his heart, Ikeda felt no pity for these laborers. These men were nothing more than targets.

He settled the reticule on one of the laborers swinging a pickax. Tall for a Filipino, the man had stripped off his shirt. Ikeda put the sights right between his shoulder blades and squeezed the trigger just as the man raised the pick for another swing. The rifle bucked against Ikeda's shoulder, and he watched with satisfaction through the scope as his target crumpled.

The rifle shot had not gone unnoticed. Many heads looked up the hill in Ikeda's direction, wondering who was shooting. Of course Ikeda himself was hidden in the rifle pit.

Sergeant Ikeda's next target was a group of laborers working near one of the trenches. They were loading bundles of brush over their shoulders and carrying them to the trench to be used to build low protective walls of dirt and brush. The laborers appeared to be moving at a snail's pace. Ikeda didn't know who was in charge of this group, but he suspected that it must be one of the softer officers. Several of those laborers would have benefited from a good beating.

He put the rifle sights on the last man in the line—the slowest one. Little did the man know that he had just seconds to live. It gave the sniper such a sense of power. A satisfied smile crossed Ikeda's face. He might stay up here all day, shooting to his heart's content.

But that was not to be the case. Major Noguchi appeared in the mouth of the bunker above Ikeda's position.

"Who is shooting?" he demanded.

Reluctantly, Ikeda rose from his hiding spot, wondering if perhaps he had taken things too far. Morosawa did the same.

Ikeda stood at attention and saluted the major. "Sir!"

"Sergeant Ikeda, you will stop that immediately!" For once, Noguchi appeared furious. However, it became clear that his anger was not motivated by any compassion for Ikeda's victims. "Stop shooting my laborers! We have discussed this, Ikeda. How will we get any work done if you keep shooting them?"

"Yes, sir."

"Watch out, or you will be the one using the shovel, Ikeda."

"Hai!"

Noguchi paused long enough to give Ikeda a long glare, then disappeared back into the bunker.

Ikeda shrugged off Noguchi's warning, but he decided not to press his luck by shooting at more of the laborers.

He looked down the slope. He could see the body fallen in the dirt. *Such a little man. He looks like a bundle of sticks and rags. No one will even miss him.* The laborers kept making nervous glances up the slope now that Ikeda had shown himself. Some of the officers waved their sticks in his direction, but he was too far away to hear whether they were cursing him or applauding his efforts in punishing another lazy laborer.

Once again Sergeant Ikeda had lived up to his reputation.

What reputation was that? A madman, a loose cannon, someone to be feared. Ikeda did not actually consider himself to be any of these things, but he liked keeping everyone off balance.

Then again, shooting laborers was little more than target practice. He yearned for the days to come, when he and his band of *sogekihei* snipers would have real targets once the Americans came ashore. Major Noguchi had confirmed that the reports said the Americans' arrival wouldn't be long now.

Ikeda would welcome that day. This hill was ready. He and his men were ready. With any luck, Ikeda might even be able to settle the score with the American sniper who had taken part in the raid.

CHAPTER SEVEN

FINALLY, the waiting game was over with the approach of A-Day on October 20, 1944. Along with thousands of other troops, the men of Patrol Easy would be going ashore to wrest Leyte from the Japanese.

Nobody knew yet how hard that job was going to be, but recent experience everywhere from Guadalcanal to Guam indicated that it would be no small task.

Everywhere aboard USS *Elmore*, preparations were being made. Deke had long since honed his bowie knife to a razor-sharp edge, cleaned his rifle, and prepared his gear. Philly still had his gear strewn across his bunk.

"Don't tell me you're already set to go," he grumped, when he saw Deke's neatly packed haversack.

"I was born ready."

"You know what? I believe you were."

The other members of the patrol were also still packing, but they seemed to have everything under control. They knew the drill. They had been through this before.

Rodeo was going to carry a walkie-talkie this time instead of a radio. Disastrously, he had dropped his radio into the sea during the first few minutes of their initial arrival on Leyte, during the raid. He still felt bad about it. He was carefully wrapping the walkie-talkie in layers of plastic.

Alphabet was giving his sniper rifle one last coat of gun oil. For the men, the smell of gun oil was like a tonic.

Yoshio had been ready since yesterday. He lay on his bunk, reading yet another Western novel. He was clearly so engaged in the pages that it was hard not to be a little envious of the fact that he had managed to escape the worry and fear of what was to come.

Like Yoshio, Deke's pack and rifle were long since ready. *What's done is done,* he thought. He wasn't going to fuss over his gear again and again like some old lady. He went around to see what he could do to help the others get ready.

The soldiers' packs comprised several parts. At the core was the canvas haversack, the actual pack itself that the soldiers carried. Canvas webbing formed the carrying straps. A pouch on top held the mess kit, which consisted of a two-piece frying pan and plate that locked together for carrying.

Anything that might rattle in any way was tied down with string or strips of cloth. They all knew that in the jungle, the slightest noise might give them away. The Japanese excelled at stealth, and the American GIs had learned the hard way that it paid to be silent. In more ways than one, how a man packed his gear could make the difference between life and death for himself and his buddies.

If anything was going to rattle and give them away to enemy troops, it was the mess kit. Soldiers had learned to silence it by putting rags between the pieces. Deke's solution was to throw them away and rely on a single spoon and his knife. Cold rations were just fine by him.

The bottom of the haversack was connected to the ammunition belt. Everyone was being given several stripper clips of rifle ammunition and even loose cartridges. Some of the combat veterans took what they were given and then some, knowing that the worst thing that could happen to you in the field was to run out of ammunition when you needed it most. They didn't feel comfortable heading into the field with anything less than a hundred rounds of rifle ammo, even if it meant lugging along a lot of extra weight.

Their entrenching tools ran down the outside center of the haversack. The tool was a small shovel with a short handle that ended with a T grip. In a pinch, the shovel made a good close-quarters combat weapon.

A bayonet was attached to the left side of the haversack—Deke had ditched his standard-issue bayonet in favor of the custom-made bowie knife. The snipers weren't going to attach bayonets to rifles with telescopic sights, anyhow.

He had to wear a helmet to avoid catching hell, but as soon as he could, he'd ditch that, too, in favor of the Australian bush hat that had been given to him by a grateful soldier on Guam. It was now strapped to the back of his haversack, ready to go.

Finally, the first-aid kit and all-important canteen hung from the ammunition belt. The canteen included a sort of cup that fit over its base, perfect for brewing coffee.

Deke watched Philly fretting over his pack and shook his head. Philly had a thing for gear—if he'd gotten something for free, he felt like he ought to keep it, even if he knew better by now.

"You ought to just leave the rest of that junk," Deke said. "All you need is your rifle, a canteen, and a knife."

"Spare socks won't hurt."

"All right, then. Spare socks."

"And maybe this flashlight. Might come in handy."

Deke shook his head. "What, so you can read your Bible at night? The only light you need at night is a muzzle flash."

Feeling antsy, Deke left Philly muttering to himself and went to prowl the corridors of the ship. Everywhere he looked, similar preparations were being made. In a way, packing gear was a good approach to taking your mind off what was to come in the morning, when they would be landing on a beach that the Japs very likely didn't want to give up. The preparations were a distraction. Sergeants moved among the men, making sure that everything was shipshape.

Harsh words caught Deke's attention as he passed a bunk room: "You stupid green bean! Didn't you learn anything in basic? For Chrissake!"

Curious, he paused long enough in the door to catch a glimpse of a young recruit with a chubby face. The man was wearing glasses and seemed to be surrounded by hard-bitten veterans. Most veterans didn't have any patience with the new men who had been bunked with them. Besides, every time they looked at them, they felt a pang for the fact that the new men were there to replace buddies who hadn't made it off Guam.

The other GIs looked on in disgust as the soldier tried in haphazard fashion to organize his gear. If Philly had fretted and fussed, this soldier looked helpless in comparison.

It didn't help that nothing about the young soldier inspired confidence in him winning any Medals of Honor against the forces of Imperial Japan. But the kid didn't have any choice in the matter. Ready or not, he'd be hitting the beach with everyone else in the morning.

Deke started to walk on but for some reason found himself turning back. He realized that he never did like to see anyone picked on. The new soldier had a job to do as much as any of them.

When he returned, he discovered that the other soldiers were in the middle of a fresh round of verbalizing disdain for the chubby GI.

"Who the hell let you into the army, anyhow? Your mama should have done us all a favor and—"

The soldiers fell silent when Deke entered, but not for long. "Are you lost, soldier? What the hell do you want?"

The soldier might have said more, but he shut up when Deke gave him a look. Maybe it was the scars, but something about Deke's presence could change the mood in a room. Just from the way that he carried himself, it was clear that he was a veteran.

"I reckoned that I'd help this fella sort out his gear, since you all don't seem to know your ass from a hole in the ground."

One of the veterans stepped forward. "That's big talk from a—"

Deke set his back foot and made a fist, figuring one good punch in the throat would take care of business—he never had been one to fight fair. But it didn't come to that. Before the other soldier got any closer, one of his buddies reached out to stop him.

"Hey, I recognize you," the soldier said to Deke. He didn't add that it was hard *not* to recognize Deke, what with his scars. "You're that sniper. I heard about what you did. Weren't you one of the guys who got sent in ahead? No offense, buddy."

Deke dropped his fist.

"You've already been there? What's it like?"

"'Bout the same as everywhere else. Hot, jungle thick as hair on a dog, and full of Japs."

The soldiers didn't look happy to hear it, but Deke wasn't going to sugarcoat it. "Doesn't sound good," agreed the soldier who had stopped the fight before it could happen.

"What do you think are his chances?" Deke jerked a chin at the chubby young recruit, talking about him like he was a steer up for auction.

"Flip a coin."

"Sounds about right." Deke reached for the kid's mess kit and tossed it aside. Thirty seconds later, he had cut the soldier's gear by half. Deftly, he assembled the remaining gear into a solid haversack that wouldn't rattle. He picked it up and shoved it into the other man's chest. "Here you go. At least now your pack won't get you killed."

"Thanks," the green bean managed to stammer.

Deke looked around at the other soldiers, who appeared sheepish, realizing that Deke had just done what they should have done themselves. "We're all here to fight the Japs," he said. "Just keep that in mind. Five minutes after hitting the beach, if he ain't dead, this kid is gonna be as much of a veteran as any of us."

At that, Deke turned and left. He didn't feel any better. The anxiety hadn't left him. He realized that the only cure for that would be when his boots hit the sandy beach and he was back in action.

* * *

SIMILAR SCENES WERE PLAYING out across the ship. Some wrote last-minute letters home, letters that might arrive weeks after they were dead and buried in the foreign sands.

Men were lined up to spend a few minutes with the chaplains, to get their souls right with the Lord and say a few prayers that might comfort them. It didn't matter if the men were Protestant and the chaplain was a Catholic priest, or vice versa. Prayer was prayer, and

God was God. As the old saying went, there was no such thing as an atheist in a foxhole.

The only lines that were bigger were at the heads. Every man was trying to empty his bowels before he had to do it on the beach with hot metal flying at him. The toilets were all in a row, no privacy of any kind, but the GIs were long past caring about that. They had lost their privacy the day that they enlisted.

A few of the more punctilious men were lathered up, standing at the sinks and shaving as they would before a big date. They knew that it might be their last chance at hot water and a razor for a long time.

Starting at three o'clock in the morning, the men had been roused for what was termed as the "Dead Man's Breakfast." The navy cooks had outdone themselves by serving up huge amounts of steak and eggs, fried potatoes, toast and bacon, canned juice, and coffee. The early-morning feast was intended to last the soldiers through the day. After that, they would have to rely on their rations, which was hardly an appetizing thought. The C rations had been designed with sustenance in mind, but not flavor.

The men ate in shifts at long tables, or standing up, in the strange twilight of the red lamps used to light the mess deck. The red light was designed not to interfere with their night vision, while the dimness was meant to hide them from any prowling Japanese in the air or on the water. Unfortunately, the Japanese Air Force was far from completely wrecked, and there were still threats of Betty bombers, or worse yet, new waves of kamikaze attacks that were so hard to defend against.

It was hard to say whether the lighting helped or hurt the appearance of the food. The smell of hot grease, frying potatoes, salt, and coffee was delicious enough, but not entirely welcome in the middle of the night. Some men were too queasy to have much of an appetite.

"What is this?" Rodeo griped, glaring reproachfully at the heap of scrambled eggs that had been reconstituted from powder. They had a slightly greenish cast in the dim lighting. "We don't even get fresh eggs?"

"Where would we get fresh eggs?" Alphabet pointed out. "In case you haven't noticed, we're on a ship in the middle of the ocean. Do you see many chickens around here?"

"Aw, quick your bellyaching, you two, and eat up," Philly said to the rest of Patrol Easy, which had found a space at one of the long tables. His philosophy on taking advantage of anything free that the military offered extended to the food. "There's no telling how long this chow will have to last us."

"Dead Man's Breakfast," Rodeo said.

"Don't say that. It's bad luck."

"What would make it into good luck?" Rodeo grumped. "That's what I'd like to know."

"How about you just shut up and eat your eggs? And give me that bacon if you don't want it."

Officers walked around the room, hurrying the men along to make space for more hungry soldiers.

Finally, one of the officers stood on a bench to speak. He wore combat gear just like the men, so it was clear that he would also be making the landing this morning. Sergeants barked for attention. Once the mess had quieted to a dull buzz, the officer stated: "Listen up, men. You eat while I talk."

Nobody argued with that. The men turned back to making short work of their plates while the officer spoke.

"I'm not going to lie. The Japs are ready for us. This won't be easy. But you've trained for this. A bunch of you have already taught the Japs an important lesson on Guam and maybe some other places. That lesson is that we win and they lose, no matter what."

If it hadn't now been a quarter to four in the morning, the officer might have gotten a cheer out of that one. This morning, all that he got were a few grunts of acknowledgment.

"The Filipino people have been awaiting this day for three long years. A bunch of them are US citizens, same as you. We're not going to disappoint them, are we?"

"No, sir!" a sergeant shouted into the silence. Nobody else joined in.

The officer went on, unfazed. He was a veteran of a few fights himself, and he knew that the men were listening, that they expected this pep talk. But hot coffee and bacon took precedent this morning.

He was aware that, deep down, every man already knew what he was expressing, down to his core, but somebody had to say it out loud.

"But you're not just fighting for the Filipinos. You are fighting for the United States. You are fighting for the man on your left, the man on your right. That's all I've got to say. Godspeed and good luck." He paused. "Oh, and one more thing, boys. Kill some Japs!"

At that, a cheer finally rang out. The sound escaped the ship and carried across the water, security protocols be damned. In a short time, the ships were going to make a whole lot of noise anyhow.

America was going ashore.

The men finished up and filed out of the mess. Some made a final dash for the head. Others did yet another last-minute check of their gear, making sure rifle muzzles were plugged against the salt water and sand. A BAR gunner went by, his weapon completely wrapped in plastic.

Lieutenant Steele appeared and gathered the patrol, which was attached to a company for the landing this morning.

"Good morning, boys. Everybody get enough to eat?"

"Sure did, Honcho," Philly replied. It was what they called the lieutenant instead of "sir," which would have made him a target for Japanese snipers.

"Good. Now listen up. Stick together. We're with C Company this morning. Our job is to take out any Japanese snipers in front of us or behind us. Leave the big stuff to them."

Deke gave the lieutenant a single curt nod. He knew what to do. They all did.

"Here we go."

They went down the cargo nets into the boats. Patrol Easy made it down just fine—or as well as could be expected when dangling from the side of a ship while laden with fifty pounds of gear. The ship swung gently back and forth in the ocean swell. The one who had the hardest time was Egan, and that was only because of the need to get his war dog into the boat. With the help of a sling and a couple of sturdy sailors above, Thor was lowered into the landing craft. Freed from the sling, the dog shook himself and barked a couple of times, as if to chase off the indignity of the process.

Despite the pep talk, despite all the training, some men had more trouble. They knew what was waiting for them on that beach. Once they were over the side, they couldn't seem to let go of the top of the cargo net and climb down to the boats. Nobody would have called them cowards—they knew they had to climb down, but their muscles weren't cooperating.

Sailors had been assigned to step on the soldiers' hands to force them to let go. It wasn't a job that any of them liked. More than once, they had to look down into the fearful, pleading face of a young soldier who was stuck fast to the top of the net. A soldier who might, or might not, live to see the sun come up. But they had their orders. The warrant officers were shouting at them to do their jobs.

The foot came down, making the young soldier let go.

Once full, the landing craft did not go racing toward the shore. Not yet. Instead, the landing craft drifted around the ship, like ducklings around a mother duck. Thankfully it was calm enough that only a few men managed to get seasick.

"What's the holdup?" Philly demanded.

"You know how it goes," Steele replied. "Hurry up and wait. Save your griping for the Japs."

Although it was warm and humid, there was a slight salt breeze that cooled everyone in the boats. Later in the day, the rising sun would make the heat nearly unbearable, but for now it was quite pleasant. Boat motors muttered all around them in the darkness, mingling exhaust fumes with the salty air. Every now and then the breeze brought clean air filtered by a thousand miles of ocean, and Deke inhaled deeply, almost understanding how some men loved the sea in the way that he loved the mountains. *Give me the land any day.*

The surface of the sea was soon crisscrossed by the wakes of the landing craft as they circled the mother ships. This was no pleasure cruise for the thousands of troops in the smaller boats. The navy had simply been waiting for the landing craft to be loaded before clearing the decks for action.

On ships all across the invasion fleet, the big guns opened up. Long trails of flame cut across the predawn sky, the flashes reflected on the calm early-morning waters of the sea. They could see the shock waves roil the surface. Men on the boats shielded their ears from the deafening noise, but the sound carried deep into their bones.

From the boats, they could just see the dark, brooding lump of land, a darker smudge on the horizon. Soon they had no trouble seeing it because the incoming shells rained down and exploded. Glowing mushrooms of flame sprouted all along the shore.

The naval barrage was an awesome sight, and any man who witnessed it would never forget that morning until the end of his days. The display of firepower was intended to wipe out any Japanese shore defenses. All that destruction was reassuring, and the men in the boats suddenly felt better.

"Good morning, Hirohito!" Philly shouted. "Bow to that, you son of a bitch!"

The boats turned and slowly picked up speed as they nosed into the waves, heading for the fire-laced shoreline.

The invasion of Leyte had begun.

CHAPTER EIGHT

In the boats, nobody had much to say, each man alone with his thoughts. The silence was broken only by the occasional shouts of the sergeants and officers. It was the way that men had been going into battle since the dawn of time. Although they were part of a massive army, they had to face their fears individually. *Will I be brave or will I be a coward? Will I live to see tomorrow? If the Japs do get me, I just hope it's quick.*

Deke glanced over at Philly, whose broad face remained expressionless. He gave Deke a nod that seemed to say, *Here we go again.*

Deke nodded back, his face grim. Then again, it was usually grim. Deke never had been the happy-go-lucky sort.

He wriggled his toes inside his boots, eager for the feel of land under his feet. He was sick of boats.

The landing craft were beginning their sprint from the ships to the shoreline. There was a considerable stretch of open water to cross because the coral reefs reaching out from shore prevented the ships from entering the shallows near land.

In the invasion-planning stage, it had been determined that there would be water deep enough for most of the landing craft to get in close to the beach—emphasis on "most." This was why the landing had been set for high tide, in hopes that the vessels could float right over the reefs. Nonetheless, it was a given that in some places the coral would be too close to the surface, and the troops would be forced to wade for shore. This was less than optimal, exposing them even longer to enemy fire while making their way through the surf.

On their run toward shore, the landing craft would be vulnerable while crossing that open water. The bombardment from the ships was intended to provide cover for the smaller vessels. For the most part, that tactic was more than effective.

Motors roaring, the flotilla of landing craft rushed toward shore. They were large, ungainly craft that wouldn't be confused anytime soon with sleek speedboats, looking more like floating shoeboxes, yet they managed to kick up a wake.

In the twilight before dawn, the sea had begun smooth as glass, almost picture perfect as the light slowly softened in preparation for another Pacific sunrise. Now dozens of wakes churned the surface.

For many reasons, from the heat and humidity to the presence of the Japanese, this part of the world seemed inhospitable to men more used to the temperate climates of Ohio or Virginia or Massachusetts, but none of them could deny that the sunrises and sunsets were spectacular when the conditions were right.

Shells screamed overhead, sending shivers up the spines of the soldiers in the boats. Artillery was never a sound they were going to get used to, even when the guns were friendly. The truly big guns were farther out, where a handful of destroyers and even a cruiser had joined the symphony like a rhythm section of kettle drums.

Despite all the noise, Philly was an irrepressible conversationalist, as usual.

"I'm just glad they're on our side," he shouted above the din of the big guns and the roaring boat motor. "I wouldn't ever want those navy boys to rain misery down on our heads."

"Yeah, it's almost enough to make you feel sorry for the Japs," Deke agreed. "Well, *almost*. The more I think about it, I'm kind of glad to see the navy boys beat the tar out of the Japs."

On Guam, many of the men recalled being on the receiving end of Japanese mortar fire, artillery, even tanks. There was nothing so frightening, such a helpless feeling, as cowering in a foxhole as enemy shells rained down, and it was not something they'd forget anytime soon.

Given the awesome firepower from the navy ships, the return fire from the Japanese was almost nonexistent, hushed by the sheer, overwhelming force of the big US guns.

That silence did not last for long.

High up on Hill 522, that Japanese bastion that Patrol Easy knew all too well from its earlier "visit," flashes filled the air as enemy artillery opened fire. That seemed to be a signal for other enemy artillery units, which also began to return fire.

Splashes erupted in the water all around them. From shore, there began a stream of machine-gun fire, the brilliant blue streaks stitching the air just above the water. The Nambu machine guns had an uncomfortably long range, reaching out to the incoming landing force. Streaks of red tracers answered from the American side.

The Japs were putting on quite a show, but deep in the belly of the landing craft, it was hard to see what was going on. These substantial vessels protected the men from rifle shots and even the machine guns that managed to reach out this far to sea.

They could hear the insistent ping of bullets hitting the metal sides. However harmless that fire might be as it bounced off the heavily built sides of the landing craft, it still sent shivers down Deke's spine as a reminder of what was to come.

Of course there was always some fool who had to climb up the side of the boat to see what was going on. Sure enough, some idiot of a green bean made his way to the gunwale of the landing craft and peered over. It was as if he didn't believe the bullets were real.

"Get down, you dumb son of a bitch!" shouted Lieutenant Steele. "Do you want to get your head blown off?"

But the warning came too late. One of the bullets found the soldier, who tumbled back into the mass of men below, dead before he landed.

"Get him off me, get him off me!" a soldier screamed as the dead man's arms managed to wrap around him like a grasping, lifeless rag doll.

"Oh, for the love of Pete," Steele muttered. He raised his voice.

"The rest of you keep your damn heads down. No sense letting the Japs thin us out before we even get there."

"Yeah, they'll do plenty of that once we get to the beach," Philly pointed out.

"Put a cork in it, Philly," Steele grumbled. "Nobody needs to hear that."

Someone propped the dead man to one side, where his body rolled back and forth as the boat went up and down in the waves.

While the men in the boats were relatively protected from the random rifle fire and machine-gun bursts that managed to reach out from shore, the same was not true of the artillery rounds that struck all around with increasing frequency, sending up geysers of spray.

A few men around Deke started to pray out loud. Who the hell could blame them? A couple more bent over and vomited, either from seasickness or out of sheer fright. Normally, during a training exercise, this would've brought curses and rebukes from the other men, but this morning, they barely even seemed to notice.

The stink of vomit drifted up and mixed with the smell of diesel exhaust, salt spray, and sweat as the landing craft continued rushing to shore and whatever was awaiting them on the beach.

Not more than two hundred yards away, one of the Japanese shells struck true and hit one of the landing craft. The initial blast blew a hole in the bottom, letting in the sea. Flames raced across the craft as the fuel caught fire. As it started to sink swiftly into the waters of Leyte Gulf, the men aboard who had survived the artillery explosion and the flames had no choice but to leap overboard and swim for shore.

Many didn't get far. It was no easy task to swim when you were encumbered by a pack, a rifle, and so much other equipment. Other men found themselves in the water before they had time to shed their gear. More than one man sank like a stone and disappeared. You could hear their final screams for help, sharp and frantic, cutting through the sounds of boat engines and artillery.

No help came. The pilot at the wheel of their own landing craft had made no effort to slow down or circle back to pick up any survivors. They struggled to swim in the wakes kicked out by the passing landing craft.

"We ought to stop the boat and help those poor bastards," Philly said, giving voice to what every man was thinking.

"We're under orders not to stop," Steele said. "We'd be sitting ducks out here. It would only be a matter of time before we'd end up just like them."

As if to prove the lieutenant's point, another splash threw spray into the open boat as a shell dove into the sea nearby.

Philly swore. "I get the picture, Honcho. Doesn't mean I like it."

"Listen, if we get hit, the best thing to do is swim away from the boat," Steele said. "It's nothing but a big metal tub. If the Japs put a hole in this tub, it's going straight to the bottom and taking everybody inside with it. Get some distance from the boat and then swim for shore."

Those words *swim for shore* were not reassuring to Deke. The lieutenant might as well have said *fly to the moon*. He tightened his grip on his rifle, then decided to sling it crosswise over his chest. If he went in the water, his arms would be freed up so that he could at least try to swim. He'd cut his pack loose. As long as he had his rifle and his knife, he'd have a fighting chance once he got to shore.

From the glimpses that he'd had, Deke could see that it was still a long way to shore. A lot farther than he wanted to swim, considering how much he disliked the water to begin with.

He would much rather run across a mile of open ground under heavy fire than be forced to swim half that distance on a calm sunny day with nothing more awaiting him on shore but a soft towel and a cool drink. But as the mountain people said back home, you made soup with what was in the pot.

For now the landing craft carrying Patrol Easy and the rest of the company seemed to be leading a charmed life. The driver had started to zig and zag as much as possible to create a more elusive target for the Japanese gunners. The problem was that the other landing craft were all doing the same thing. Considering that they were not spread far apart, colliding with another vessel became a real hazard.

Some of the men shouted a warning as another landing craft came within spitting distance, then veered away. A geyser appeared in the space that had suddenly opened up between the two vessels. A few seconds earlier and the Japanese gunner would have gotten the two-for-one special.

"I guess we should have done a better job taking out that Japanese fort," Philly said, referring to the raid on Hill 522.

"Just be glad we knocked out those really big guns," Deke replied. "Otherwise I reckon they'd be doing to the cruisers and the rest of the ships what they're doing to us right now."

Those ships hadn't fallen silent and were still pouring fire down upon the beach and hillsides, wherever a Japanese gun revealed itself with a bright stab of flame. The morning light was growing so that the ships and the landing craft were becoming easier targets for the enemy.

At the same time, as the details of the shoreline became more visible, the heavy vegetation gave nothing away about the Japanese positions, but only delineated the jungle, mountains, and the well-defended obstacles, such as Hill 522, that the soldiers would face once ashore.

As their landing craft motored closer, the rate of fire increased. The Japs were throwing everything they had against the boats. More bullets rang against the metal sides. A few feet off to Deke's left was the ladder leading up to the helm. He looked up to see how the helmsman was faring in the angry maelstrom of fire.

It wasn't a job Deke envied. The helm sat up high enough to enable the pilot to steer a path through the waves. At the same time, that higher position made the helm a target. Each pilot did have partial metal shielding that provided at least some protection. But the man needed nerves of steel, because he was exposed almost directly to the enemy fire. As they came in range of the beach itself, the small-arms fire became more worrisome. Individual bullets began to ping like deadly hail off the pilot's metal shield. Say what you wanted about the Japs, Deke thought, but there was nothing wrong with their marksmanship.

Some of the soldiers envied the pilot because he wouldn't be going ashore. But there was no denying that the pilot was in the line of fire. The pilot ducked down but kept the vessel on track, brave son of a bitch that he was.

Suddenly the pilot slumped. He'd been hit. Deke stared in amazement. In his opinion, that bullet had been too precise to have been a lucky shot. One in a million. His mind went to the Japanese sniper they'd run into on Leyte. It was just the kind of shot that a sniper like that might make.

After all, it was exactly what Deke would have done in an enemy sniper's shoes—target the incoming boat pilots. It made him uncomfortable to consider that he and the Japanese snipers shared similarly devious minds.

For a few moments the boat forged ahead into the waves, but its path to shore could not continue for long without someone at the helm. The course of the vessel began to veer wildly into an arc, cutting across the paths of other incoming landing craft. Soon the boat bucked like a riderless horse as they turned sideways into the waves. The men in the craft lost their footing and stumbled against one another.

The deck had gone all *si goggly*, which was the mountain people's word for something off kilter and unbalanced. He and Philly fell together, doing an awkward dance as they struggled to keep their balance. Adding to the pandemonium was the fact that more and more men around them were becoming seasick. All that food they had eaten at breakfast was making its return—and not in a good way.

The nauseating smell seemed to make seasickness contagious. Deke wrinkled his nose and felt the bile rising in his own belly, but he tried to ignore it. He focused on the situation at the helm. Somebody needed to steer this boat.

Above them, another sailor grabbed for the helm, but he was also shot down—helping to confirm Deke's theory that a Japanese sniper was responsible. For a fleeting moment, he considered getting into position so that he could shoot back, but the prospect of hitting anything from the wildly bucking vessel wasn't promising.

He looked around, wondering what the hell else he could do.

It just so happened that Deke was one of the soldiers closest to the ladder that led up to the platform that the helmsman had occupied. Nobody else seemed to be paying attention to what was going on at the helm, because they were too busy being thrown around the boat.

"Who the hell is driving this thing?" Philly demanded as he tugged and pulled at Deke, who was doing the same back to him. "It's like the pilot had a few drinks this morning. Either that or he's got it in for us dogfaces."

"There's nobody at the helm," Deke tried to explain, but he doubted Philly even heard him.

Together he and Philly somehow had an equilibrium that kept them on their feet while other men were tossed willy-nilly around the boat. Some men were getting bruised up pretty good when slamming against the metal interior.

Deke kept hoping that someone else—anybody but him—would go up that ladder to the helm, but everyone else seemed preoccupied with staying on their feet despite the wild motions of the pilotless craft. Lieutenant Steele was busy shouting at everyone, trying to keep order while struggling to stay on his feet.

"Dammit all to hell," Deke said. He turned to Philly. "Watch my gear, will you?"

"Watch your—where the hell do you think you're going?"

Deke didn't have time to explain. He reached for the ladder leading to the deserted helm. Before starting up, he shrugged out of his pack. The boat pitched wildly, but he managed to climb the rungs, even when his feet kept slipping off.

Deke knew less about boats than the average soldier, and he didn't want to know any more, but he reckoned that he could steer the thing. Somebody had to do it.

A shell plunged into the sea not more than fifty feet away. If the Japanese gunner's aim had been a little better, Deke's efforts would have been for naught. They'd have been a smear of burning flotsam and jetsam on the surface of the sea.

He reached the helm, but there wasn't a lot of space, and he had to shift one of the bodies out of the way. Easier said than done—the dead man was heavy as a sack of feed corn. In Deke's experience, there was nothing heavier than a dead man.

The body of the dead helmsman finally slid out of the way. *Sorry about that, fella.*

Deke barely had time to feel bad about it, though. Keeping his head down—just in case that Japanese sniper still had them in his sights—Deke reached for the controls and straightened out the vessel's course. He soon had the vessel running right for shore instead of sideways to the beach and foundering in the waves. Deke didn't know what he was steering for, but he figured that as long as he could run the landing craft up on the beach, hopefully not tearing the bottom out on the coral reef in the process, then they would be doing just fine.

It was a big beach, after all, and an even bigger island. Pretty hard to miss.

Then again, the helmsman had understood how to zigzag so that the landing craft made a more difficult target. Deke supposed that the best he could do was run straight for shore. As far as he was concerned, the sooner they were off the water, the better. The Japs were tearing them up out there.

Lieutenant Steele spotted Deke at the helm and gave him the "OK" symbol. Philly spotted him and shook his head in disbelief. No matter —the boat was now heading in the right direction. So far, so good. Deke was actually managing to drive this boat.

Deke realized that he had been holding his breath. With a sigh of relief, he let it out.

But Deke's relief was premature.

Deke had no way of knowing it, but up on Hill 522, the Japanese gunner was adjusting his sights. The gunners were skilled and had practiced on floating targets on this very stretch of sea. The previous round had fallen short by a few dozen feet. The artilleryman wasn't going to make the same mistake again.

The next shot hurtled from the Japanese position.

The landing craft took a direct hit.

CHAPTER NINE

ONE MOMENT DEKE was at the helm, but an instant later he found himself thrown through the air. He hit the water with a shock that forced the breath out of him. He took a gulp of sea water that made him choke and sputter, the salt water burning his throat and nose like acid. If he'd been knocked senseless like some of the other soldiers, he wouldn't have stood a chance.

Deke's survival instincts kicked in automatically. His legs kicked and his arms scrabbled at the water. At first he didn't even know which way was up and which way was down, but his brain dimly differentiated that he should flail in the general direction of the brighter water.

Deke surfaced, sputtering, coughing, and desperately trying to catch his breath. It had all happened so fast that he was completely disoriented. It took a moment to register what had happened.

All around him other men struggled to stay afloat. Every last man had gone into the water. The shell must have split the landing craft wide open.

Deke had already shed his pack before trying to reach the helm, but other men weren't so lucky. Some clawed their way to the surface, only to be dragged back down by the sheer weight of their gear. Essentially they found themselves drowning not once, but twice. The ones who had the presence of mind to do so managed to free themselves from their packs, but it wasn't easy to do in the water. There were too many straps to get your arms through. Others panicked and quickly sank into the depths for good. Some were burdened with their rifles. It went against an infantryman's every instinct and training to let go of his rifle, even when it was a matter of survival.

Considering how much he disliked the ocean, it was Deke's worst nightmare. He could see the shore from where he floundered in the sea. The beach couldn't have been more than two hundred yards distant, just beyond where the surf foamed on the coral. Already the strongest swimmers were heading ashore. When Deke bobbed up on a wave, he spotted the figures of men crossing the coral shallows, where other landing craft had taken them as far as they could. A few soldiers had even reached the beach itself and thrown themselves flat in the sand, returning the Japanese fire. But to a man struggling in the water, all that looked like a million miles away. Keeping his head above water was the only concern.

Dear Lord. Don't let me drown.

He looked around in the water for any sign of Philly, Yoshio, or anybody else from the squad. The last time that he had seen Yoshio had been just to one side of Philly, lost in his own thoughts. Lieutenant Steele had been caught up in trying to manage the chaos as the vessel veered out of control, right before Deke had taken the helm. Where he'd ended up was anybody's guess.

Rodeo and Alphabet, along with Egan and his new war dog, had been mixed in there somewhere. He just hoped to hell that they had all been thrown clear rather than trapped in the wreckage of the landing craft. Trying to find them at this point would be impossible. The best that he could hope for was that they had survived and would regroup on shore.

Foundering in the waves, the vessel was going down fast. Already it was half-submerged, with the incoming waves washing over the twisted metal. Toward what had been the stern, angry orange flames danced on the hulk and spread out over the water. Screams indicated that the flames had come for a few of the survivors.

That Japanese shell had done a number on the landing craft. A few bodies floated on the water. *Those poor sons of bitches.* For these men, the invasion had ended almost before it had gotten started.

But Deke was alive and he wanted to stay that way.

There were other nearby swimmers, struggling like Deke to stay afloat. Even if they had shed their gear, the weight of a waterlogged uniform, water-filled combat boots, and a steel helmet made treading water difficult. Some lost their fight against the sea and disappeared under the surface for good, leaving barely a ripple.

Deke was keeping his head above water, but he wasn't sure how long he could keep that up. On the landing craft, he had swapped out his helmet for the bush hat. The chin strap had gotten wrapped around his neck, keeping him from losing the hat. Although he wasn't burdened by a pack, the weight of his clothing alone weighed him down.

Desperately, he looked around in the wreckage for something to help keep him afloat. Most of it was useless trash, unidentifiable bits and pieces. Finally he spotted just what he was looking for—a life vest. The soldiers had not been issued the kapok-filled life vests, so this one must have been intended for the navy crewmen piloting the landing craft. Sadly, the pilot wouldn't be needing it.

The vest was charred, and one of the kapok chambers was already soggy, but for Deke it was literally a lifesaver. He clutched at it and started for shore.

He had managed just a few awkward strokes when he heard the desperate shouting coming from the wreckage.

"Help! Please, somebody help! I'm trapped!"

It went against all of Deke's instincts to swim back toward the wreckage rather than toward shore, using up his limited reserves of strength. But if he could help, he would. He couldn't think of a worse fate than being trapped among the twisted steel and going down with the ship.

Paddling through the water, he reached the sinking vessel. The burning pool of fuel seemed to be spreading and moving in his direction, which was worrisome. He nudged aside a man floating facedown in the water, then came face-to-face with the man who had been doing the shouting.

Instantly he recognized the eyeglass-wearing green bean whose shipmates had been giving him a hard time about packing his gear. The green bean's head and shoulders were out of the water, mainly because his feet must have been supported by the wreckage of the vessel. But if that twisted metal was keeping him from sinking—at least for the moment—it also kept him trapped.

"I can't free my legs," the green bean said. "Something has got them pinned."

"Maybe I can pull you," Deke said.

Deke grabbed the soldier's arms and tugged, but it was awkward because he couldn't get any leverage in the water. Deke gave up and let go. The vessel was settling lower. Already the water was up to the young soldier's chin.

"It's no use," the soldier said. From behind the lenses of his water-streaked glasses, he looked at Deke with a calm stare. "Get out of here before you get sucked down."

"I ain't leaving yet," Deke said stubbornly. He unslung the rifle and shoved it toward the green bean, along with the charred kapok vest. "Hold these."

There wasn't much that frightened Deke, but what he did next was terrifying. *I must be a damn fool.* He took a couple of deep breaths and slipped his head under the surface. It took some nerve to keep it there. He could hear the underwater sounds of the vessel popping and creaking as it went down. He forced himself to open his eyes, even though the salt water stung. He needed to see what he was doing.

He followed the soldier's legs down. Sure enough, a metal strut had fallen across the soldier's shins, pinning him in place against the side of the landing craft. Deke couldn't identify what role the strut had played because it was hard to make any sense of the wreckage.

And no wonder. He could see a jagged hole where a piece of shrapnel had torn through the vessel's hull. If the shell had struck another couple of feet closer, the green bean wouldn't have had any legs to worry about.

Deke grabbed hold of the strut and tugged, but it didn't budge. He saw that the trouble was that he was coming at it from too high up and couldn't get any leverage.

It was clear what he had to do next if he had any hope of freeing the soldier. Inwardly he groaned. Once again going against every instinct, he sank deeper into the sea until he could get his own feet braced against the steel sides of the vessel. He grabbed hold of the strut. Already he could feel himself running out of air. The wreckage lurched around him, settling lower in the water. He was only going to get one chance at this.

Once again he pulled for all he was worth. At first nothing happened. Deke put his legs into it, the effort forcing out the last of the air in his lungs. Then ever so slowly the strut moved.

Half an inch. That was it, and it wasn't enough. The soldier was still pinned.

Deke's lungs screamed for oxygen. He tugged. Another half an inch.

This time it did the trick. The young soldier wiggled his legs free, and Deke clawed toward the surface.

He came up, gasping for air, but his wet uniform and heavy boots threatened to pull him back down.

The young soldier was gripping the charred life vest. He got one arm around Deke. The tables had turned.

"I've got you," he said.

Together they started toward shore. It turned out that the chubby young soldier was a strong swimmer, his ample baby fat helping to keep him afloat and masking what must have been muscular arms and legs. The soggy life vest was better than nothing.

He gave a few final kicks. Deke was relieved to feel the solid coral under his feet, so much so that he could almost ignore the bullets zinging past them. They reached the sandy shore and flung themselves into a shell hole, finding what shelter they could. Most of an intact company seemed to be doing the same thing in other holes nearby. Deke didn't know who they were, and he didn't much care.

The naval bombardment had abated once the invasion force reached the coral reef. It had left behind a beach that looked as if it had been plowed by a drunken giant. Shattered trees from the line of jungle at the edge of beach were strewn far across the sand. However, the bombardment hadn't seemed to do much to dampen the Japanese defenses. Machine-gun fire zinged through the air above the sand. The sharp crack of rifle fire filled Deke's ears.

"I'm Dickie Shelby, by the way." The green bean made the introduction as if they were at a church picnic, not on a beach with hot lead flying. Private Shelby seemed on the verge of sticking out his hand, but he thought better of it when he saw Deke's look.

"Don't care," Deke said.

"You're that sniper fella. You helped me pack back on the ship. I heard about you. What are you gonna do now?"

"I'm gonna go kill some Japs, that's what. So are you. That's why we're here, you know."

"How do we do that?" the green bean asked.

"Keep your head down. Stick with this company. Listen to the sergeant. Do what you're told if a veteran like me tells you to do it. He'll be trying to keep you alive. I didn't save your ass to have you get killed in the first five minutes of being on this beach."

The green bean nodded. Deke got the sense that he was going to be all right.

"What about you?" the soldier asked.

Deke patted his rifle, which had made it to shore wet but functional. The Springfield could take a lot of punishment—and give plenty too. "I'm gonna shoot some Japs, that's what. Good luck."

CHAPTER TEN

DEKE LEFT him there and went in search of Patrol Easy—hoping against hope that at least someone had survived the sinking of the landing craft. He hadn't seen any of them in the water, which wasn't surprising, given the chaos of the sinking. He refused to believe that they were all gone.

He ran down the beach, keeping at a crouch, running parallel to the surf line. Once or twice he had to step over a dead soldier. He tried to stay below the sandy ledge that had been cut by some previous storm, because it offered cover from the Japs in the tree line. They were watching, all right, because whenever his head popped above the sandy shelf, a flurry of bullets kicked up sand. No matter how many shells had been thrown at the beach, it hadn't seemed to do a bit of good. They had hidden themselves away like spiders in a woodpile, only to come out when the barrage ended.

He followed his own advice and kept his head down.

Everywhere he looked, it was pandemonium. This sector was known as Red Beach, and it had encountered heavy Japanese resistance. What the men here didn't know was that other landing zones had been uncontested or very nearly so, with soldiers coming ashore with little or no enemy fire to greet them. It was luck of the draw, considering that other units had gotten off easy, and their only choice was to fight back and eliminate the enemy threat.

Staying on the beach wasn't an option. The Japs would just pick them off.

Part of the issue was that Hill 522 served as an anchor for Japanese resistance on this stretch of beach. Even without the battery that Patrol Easy had eliminated, Hill 522 remained a veritable fortress.

Deke ran along the shore without any destination in mind, hoping that he would spot another member of Patrol Easy. He didn't see anybody. Maybe he should have gone in the other direction? Then again, maybe nobody else had made it off the wrecked landing craft. For now, he pushed that thought from his mind.

Sand had stuck to his wet uniform and even his boots, adding extra weight and effort to every step.

Feeling winded, Deke realized that his efforts to find any survivors from his patrol might be futile. The loss would be a bitter pill to swallow. They had endured so much together that he didn't dare to think of them as dead. Philly, Yoshio, Rodeo, Alphabet, Egan, and his new war dog, and even Lieutenant Steele, who seemed indestructible in Deke's mind. Maybe he should have tried to find them in the wreck instead of helping that useless four-eyed green bean.

"Dammit!" he shouted in frustration.

He still held out hope. The alternative was too awful to contemplate. But for now he had to make sure that he lived through the next ten minutes on this beach.

He decided to attach himself to a group of soldiers that was rallying around an officer. The man could be heard shouting orders even above all the fireworks on the beach.

To Deke's surprise, he saw that the officer wore a camouflage uniform. It was none other than Colonel Woodall. Some of his sniper squad was spread along the sand. Their bravado from the ship was gone, however. Most of them had their heads down, too scared to move.

Deke didn't blame them. This wasn't shooting at paper targets on the firing range. These men might be well equipped, and they might even be crack shots, but they had never been under fire before. Instead of shooting back at the Japs, they kept their faces buried in the sand.

Woodall was having none of it. This assault on the beach wasn't his first rodeo. He screamed at the men to fight. He appeared to be a brave son of a bitch, but foolhardy. He stood up and waved the soldiers forward.

"Get off this beach!" he shouted. "If we don't get off this beach, we're going to die here. The Japs will chew us to pieces."

His warning was punctuated by a fresh burst of machine-gun fire. The Japs had gotten some of their knee mortars into play, and they were now walking their fire closer to the sandy shelf where the troops were taking cover.

Colonel Woodall grabbed a man by the shoulder and shoved him forward. After a couple of dazed steps, the man figured it out and ran toward the tree line. Other soldiers started to get the message and began to rush toward the tree line, where the beach sand ended and the jungle began. At least there was cover there. It was also where the Japanese were hidden, and it would be up to the soldiers to push them out.

Deke saw the officer standing tall despite the bullets spitting at the sand around his feet. There was brave, and there was foolish. *Get down,* Deke silently urged him.

Too late.

Colonel Woodall spun around, clipped by a bullet. He fell back onto the sand.

Deke ran over to see if he could do anything for Woodall. To Deke's relief, the bullet appeared to have grazed Woodall's shoulder with enough force to knock him off balance, but it hadn't done any serious damage.

"Sir, are you all right?"

Woodall looked up and recognized Deke instantly. "You're one of Steele's snipers. What are you doing here, soldier?"

"Lost my unit, sir. The landing craft got hit."

Deke began helping Woodall to his feet, but the colonel shook him off.

"I'm all right. Never mind about me. Start shooting some Japs."

Incredibly, Woodall managed a small smile. "Private, just remember that they're not seagulls."

"Yes, sir."

Side by side, they sheltered behind a sand ledge and studied the tree line ahead. Most of the enemy fire appeared to be coming from a single spot.

"Those Japs can sweep the whole beach from that point," Woodall said. "They've got us pinned down."

"They must have a pillbox set up."

"We'll have to rush them."

"I may have a better idea, sir."

Deke set his rifle across the sand, aiming at the muzzle flashes. The gunners themselves were well hidden, but it was clear enough where he had to shoot. The gunner would be right behind the gun, aiming down the beach. As he watched, a trail of tracers sizzled across the beach, and the fresh burst of unseen bullets churned up the sandy ledge where the troops had taken shelter.

Deke squeezed off a round, worked the bolt, fired again. The machine gun fell silent. Although there was still plenty of fire from hidden rifle pits, the biggest threat had been from the machine gun.

Woodall sprang up again. He shouted at his men: "Go! Go! Get the hell off this beach!"

Deke didn't need to be told twice. He wanted to get into the jungle itself, where there was cover, instead of being stuck out here in the open. It might only be a matter of time before the Japs got another man on that machine gun or they managed to zero in on those mortars.

He sprang up and ran for the trees, screaming a bloodcurdling rebel yell. The rest of the soldiers followed.

The colonel had stayed behind, forcing reluctant men to their feet and urging them forward. The men weren't all his scouts, but soldiers from units who had gotten mixed up in the confusion of the landing. No matter—the colonel was getting them into the fight.

Deke reached the trees and got in among them, rifle at the ready. He spotted a Japanese infantryman falling back to another spider hole and shot him between the shoulder blades. He worked the bolt just in time because another Japanese appeared. This one ran right at Deke, screaming bloody murder. He was so close that Deke could see his angry, contorted face. The Japs were shorter and smaller than the Americans, but that didn't make them any less dangerous. This one also had a bayonet on the end of his rifle. He looked eager to sink the pointy end into the nearest American.

Deke shot him in the chest. The Japanese soldier went to his knees but was still moving, so Deke shot him again for good measure. This time the enemy soldier lay still. Deke kicked his rifle away, just in case.

He pressed deeper into the trees, moving more slowly and cautiously. The enemy fire seemed to have slackened, but that didn't mean this sector wasn't crawling with Japs. He knew from experience that their preferred tactics included keeping hidden until the American troops had gone by, and then ambushing them from behind. They were sneaky bastards, every last one of them.

Now that he was in among the trees and jungle growth, he marveled at the sheer amount of destruction. The naval bombardment had shattered trunks and torn the undergrowth asunder. It looked as if the worst hurricane you could imagine had swept through, turning trees into matchsticks. Everything had been chewed up and spit out.

Many of the trees closest to the beach were palms, now missing most of their fronds so that they resembled irregularly spaced telephone poles. Similar to Guam, the forests on Leyte were substantial, with massive hardwoods climbing up the slopes farther inland. The hurricane winds of the bombardment had still managed to shatter and twist these sturdier trees.

And yet the bombardment had not been enough to entirely thwart the Japanese defending the beach itself. They had either been dug in deep, unaffected by anything but a direct hit, or they had rushed into position as soon as the bombardment stopped.

The navy had put on one hell of a fireworks show, Deke thought, but in the end it hadn't amounted to a hill of beans.

He looked around and detected motion among the trees. In his frenzy to get at the Japs, he had outpaced the rest of the soldiers. Now, among the shattered trunks, he could see other GIs doing the same thing as him, cautiously advancing.

Take a step. Look around. Take another step. Rifle at the ready. See a hole?
Lob a grenade or empty a clip into it. Keep going.

The sight of more American soldiers reassured him. He was no longer out here alone. Maybe, just maybe, they had taken the beach.

With the worst of the Japanese threat eliminated, Deke decided that he'd done his job for now. Colonel Woodall led his company, including his scouts, deeper into the jungle.

"Spread out, men," he heard Woodall shout. "Keep five-yard intervals. Don't make it any easier for the sons of bitches."

Considering what a target Woodall had been on the beach, Deke was a little surprised to see that he was still alive. Not only was he brave, but he was lucky.

That didn't mean Deke was going to stick with this unit. He still hadn't given up hope that he could find somebody from Patrol Easy. The Japs in this section had been cleared out, so Deke turned around and headed back toward the beach. A couple of other GIs he passed gave him a look because the only men going to the rear were wounded, but they didn't say anything. There weren't any sergeants or officers close enough to give him a hard time. Other than Woodall, Deke realized that maybe the other officers were all dead.

Deke retraced his path, knowing that it was probably the route least likely to have any hidden Japs. On the way he passed the two Japs he'd shot. At first the enemy soldiers resembled bundles of rags rather than dead men. The dead always looked smaller, but these dead Japanese looked almost childlike, much smaller than the American soldiers.

He tried to register some emotion as he stepped around the Japanese bodies and realized that he didn't feel a damn thing. Well, that wasn't quite true. What he did feel was anger. They were the ones who had started this war in the first place. They were the reason that so many Americans were already dead on this beach—them and their emperor, Hirohito. Deke wouldn't mind getting *him* in his sights.

Back on the beach, more men and material were being ferried ashore. The Japanese fire hadn't been entirely suppressed. Shells still splashed into the sea. Rifle shots still rang out. From time to time, sniper fire claimed a stretcher bearer or officer. Perhaps out of sheer perversity, the Japanese snipers loved to target stretcher bearers. It didn't make any damn sense to Deke.

High up on Hill 522, Japanese artillery still fired, dropping a few shells on the beach but mainly targeting the incoming craft. Before long somebody would have to take that hill. Deke pitied the poor bastards who got sent up there. He had seen those defenses and knew that it wouldn't be an easy fight. The entire hill was one big fortress. If they hadn't seen many Japs near the beach, he suspected that it was because they were all up on that hill, dug in and waiting for the Americans.

Despite the sniper fire and occasional shells, supply depots were already being established. The army organization of beachheads was like a well-oiled machine at this point. Bullets and bayonets got you only so far. In the end, logistics would be what won the war.

Tarps had been set up to provide shelter from the tropical sun and wind. Under them, medics were at work trying to save the wounded. Those who hadn't made it lay stretched out in neat rows, field jackets or blankets covering their faces, their exposed boots pointing toward the sky. *Poor bastards.* Every man who passed the dead knew that it might just as easily have been him stretched out and awaiting the graves registration detail.

Deke wandered the beach, avoiding anyone who looked as though he might be in charge of something. He was still hoping to catch a glimpse of a familiar face from Patrol Easy.

He was passing a temporary HQ of some sort when he heard somebody shouting: "Button up! Button up!"

Curious, he slowed his pace. The term "button up" was the universal warning when the brass was around. Basically it was a reminder to make yourself presentable and act like a soldier.

Considering that they were still taking enemy fire, he wondered what high-ranking officer would be foolhardy enough to come ashore. That was when he heard another soldier say, "Holy mackerel, that's MacArthur!"

Down the beach, he could see a couple of officers walking purposefully toward the temporary HQ. One of the men had a pipe stuck in his mouth. Up and down the beach, soldiers' mouths fell open in awe.

It was rare for a GI to see someone as exalted as MacArthur—much less to see him on the beach when enemy bullets still flew. Deke wasn't sure if the general was brave—or foolish. Who was going to run the army if he got himself killed?

Deke didn't stick around to see more. In his experience, officers attracted trouble like a flagpole in a lightning storm. You didn't want to go stand under it in a storm. He took one last good look at the general, then turned around and started back in the other direction.

It was a good thing he did. He had barely left all the commotion with MacArthur behind when he spotted a familiar face—several faces, as a matter of fact. Patrol Easy had made it to shore after all. They looked like drowned rats, but they were alive.

"I'll be damned, look who it is!" Philly shouted, catching sight of Deke. "We thought for sure that you were dead."

"You ain't gettin' rid of me that easy."

Philly slapped him on the shoulder, clearly pleased and relieved to see Deke alive. The thought hadn't even occurred to Deke that the survivors might have been wondering what had happened to *him*. No matter. Against all odds, they had all made it to shore and found one another.

Lieutenant Steele gave him a nod. "Thought we lost you when the landing craft went down," he said. "Knowing how much you love the ocean, you were the last person I expected to swim to shore."

"Swimming beats drowning."

Their reunion was cut short by the arrival of a courier who had a message for Lieutenant Steele. Quickly, he scanned the orders and turned back to his men.

"Don't get too comfortable, boys," Steele said. "We're being sent to help take out Hill 522. Somebody decided that we're just the ones for the job, considering that we've been there before."

"How about that, Deke?" Philly said. "It turns out that you're just in time to get killed for real this time."

CHAPTER ELEVEN

FOR ONCE THE snipers had been chosen because someone up the chain of command realized that Hill 522 would be familiar territory for them, considering that they had been involved in the raid to eliminate the battery just a short time ago.

Their assignment to the assault was a rare example of common sense, extraordinary as a blue moon, but the way that Deke and the rest of Patrol Easy saw it, it wasn't a decision that worked in their favor.

They had barely made it off that hill alive last time after accomplishing their mission by knocking out those powerful guns. It was anybody's guess if they could survive that hill a second time.

"That hill is damn well defended," Philly said. "The Japs have been up there this whole time, digging in. Waiting for us."

"Mmm," Deke murmured.

"We're just lucky, I guess," Philly continued. "First, we help take the beach. Then we get to lead the assault up that hill. Next thing you know, they'll be sending us to be the first guys to knock on Hirohito's palace door."

"Mmm," Deke murmured again. He was only half listening. As

usual, Philly talked too much. He was like some radio program that droned in your ear like background noise.

But Deke was willing to cut him some slack long after he would have told another man to stop flapping his gums. He recognized that talking was Philly's way of letting off steam, of dealing with the nervousness, the fear of what was to come.

Deke preferred to keep busy. He was once again honing his bowie knife, which was already sharp as a razor, but the simple act of scraping blade against stone was enough to occupy his mind. It was a soothing sound, but one with a deadly purpose. Better than talking, that was for sure.

Philly went on: "Why can't the army give us a nice, easy job, like sitting up in a tree and picking off Japs from a safe distance? Isn't that what us snipers are supposed to do?"

"Maybe that's because they know you can't actually hit anything unless you're close enough to poke it with a stick."

"Aww, listen to you. You're not the only one who knows how to shoot. I told you that story about how I won my girl a stuffed bear at that shooting gallery on the boardwalk in Atlantic City."

Deke couldn't help but smile. "A stuffed bear?"

Philly waved his hand dismissively. "Yeah, yeah, you mountain people want trophy bucks or whatever, but I tell you what, that stuffed bear was enough to get me laid that night. I gave her that bear, and she had her panties off like there were ants in them. Then there was the time—"

Deke tuned him out, returning to his own thoughts. Besides, Philly wanted everybody to believe that he had considerable experience with women, which Deke took with a grain of salt.

He didn't need to jabber about things like Philly did, but the truth was that Deke dreaded the return to the hill. It wasn't fear, exactly, but something he'd rather not do, like put up hay on a ninety-degree day in July.

Deke knew that he, Philly, and Yoshio had indeed barely escaped just ahead of the Japanese during that raid, and it was a good thing, too, or the Japs might have cut off their heads as they'd done to the Filipino guerrillas they'd captured.

It was on that hill that he had encountered the Japanese sniper who had nearly taken him out with a lucky shot or two. Deke wasn't afraid of the Japanese sniper, no more than he was afraid of any man, but he had a healthy respect for the man after that encounter. Would the Japanese still be on that hill? It seemed to be where he was stationed. Deke reckoned they would find out soon enough.

* * *

"ALL RIGHT, BOYS, LET'S GO," said Lieutenant Steele, leading the way as they trudged inland.

"You taking us to the USO, Honcho? Cold beer, steaks, and broads?"

Steele shook his head, suppressing a smile. "Shut up, Philly. And keep your eyes open. There are still plenty of Japanese around. You know as well as I do that we're headed back to that hill. Last time we stopped by for a visit. This time we're going to plant the flag on that son of a bitch."

Hill 522 was located roughly a mile from the beaches that were rapidly filling with more American troops and supplies. Despite the incursion, the Japanese were far from defeated. From the heights of Hill 522, Japanese artillery still fired, harassing the troops coming ashore.

General MacArthur was already on the beach, fulfilling his promise to return to Filipino soil. For all the sensation that the images of his landing would cause back home, scarcely any of the troops had actually witnessed the landing. They had heard about it only through rumors and excited whispers.

"Hey, you better look out," soldiers warned one another. "MacArthur is somewhere here on the beach. General MacArthur himself, fellas. Goddamn!"

The rank-and-file soldiers had mixed emotions about MacArthur. Sure, Mac was known as a capable general. But he had a reputation for being aloof. He wasn't one to mix and mingle with the troops. It was hard to love him the way the men in Europe cheered for General Patton or the navy boys loved Admiral "Bull" Halsey. Those two had made plenty of mistakes, but a little charisma went a long way in the public eye and in the hearts of the men.

Still, it heartened the men to know that their general was willing to take risks in securing the beach alongside them. But that was MacArthur for you. Everyone knew how much he loved the Philippines. He'd made a promise to return, and he had kept it. Any GI had to respect that.

MacArthur had also put the word out that he wanted any American POWs to be liberated as quickly as possible. Small squads and patrols were being sent into the countryside for that purpose. Of course, the Japs tried to keep the camps secret. There were even dark rumors that they had killed all the POWs in some camps rather than see them given back their freedom.

One more reason to hate the Japanese, Deke supposed.

Some of the patrols to find the POW camps were led by Filipino guides who had only a rough idea of where the camps were hidden. There had been rumors that Patrol Easy would be sent out to help liberate these camps, but that wasn't going to be the focus of Patrol Easy today. No, not with the enemy still in command of most of the island. Everybody knew that the Japs had to go first before the mopping up began, and that mopping up included liberating POWs.

Along the way from the beachhead to the base of the hill, Deke passed familiar territory. He could see the town of Palo in the distance, straddling the muddy Bangon River, the waters silently flowing, oblivious to all the human drama on its banks. Now and then a corpse floated past. They crossed an ancient stone bridge across the Bangon that the Japanese had not managed to blow up, although it showed damage from the naval bombardment. The bridge was still sturdy enough for tanks to get across, and a couple passed the patrol, racing ahead toward the hill.

"Go get 'em, boys!" Philly shouted after them. "The more Japs you kill, the fewer that we've got to worry about."

"Shut up, Philly," the lieutenant said wearily. Unlike Deke, Lieutenant Steele couldn't seem to tune Philly out.

Beyond the town, jungle growth encroached between the river and the base of the hill, but the trees and other vegetation had been badly tattered by the bombardment that had so effectively carpeted the beach area and then reached inland.

They passed among shattered trunks and trees that stood barren as poles, having been stripped of their branches and foliage. If only the bombardment had managed to wipe out the Japanese. They heard shots and firing in the distance, a reminder that the barrage had done little to soften the Japanese defenses deeper in the hills or deep underground. Unfortunately, the job was going to take boots on the ground.

"I sure wish we had that priest and his Filipino buddies to help us out," Philly said, referring to Father Francisco and the guerrilla fighters who had assisted them during their earlier mission on Leyte. "It would make the job that much easier."

"We know where we're going," Deke said. "We also know what waits for us up there, and it ain't good. You know the drill, same as I do. Just keep your eyes open and keep your head down."

"You don't have to tell me twice," Philly said. "As a matter of fact, I'll even let you take point. Somehow I think you have a better chance of keeping us from getting killed."

Deke didn't disagree, although he didn't welcome being the first one who would encounter any surprises that the Japanese had in store for them. Then again, it was the lieutenant's call. He caught the lieutenant's eyes, and Honcho gave him a nod.

"Deke, you take point. Everybody else look sharp," Lieutenant Steele said in a harsh whisper. "There could be Japs anywhere—hidden pillboxes, spider holes, you name it. Anything that moves, shoot first and ask questions later."

"You got it, Honcho," Philly said.

Lieutenant Steele turned to one of the sergeants from the company being sent to the hill. "Make sure everybody spreads out. Don't bunch up and make the job any easier for the Japs."

The sergeant nodded and passed the order so that the men behind him fanned out in both directions, watching for anything that could be a sign of the Japanese.

"Where the hell are those other snipers?" Philly wondered. "You know, Woodall's Scouts. It seems like they managed to disappear just when we could use them."

"Don't worry about them," Deke said. "You just worry about your-self. I reckon they're off on another part of the island doing the same thing we are. There's an airfield to secure and another hill not much different from this one that needs to be eliminated."

Philly snorted. "I wouldn't be surprised if they were all on the beach, guarding some general's personal supply of booze."

"I fought with those boys this morning. They weren't so bad."

Philly just shrugged. Deke slipped past Philly into the point posi-tion, leading the way through the shattered landscape toward the base of Hill 522. He was soon a good fifty feet ahead of the rest of Patrol Easy. Behind them came the company that had been assigned to the task. Egan was there with his war dog, the two of them covering the flank. If there were any Japs out there, Thor would sniff them out.

Each one of Deke's senses was on high alert. He might not be around in the next minute if he got unlucky, but there was something about pressing alone into the landscape, rifle at the ready, that made him feel incredibly alive. In some ways he'd been born for this moment.

He realized that he felt no fear. He was right at home, wandering through the jungle, eyes peeled, senses alert to any sound or motion that seemed out of place.

It wasn't much different from hunting back home, and yet there was a world of difference because it was anybody's guess who was the hunter and who was the hunted. In some perverse way, he found that even more thrilling.

However, he knew better than to share that sentiment with anyone else and the patrol. They would have thought that he'd lost his mind if he admitted that some part of him actually liked being out here in the jungle. The only one who might understand how he felt was Lieu-tenant Steele. He glanced back and saw the lieutenant moving with equal stealth through the jungle.

The lieutenant had only one good eye, so his head scanned slowly back and forth across the jungle undergrowth, his twelve-gauge shotgun held at the ready. At close range here in the underbrush, the twelve-gauge with its load of buckshot would do more than its share of damage to any of the enemy dumb enough to show themselves.

On the ground ahead, something didn't look right. Deke used the muzzle of the rifle to push aside a pile of leaves to reveal a hole that went down into the ground about four feet. The leaves had been meant to disguise it, but he couldn't see any wires or other signs of a booby trap. The hole was so narrow that Deke, lean as he was, would have had trouble fitting into it. He studied the hole for a moment as Philly caught up.

"What do you suppose that is?" Philly asked quietly. "Are the Japs expecting us to step in there and break a leg?"

"No, I've seen a few others out here. That's what the Japs call a spider hole. It's just big enough for them to hide in and pop out to shoot you in the back."

"That's just great," Philly said, looking around. "I'll bet this whole place is covered with them. I guess it's a good thing for us that the bombardment scared them off."

"Ain't likely," Deke said. Deep down, he didn't think that the Japs had run off. He supposed that the Japanese had elected to defend certain fortified locations, such as the hill.

The enemy would be dug in deep. Waiting.

They were now moving toward the base of the hill and whatever awaited them there. The ground rose steeply, and they were forced to climb.

He lowered his rifle and looked around cautiously. He recalled that the Japanese had not bothered to clear the undergrowth around the steepest part of the base, cleverly leaving it as part of the hill's natural defenses. It was tough enough for a man on foot to traverse the hill. There was no way that a tank was getting up here.

Deke slung his rifle over his shoulder, then began to ascend the hill, hand over hand, using bits of stump, vines, and even rocks for handholds. Glumly he realized that the Japs could roll rocks down on the GIs, and it might be enough to stop the advance.

Apparently Philly had the same thought. He caught up to Deke, who had been slowed by the steep slope. "I don't like this, Deke. We're sitting ducks if they so much as roll rocks down at us."

"Yeah," Deke admitted. "How about if you go up there and ask them real nice not to do that?"

Philly just snorted and kept climbing.

Deke slipped, and his boot came down hard, going out from under him so that his ankle crunched on a sharp rock. He winced, first at the noise and then at the pain, looking down to see if he'd cut himself, but he didn't find any blood.

He wasn't the only one struggling up the hill. Off to his right, Yoshio's boots slipped on the slick dirt, and he fell heavily with a grunt.

Somebody muttered, "Quiet, goddammit!"

Yoshio glanced in Deke's direction, looking stricken. Deke shrugged. They all knew that they'd be better off if the Japs didn't hear them coming up the hill, but it was easier said than done.

Deke held on to a tree root and stopped climbing, listening for any clue that the Japanese had heard them. They could hear small-arms fire in the distance and even the *crump, crump* sound of artillery, but nothing from the hill itself.

Quiet, Deke thought. Maybe too quiet.

They had no choice but to continue. Deke started climbing again.

After a few minutes of hard going, he reached the top of the sharp incline, to the point where the hill began a gentler slope across open ground. Oddly, there was still no sign of the Japs. Where the hell were they?

There was no firing, yelling, or movement of any kind. He'd had some idea of what to expect, but this wasn't it. Deke gestured to Philly to stay down, keeping to the brush that clung to the forest's edge.

Once at the top, Deke found that he could go no farther without exposing himself. He had reached the open part of the hillside, where all the trees had been cleared away to give the defenders open fields of fire. From their raid, Deke and the others knew that the hillside was laced with trenches, some of them cleverly interconnected. Other than the batteries near the summit, still raining shells on the beaches and even reaching out to the ships offshore, there didn't appear to be any Japanese activity.

Philly crept closer and knelt beside him, both of them taking advantage of the natural cover. "See what I mean?" Philly asked. "I'm telling you that the Japs pulled out."

"I don't think so."

"How can you be so sure?"

"Just trust me for once."

Deke studied the empty ground, which didn't look right. He knew that the Japs must be out there, unseen. Unless they were deaf, dumb, and blind, they would have had plenty of warning that the Americans were on their way up here.

He remembered once, as a boy, there had been a mean old bull that ruled over Old Man McGlothlin's pasture. The pasture had been a shortcut to the one-room schoolhouse that Deke sometimes attended when farm chores permitted. When he and Sadie crossed that field, the bull snorted and pawed the ground, but he didn't charge.

Some part of Deke had been disappointed. Running from the bull would have helped to liven up the otherwise routine walk to something as boring as school.

"For all that noise, that bull don't amount to no more than a fart in the wind," Deke had said.

"That's probably just what that bull thinks about you," Sadie had said. "He reckons that such a skinny beanpole ain't worth chasin'. Now if you wanted to stir that bull up, what you'd have to do is wave a red flag at him."

"Go on now," Deke had said. "That ain't true."

"Try it and see. Wave something red at that bull just once and you'd better run."

Deke hadn't had anything red that day, but the next time they'd crossed that pasture on the way to school, he'd surprised Sadie by pulling out a red bandanna. "You know what you said the other day about that bull?"

"Deke, don't you dare!"

But Deke hadn't been able to resist. There was the bull, snorting and pawing the ground as always from halfway across the pasture. Deke had waved the red handkerchief at it.

At first nothing had happened. But then the old bull had begun to trot toward them, huge slabs of meat and muscle vibrating powerfully down his sides. Deke had begun to have second thoughts about the wisdom of his actions, but it had been too late for that. The bull had lowered his horns, bellowed with rage, and charged.

"Run, Sadie!"

"Run, Deke!"

Barefoot, they'd flown across the pasture, the bull snorting and bellowing right behind them. It had been a near thing, but they'd gotten across that field and over the fence ahead of the bull, who'd pulled up short at the fence and stood snorting in frustration. Deke and Sadie had jumped off the fence and tumbled into the deep grass on the other side, laughing their fool heads off.

He reckoned that now the Japanese were the bull, and Deke was the handkerchief.

"Here we go, boys," he muttered. "I sure hope you're ready."

Light as smoke, Deke stepped out of the underbrush and into the clearing.

At first nothing happened. Deke held his breath, imagining that some Japanese was using the time to line up his sights on him.

Then again, that was the whole idea. He gave the hidden Japs what was known back home as a "hillbilly wave," the big arm swing of a mountain howdy. In the old days, it had been meant to show that you had only one hand on your rifle and weren't planning on shooting anyone.

The enemy wasn't so welcoming. Almost immediately, the firing began.

The Japanese were there, all right, but they'd just been waiting for that red flag. Deke had sprung the Japanese trap.

As he looked up the hill, a muzzle flashed from within a hidden pit. The bullet whizzed past him, and he ducked behind a rock. He was so close that he heard the click of the Japanese soldier working his rifle bolt, giving Deke a target for his own rifle. He fired without thinking, acting out of pure instinct and adrenaline, then looked to see that he'd hit the Japanese soldier. The man was slumped over the barrel of his rifle, a look of surprise frozen on his face.

If only all the Japs would die that easily. Back home there seemed to be this idea that the Japs were all near-sighted, buck-toothed, terrible shots, and no match for a real American. That was all propaganda to reassure Americans that there was no doubt they could win the war. By now Deke knew there was nothing further from the truth about this terrible enemy.

"Get into those trenches!" Steele shouted. "I want fire on those positions on the hill."

Deke bent low and ran forward into the storm of lead as he might run into a hurricane wind. A couple of men went down. The only reason there weren't more casualties was because the Japanese were shooting downhill, resulting in a natural tendency to shoot high.

It worked both ways. Firing up the hill, many of the GIs were shooting too low.

"Aim lower!" Steele shouted.

While the nearest trenches did offer cover, the trouble was that they were still occupied by Japanese. Deke tumbled into a trench, finding himself face-to-face with two enemy soldiers. They were screaming at him in Japanese. He wasn't sure what they were yelling other than that it probably wasn't, "How do you do?"

Deke fired from the hip, the .30-06 slug taking out the nearest Japanese. The soldier behind the one that Deke had just shot opened fire. Deke felt the bullet give a hard tug at his hip. Was he hit? No time to think about that. He worked the bolt and fired at point-blank range, hitting the Japanese in the chest. Powder burns from Deke's muzzle flash smoldered on the brown tunic. The man collapsed like a rag doll.

Behind Deke, the other members of Patrol Easy were dealing with enemy troops in the trench in similar fashion. It was a bloody, desperate fight as enemy soldiers sprang from hidden alcoves carved into the walls of the trench. The attacks were savage, and no quarter was given on either side. For the Japanese, this wasn't a nameless dirt trench at all, but the very doorstep of Japan. They would die defending it.

Philly was screaming bloody murder and blasting away with his rifle. When the empty clip spun away, Philly dropped his rifle and pulled his knife. He slashed wildly, the blade knocking aside a Japanese muzzle that was pointed at him. The enemy soldier let go of the rifle and turned to run, but he didn't get far before Deke's bullet cut him down.

Over and over again he heard the deep boom of Honcho's shotgun. Thor barked madly.

Out of the corner of his eye, Deke caught a glimpse of Yoshio using his rifle butt to smash a Japanese soldier in the face. *Damn, didn't know the kid had it in him.*

He heard curses in English, enraged shouts in Japanese, and gunshots, then an uneasy silence in the trench itself, even as the enemy higher on the hill kept firing. Most of the Americans were now under cover, so the shots were wasted.

Deke reached for his hip, which felt wet. Blood? Something had struck him there, but he didn't feel any pain. He glanced down and saw with relief that his canteen was leaking water thanks to a bullet hole that went right through it.

"Don't that beat all," Deke muttered, feeling a sense of relief.

"I must have shot three of those yellow bastards," Philly said. He sounded pumped up, full of adrenaline from the fight. "They just don't know when to quit."

Deke thought about his father, who had fought in the trenches in the Great War. Had it been like that for him? No wonder his father had been content to return to his mountain farm and never speak of what he'd seen and done.

Deke looked around and took stock. He spotted Yoshio, Lieutenant Steele, and the rest of the squad. Egan had hold of his dog, still straining at his leash as if ready to run after the Japs, so they had both made it through.

The local mosquito population began to swarm as darkness approached, buzzing in Deke's ears. They had hatched by the thousands in the water festering in the bottom of the trench. The soldiers' arrival only stirred them up.

"Damn, but I swear these skeeters are as bad as Japanese dive bombers," Deke said.

"Huh, I haven't even seen a mosquito," Philly lied, scratching his fresh bites. "You country boys must taste sweet to them."

After a while, Deke gave up even trying to slap the mosquitoes away. On his exposed neck and arms, it soon felt as though even his bug bites were getting bites. It just added to the misery of holding this trench.

Deke's eyes went to a prone body, one of the GIs from B Company who hadn't been lucky enough to survive the attack. Deke dug through the fallen soldier's gear for spare ammunition and then took the dead man's canteen. Deke figured he would need the items more than the dead soldier.

They had managed to take the trench, gaining a foothold on Hill 522. However, taking the rest of the hill promised to be an even tougher, more miserable fight.

CHAPTER TWELVE

THAT MORNING, from the crest of Hill 522, Ikeda had watched with a sense of awe at the American landing craft racing toward the beach. So many boats!

"It looks as if the entire American fleet is here," said Morosawa, who was watching the spectacle through binoculars. In many ways, Morosawa was his right-hand man. Like Ikeda himself, Morosawa and the other highly trained *sogekihei* were eager to meet the enemy.

"They say this is only a part of their fleet," Ikeda replied.

Both men thought about that. It seemed impossible that the Americans could have even *more* ships. "I wish they would come within rifle range," Morosawa said.

"Be patient, Kazuyuki. Our rifle barrels will be hot soon enough."

They had been expecting the invasion for many long weeks, but Ikeda realized that his imagination had not been the equal of the actual sight of Leyte Gulf packed with ships and the skies filled with enemy planes.

From their vantage point, many of the Japanese troops watched anxiously. They had emerged from their deep shelters, unscathed, after the massive American bombardment. The defenses that they had labored to build had worked perfectly.

"Remember your duty!" shouted Major Noguchi, passing by in his dress uniform, complete with sword. The major caught Ikeda's eye and nodded. "Look around you at these defenses that we have built! The Americans will break upon them like waves on the rocky shore!"

Ikeda was so used to seeing Noguchi in his simple work uniform, often as dusty as the laborers and carrying a shovel, that it was strange to see the major in his formal uniform. The crisp officer's dress uniform looked out of place against the backdrop of rugged logs and fresh earth that composed the hill's defenses, but then Ikeda understood. *Major Noguchi planned to die here today.*

Noguchi had poured all his energy into the defenses of this hill. Now that the hour of battle had come, the officer planned to defend the hill to the end, all while wearing his funeral best. Ikeda watched the major closely but saw no trace of sadness or fear. Major Noguchi looked calm—even happy—his energy focused on the battle to come.

Not every Japanese soldier shared in the fervor to die for the Emperor. For them, ample amounts of liquor were circulating. It was easier to be brave when inebriated. The sight of so many ships, planes, and soldiers arrayed against them felt overwhelming.

"Drink up, Ikeda!" said another gunsō, offering him a drink from a bottle. "Our ancestors will understand if we arrive a little tipsy."

Ikeda shook his head at the offer of a drink. "I need a clear head for shooting. How would I hit a target if I am drunk?"

"Suit yourself! More for us!" the gunsō said with a laugh, moving on. Clearly he was already feeling the effect of the alcohol.

Unlike many of his comrades taking deep drinks of liquor, Ikeda felt no fear at all, but only a sense of elation. The long-awaited battle had finally begun. After weeks and months of preparation, they would fight. Their forces had been unleashed.

During the course of the morning, the battle had unfolded, beginning with the beach landing. Now that it was past midday, the Americans were pushing inland. Ikeda had been expecting the enemy to attack the hill for a while. Having skirted the town of Palo itself, which was still held by a handful of Japanese troops, the Americans were finally pushing up the slope.

His pulse raced, his eyes hot and dry as they flicked from one patch of ground to the next, eagerly seeking out targets. There were so many that it was difficult to pick out just one. He sought out officers in particular because they were the most valuable targets. It was exactly what he had been trained to do.

His initial euphoria at the sight of the Americans—at long last, the real fight had begun—had soon vanished. If he had been excited by the American attack on Hill 522 itself, that moment was long past. Now Ikeda spent his time watching and waiting for the enemy to show themselves. He had come to realize that he would need to use all his sniper skills if he was going to turn the tide against the onslaught of Americans.

What had seemed like child's play at first, with so many targets to choose from, was turning out to be far more challenging than he had first imagined. The Americans fought hard, even if they did not have the same willingness that the Japanese did to sacrifice themselves.

High on the hill, Ikeda saw the line of Americans emerge from the surrounding jungle. His attention was soon drawn to one American in particular—a lone soldier in a wide-brimmed hat who stepped out of the jungle shadows and into the light.

Something about the man's figure looked familiar. Had Ikeda seen him before? And then in a flash of recognition, he knew—this was the same American soldier he had encountered during the earlier raid on the hill. Most GIs wore helmets, but this soldier wore a hat like the Australians—or maybe like a cowboy. The American sniper stood there for a moment, alone, as if taunting Ikeda, although that was impossible. The American couldn't possibly know that Ikeda was there. Or did he?

Ikeda was so taken aback that he didn't have time to shoot before the American launched himself at the trenches, jumped down, and disappeared. Incredulous, Ikeda cursed. He had missed his chance.

More American soldiers poured from the underbrush. Ikeda fired, but running shots were never easy, even for a skilled marksman such as himself. He fired again and again. Some of his targets fell and did not rise again, but others kept going and disappeared into the trenches.

Within seconds, there were no more targets. This must be an

advance force, he thought. The Americans couldn't be so arrogant that they actually thought that they could take his hill with a relatively small number of men—no more than a company. To take this hill, didn't they know that they would need an army? The Americans were in for a surprise if they thought that this would be an easy fight. Such arrogance!

The thought angered him. He kept the rifle sights trained on the trench, but no targets presented themselves.

Morosawa nudged him. The other sniper was smiling. He held up two fingers. "I got two."

"Well done, Kazuyuki." Ikeda nodded in approval, then turned back to his rifle scope. If his *sogekihei* squad member had already shot two, then Ikeda had some catching up to do.

* * *

PATROL EASY HAD TAKEN the first trench alongside B Company, anchoring the right flank. Peering over the lip of the trench, Deke could see the summit of Hill 522, with its cave-like artillery emplacement near the top. That was their destination if they hoped to silence the battery that was tearing hell out of the beach and landing craft.

As he watched, a tongue of flame and smoke licked from the mouth of the cave. The shell was headed for the vessels ferrying men and supplies to the beach. Deke wondered if this same battery had sunk the landing craft carrying him to shore. If so, knocking it out would be sweet revenge.

Now what? They needed to knock out that battery. *Just a few hundred feet to go,* Deke thought.

Not far. A man could easily stroll that distance in a few minutes and toss in a couple of grenades. But this was no walk through a field of daisies.

Might as well be a hundred miles away.

With their Nambu machine guns, the Japanese had cleverly set up overlapping fields of fire that would mow down any squad that attempted to advance. No, there would be no strolling. The only way across that killing field was crawling on your belly, one desperate yard at a time.

Deke wasn't looking forward to it. Meanwhile, every Japanese in the neighborhood would be trying to pick them off.

He heard a sneeze and realized that it had come from somewhere up ahead, beyond where the GIs had advanced. Startled, he realized that he'd just heard a *Japanese* sneeze. It was a reminder of just how close they were to the enemy.

"What do you think, Deke?" Philly asked. He crouched in the trench a few feet away, peering over the rim at the same no-man's-land that Deke was looking at. "I've got to admit, I'd rather walk down the worst dark alley in Philadelphia at midnight than try to cross that patch of ground."

"An alley at midnight? You know me, being a country boy and all, I ain't sure which is worse, an alley or this hillside. I never had much use for cities. What I do know is that we've got to take this hill, Japs or no Japs."

"I was afraid you'd say something like that."

"What we're gonna do is pick off these sons of bitches one at a time."

"You seriously think you're going to shoot all those machine gunners?"

"Ain't got much choice." Deke spat a mouthful of dry grit into the sandy soil. "You got a better idea?"

"Yeah, how about a boat ticket back to Hawaii?"

Deke snorted. "You just watch how it's done. Oh, and keep your head down. You too, Yoshio."

The young Nisei interpreter nodded grimly.

"Those Japs are all dug in," Philly said. "We can't even see them. How are you supposed to shoot 'em if we don't even know where they're shooting out of?"

It was a fair question. For some reason it prompted a boyhood memory. Deke recalled, as a young boy, watching a calf being born. He had already been witness to the barnyard amour that resulted in pregnant heifers and sows, so he knew how those babies got *in*. Children learned about the "birds and bees" quite young on the farm. He remembered asking his father how *people's* babies got out. His pa had just grinned and said, "The same way they got in, son." That had been an eye-opener for the young Deacon Cole.

He thought about that now. "You know how bullets get *in*, Philly? The same way they get out."

"I'll just pretend that I know what you're talking about."

"Listen, you two watch the trench on both sides of us and make sure no Japs come sneaking up."

Deke settled behind the rifle, welcoming the familiar feel of the smooth stock against his cheek and the way that the stock fit into his shoulder. Until now, there hadn't been any need for precision shooting. They had taken the trench by brute force.

Through the scope, the Japanese lines sprang closer. He was able to pick out details—a rock that hid a Japanese soldier here, a sandbag with a rifle barrel poking out there. Plenty of targets, all within sneezing distance.

He realized that during their whole time on the ship, this was just what he had been waiting for. Hell, this was what he'd been *born* for. Deke wondered sometimes if there was something wrong with him because he liked this so much. Other men found themselves paralyzed with fear, but not Deke. Sure, he might die in the next few minutes, but until that moment came, he had never felt so keenly alive.

Hidden behind the scope and the stock, a hint of a smile crossed the good side of his face. It wasn't a pleasant smile, but one that hinted at meanness. Deke tried to be a good person in his own way, but the war had opened up someplace hot and cruel in more than one man, a bit of hellfire seeping out the way that lava spills from fissures in the earth.

It wasn't long before a burst of fire erupted from the slope above, trying to flush out the Americans in the trench. The bluish tracers streaked through the air just inches above the dirt. Bullets pockmarked the area all around the trenches where the Americans had taken shelter, forcing them to keep their heads down. Their attack was completely stalled.

Deke couldn't see a target, so he was relying on instinct. He could see the dark hole, some kind of bunker, that the shots had erupted from. But there wasn't anyone to shoot at.

How does a bullet get in? The same way it gets out.

He lined up on the dark hole and squeezed the trigger. The merciless *tap, tap, tap* of the Nambu abruptly fell silent.

"You got him!" Philly shouted.

"Don't get too riled up," Deke said. "There's a lot more where he came from."

Unfortunately, that was more than true. Fire from the machine guns and entrenched Japanese troops forced the GIs to keep their heads down. They kept up constant return fire, but with little effect. The *tap, tap, tap* of the Nambu continued to echo across the hillside.

The day's shadows lengthened as the sun began to settle toward the horizon, becoming an angry red ball over the hill's shoulder so that they were shooting into the glare, making their task even harder.

After his initial luck against the enemy, Deke couldn't seem to pick off any more machine gunners. Maybe they had gotten wise to him and had withdrawn deeper into their hidey-holes. He settled for whatever targets he could find, Philly calling some of them through the binoculars. The Japs were close enough that he caught glimpses of enemy faces through the scope. He pulled the trigger again and again.

He took a breath, and the gunpowder's lingering acrid taste remained on his tongue and clung to the back of his throat. The smell and taste were not altogether unpleasant, as anyone who loved shooting could tell you.

On the other side, the Japs were doing the same, plying their own deadly trade. They had the advantage of deep defenses, located higher up than the trench. Like the Americans, they clearly had a few snipers at work. The enemy snipers watched and waited. Not all the soldiers who were part of the US assault force were as experienced as the men of Patrol Easy. More than one exposed himself too long after taking a shot, only to fall prey to one of the Japanese snipers.

In particular, many of the most accurate shots originated from a stretch of the enemy defenses almost directly across from Deke. There would be a shot, then a sudden cry or curse, or worse yet—an empty silence as a soldier fell dead instantly.

Deke couldn't help but think of the sniper that he had tangled with on his last trip up this hill. Could it possibly be the same Japanese sniper?

"I'd like to shoot that bugger," Deke said. "He's got us pinned down good."

Philly stared through the binoculars. "No sign of him."

During lulls in the fire, they could hear murmured snatches of Japanese voices.

"Yoshio, what are they saying?" Deke asked.

The interpreter cocked an ear in the direction of the Japanese lines to listen but finally shook his head. "They are too far away to hear."

"Why don't you ask them to surrender?" Philly suggested.

Yoshio stared at him as if he might have cracked, but then a slow smile spread across his face. "Why not?"

He started to raise himself even with the top of the trench, but Deke tugged him back down. "Easy there, cowboy. Keep your head down."

Yoshio stayed down, gathering his words.

* * *

As YOSHIO STUDIED the Japanese trenches during this lull in the fighting, Deke studied him in turn. He thought that it couldn't have been easy to be in Yoshio's shoes, fighting against people whom you might even be related to in some way. Sure, Yoshio called himself an *American*, but there was no denying the fact that he was also *Japanese*. Like it or not, Yoshio had a lot more in common with the enemy than he did with Americans from city tenements or the hills of Tennessee.

Also, Yoshio was not a natural-born hard case like Deke, or even a tough-talking city boy like Philly. It didn't matter that Yoshio was roughly the same age as Deke. From Deke's point of view, Yoshio had a naivete or innocence that made him seem younger than his years.

If Deke had known Yoshio's whole story, he might have reconsid-

ered. He didn't know how Yoshio's family had worked hard on their
West Coast farm, trying to be good neighbors, but had also been held
apart because of their Japanese heritage.

For Yoshio, no matter how much he wanted to be seen as American
or how much he considered himself to be one, he and his family were
always segregated because of the color of their skin and their distinctive Asian features. Then had come the war, which made matters
worse. His family, along with other Japanese Americans in their
community, had been forced off their land and into internment camps
—perceived as a threat by their neighbors and their government.

In the early days of the war, there had been real fears about a
Japanese invasion or sabotage on the heels of Pearl Harbor. In hindsight, the internment camps would be viewed as a terrible injustice.

Yoshio had seen the heartbreak of his mother having to choose
what few family heirlooms she could take with her into captivity.

Some of their non-Japanese neighbors had been helpful, even
embarrassed by what was taking place. They promised to maintain the
property for however long this nightmare lasted for Yoshio's family.

Those were the decent people.

Others had been greedy, offering to purchase the land for a ridicu-
lously low price or hoping to get a bargain on the family's household
goods. When moving day came—a hurried affair carried out under the
watchful eye of armed soldiers—some neighbors had shown up to help.
Others came looking for bargains, not much different from crows or
buzzards picking over a roadkill.

What they could bring with them was limited to a single suitcase.
There wasn't even enough room to bring extra clothes or bedding. A
lifetime of possessions and all the farm equipment had to be left
behind.

Yoshio had watched his mother agonize over bringing a teapot and
cups that had come all the way from Japan, brought over by her grandparents. The delicate porcelain had occupied a place of honor in the
house and been used only for special occasions. The space in the suitcase would have been better put to use for warm clothes rather than a
teapot.

One of the neighbors, a man whom Yoshio had never particularly liked and who had a big house at the edge of town, had sensed his mother's dilemma as she cradled the teapot in her hands.

"I'll give you two dollars for that," he'd said. He wore a smug smile. "Where you're going, you can probably use the money."

His mother had glared at the man in a rare show of anger. Her eyes said it all. *Two dollars for an heirloom that is priceless to my family?*

The man appeared oblivious. When his mother didn't respond, he'd said, "All right, you Japs drive a hard bargain. I'll give you three dollars if you toss in that stack of plates over there."

To Yoshio's astonishment, his mother hadn't said a word but had raised the teapot over her head, preparing to smash it to the wooden floor. Yoshio held his breath.

Another neighbor stepped forward, a widow who had a plot of land and a modest house down the road from his family. She held out her hands to Yoshio's mother. "Let me keep it safe for you," the woman had said. "When you come back, I'll have that teapot waiting for you."

With a nod, his mother had handed over the teapot. The neighbor took it with the same care that women used cradling an infant.

That day had been a display of human nature, the good with the bad.

His father had stood mutely, looking out at the fields, saying goodbye to the land. And then they had been taken by truck and train to a distant camp and forced to live in canvas tents and rough barracks. The food was of poor quality, and there wasn't enough fuel to heat their shelters. To make things worse, no provisions had been made for young children to attend school. A few of the young women organized classes so that the children's reading, writing, and math skills did not languish completely.

Yoshio had volunteered to fight, joining the ranks of the Nisei, not only to do his duty to his country, but also to prove a point. He was just as American as any man in this army. The road hadn't been easy. The drill instructors had been extra hard on the Nisei recruits and reluctant to let them train with actual rifles, as if they still didn't trust them. Maybe some of the soldiers nearby still didn't trust him.

This was the "kid" whom Deke fought beside.

Now Yoshio served as their ears on this hillside, trying to piece together the snatches of conversation overheard from the Japanese. If any prisoners were taken, it would be Yoshio's task to interview them to gain any nuggets of intelligence. He'd had a chance to talk with some of the Japanese captured on Guam, but so far there had been precious few prisoners taken on Leyte.

Most Japanese troops would rather die by their own hand than surrender. It was a brutal fact of war that some American troops didn't trust the Japanese who tried to give themselves up. They were simply shot. In fact, it was often only the badly wounded who fell into American hands. The GIs weren't afraid of them, and they were too weak to take their own lives.

* * *

FOLLOWING Deke's advice to keep his head down, Yoshio leaned back against the trench, took a deep breath, and shouted something in Japanese.

There had been snatches of conversation drifting toward them previously from the enemy trenches, but now a stunned silence followed.

Curious, Philly asked, "What did you say to them?"

"I finally did what you suggested, Philly. I asked them to surrender."

"Well, it's about time somebody listened to me," Philly said. He nodded in the direction of the enemy trenches. "They're pretty quiet all of a sudden. Maybe they're thinking it over."

The silence did not last long. A shouted reply came from the Japanese side, followed by a fresh flurry of gunshots.

"What did he say?"

"He said that I am a traitor to the Emperor."

"I can think of worse insults than that."

"You don't understand," Yoshio explained. "For a Japanese, there is no worse insult."

"You don't look none too bothered by it," Philly said.

"That is because I am not Japanese. I am an American. What do I care about the Emperor?"

From over on the enemy's side, there came more shouts and gunshots.

Deke grinned. "Nice going, kid. I reckon you managed to rile them boys up."

CHAPTER THIRTEEN

THE STALEMATE between the Japanese and the GIs continued as the shadows on the hill deepened. On the American side, they knew it couldn't last for long. The hill needed to be taken. They would have to keep pushing. There were constant radio messages demanding progress updates.

"They've got a timetable they want us to keep back at HQ, huh? Well, the Japs have got a *different* timetable. We'll take this hill when we've taken it, that's when, and not a minute sooner," an officer grumbled under his breath.

But it was not how he replied over the radio.

"Yes, sir!" The brass didn't want to hear any griping or excuses. Up on Hill 522, the officer's official reply was simply, "Situation progressing."

He clicked off before he heard any response. There was an unwritten rule that an officer who hoped to keep advancing in his career knew to say as little as possible while expressing a can-do attitude. That and not getting killed by Japanese snipers was a good strategy for moving up the ranks.

With night coming on, the idea of progress on the battlefield seemed optimistic. All the while the enemy gun battery kept up its fire, wreaking who knew how much havoc on the American forces on the beach below.

Each concussion of the enemy guns served as a reminder of unfinished business. The Japs still held the hilltop. The big ships of the American fleet kept silent for fear of dropping a shell on the heads of their own troops on the hill.

From time to time, an American plane swooped in low and hammered the hilltop, trying to knock out the battery. The sight brought cheers from the GIs assaulting the hill, but their joy was short lived. Despite the efforts of the bravest pilots, the cave was too deep and well defended by antiaircraft guns. After tangling with the Japanese defenders on Hill 522, one or two planes limped away, trailing black smoke.

"We've got to take this hill," said Philly, hunkered down in the trench.

"Sure we do, but there are a whole lot of Japs who don't want to give it up," Deke pointed out.

"The Japs didn't stop us the last time we were here," Philly said. "They won't stop us now."

Deke didn't say anything. He knew that Philly was right, but he couldn't help remembering the sight of those headless corpses of the Filipino guerrillas who had died here that last time. The Nips were ruthless, all right. They would be a tough nut to crack.

As if to serve as a reminder that time was wasting, the shadows cast by the overripe sun elongated into dappled fingers that stretched across the killing field. The shadows created a perfect camouflage for the Japanese infiltrators who began to creep toward American lines.

These enemy troops were armed with hand grenades rather than rifles, their only goal being to move close enough to toss the grenades into the trenches occupied by the Americans. Now and then a Japanese soldier popped into view as he got to his knees to hurl a grenade. Heck, the Japanese could just about roll the grenades down at the Americans.

Sometimes the Americans got lucky and shot the enemy soldier before he could release the grenade. The enemy grenades also had one major shortcoming. While American grenades were activated by pressing on the charging handle and pulling out the pin, the Japanese version was activated by a sharp knock—usually against a rock or even more often against a soldier's own helmet. The telltale sound gave the Americans warning of each grenade attack.

To see a Japanese soldier hit himself in the head before hurling his grenade was almost a comical sight, except for the fact that the grenades often made it into the trenches and exploded with devastating effect. The Japanese fragmentation grenades were somewhat weaker than what the GIs used, but you didn't want to be anywhere near one when it went off.

Meanwhile, the Japanese sniper somewhere across from them kept up his harassing fire. He had claimed more than a few American lives —he seemed to shoot the instant some poor GI made the mistake of sticking his head up from the trench or out from behind a rock. The GIs couldn't stay down all the time because they had to keep a lookout for infiltrators and defend against them.

Deke knew the Japanese sniper was hidden in the adjacent trenches, but he hadn't been able to get a bead on him. The sniper must have been dug in and well hidden. Considering that the Japanese had been up here building their defenses on this hill for weeks or even months, he would have had plenty of time to create the perfect sniper's nest.

An unsettling aspect of this fight was that the Japanese were close enough to be heard in the American lines, and the inability of the American troops to press forward had made the enemy bold enough to taunt them.

From time to time they heard the taunts in broken English:

"Hey, Charlie! How you doing, Charlie? Listen good now. We going to kill you."

"You Japs stink like rotten fish," one of the GIs shouted. "I can smell you from here."

"American, you smell like rotten meat. Perhaps we are already smelling the rotting corpses of your friends that we have killed. You will rot next to them soon."

Off to Deke's right, Philly couldn't resist responding. "I'd like to see you try!"

The gibe was followed by a bullet that cut the air not far from Deke's head.

Philly swore. "That was close."

"Best keep your head down, Philly," Deke said. "Don't let these Nips get you all hot and bothered. It's just what they want."

"I am crack shot," the Japanese voice called in heavily accented English. "Put your head up and I will show you."

The voice seemed to be coming from the vicinity of where the Japanese sniper was hidden. With a jolt of realization that struck him hard as a bullet, Deke realized that it must be the Japanese sniper himself who was taunting them.

"Son of a bitch," Deke muttered, leaning into the rifle and hoping for a shot. "I'd sure like to nail that Jap's hide to the barn door."

Judging by the growing number of taunts, several Japanese had at least a passing knowledge of English. But the language barrier was lopsided. On their own side, Yoshio was the only one who knew the enemy's language.

Overall, it was a bizarre experience to be trading insults with the enemy. They were no longer anonymous Japanese soldiers, targets in their rifle sights. The exchange of prickly words had made the fight personal in an entirely new way.

Between the verbal barbs and the sniper's bullets, Deke decided that he'd had enough. The enemy sniper was too dug in for him to see. He needed to goad the sniper into showing himself, but how?

He decided that he would try putting his hat on a stick so he could draw fire with it. He reckoned the sniper was too smart for old tricks, but you never knew. Before he tried the hat trick, Deke had a better idea. He turned toward Yoshio.

"Hey, kid. You said that they hurled a big insult at you by saying that you were a traitor to the Emperor."

"That's right. As if I had anything to do with the Emperor in the first place."

"What would be a big ol' insult to shout back at the Japs?"

Yoshio smiled. "Oh, I could think of a few."

"Like what?"

"How about calling them barbarians? They would hate that. Even the lowliest Japanese soldier believes that Americans are inferior savages, so they would be truly insulted."

"Sounds good to me. Go on and give it to them in their own language."

Nodding, Yoshio took a deep breath and let loose a diatribe in Japanese. He fired words at the same rate as a machine gun. Deke couldn't understand any of it, but he supposed it was sufficiently scathing, judging by the increased rate of fire in their direction once Yoshio had finished.

"Hey, Charlie! Show yourself! I promise not to shoot."

Yoshio wasn't falling for that. He settled deeper into the trench, a big grin on his face. "That felt good."

Deke decided to join the fun. He shouted, "Y'all couldn't hit the broad side of a barn."

In response, a single shot cracked overhead. "How about that, Charlie? That close enough for you?"

"You missed!" he taunted.

"Put up your head and see if I miss again."

"Who are you?" Deke shouted.

There was a moment's hesitation. "I am Gunsō Ikeda."

Deke glanced at Yoshio, who explained, "*Gunsō* means that he's like a sergeant. Sergeant Ikeda."

Deke raised his voice. "Sergeant Ikeda, huh? This here is Private Deacon Cole, United States Army. I reckon we've met before, on my last trip up this hill. Stick your own head up and see what happens."

There was a long pause as the Japanese sniper processed what Deke had just said. "You! You were a raider? Cowardly American!" As if to punctuate the words, a bullet spit gravel and dirt from the lip of the trench.

"Aw, you missed again." He looked at Yoshio once more. "How was that? You reckon I got him riled up?"

"Not bad, but this is better." Yoshio added his own stream of invective in Japanese. The sniper responded in kind.

Deke was curious. "What did you say to him?"

"I said that his ancestors must have, uh, you know . . . *consorted* with goats, or possibly sheep."

"I'm impressed, kid. That was a pretty good insult. I reckon he didn't like that."

"He said that if he catches me, he will gut me like a fish while I am still alive."

"Sounds to me like he's an irritable son of a bitch. I believe he'd make good on that threat. Just to be on the safe side, you'd better not get caught."

Throughout the verbal exchange with the enemy, both Deke and Philly had been watching the Japanese position carefully. The enemy sniper already knew where they were, but now they had a better idea of where he was hidden. Philly had binoculars pressed to his eyes.

"Talk to me, Philly."

Philly needed to paint a picture in words. "See that pile of three rocks, with the one rock that kind of has a black splash on it? Maybe dried blood or something? It's right across from us, but more like the one-o'clock position than high noon."

Deke's eye stared intently through the scope. "I see it."

"I'll bet there's a rifle pit behind those rocks. He's got to be in there."

"Keep an eye on him. Let me see if I can stir the pot."

Deke now had a better idea of where the sniper was hidden. Again he was reminded of the fact that unlike the Americans, the Japanese defenders would have had time to prepare. The enemy sniper could have made the smallest of openings through those rocks for his rifle barrel. The enemy sniper had every advantage.

Peering through the scope, Deke spotted a dark crevice at the base of the rocks.

He became aware that the air tasted dry, parched. Just like how his throat felt after the brisk hike up the hill. But there was no time to take a drink now. He felt an insect buzzing in his ear but ignored it. The only thing that mattered in all the world right now was the image in his telescopic sight.

Through the lens, he studied the crevice. It looked to him like it might be the perfect hiding place. If he'd been in that Japanese sniper's shoes, it was just where he'd be.

How does a bullet get in? The same way that it got out.

To Deke's eye, the crevice suddenly resembled a crooked smile, its dirty lips seeming to brush against the scope, kissing the glass for a moment.

He put his sights on the crevice, looking for a way in.

* * *

AT FIRST, upon hearing the taunts from the American, Ikeda felt furious. He knew enough English to understand the insults, and as if to be certain that he had not missed anything, that traitor of an interpreter had added insult to injury in Japanese.

Suddenly, shooting the other man didn't seem to be enough. Ikeda wanted nothing more than to run down that slope and bury his knife deep into the other sniper, not to mention the interpreter.

At least he knew the sniper's name: Deacon Cole. What kind of a name was that? In Ikeda's mind, most Americans were named Jimmy, Bill, or Charlie. The names all sounded similar, just as the white faces of the Americans all looked the same to him.

But then a wry smile came to Ikeda's face as he realized the sheer audacity of shouting insults at him even as the enemy's position was peppered with machine guns and mortar fire. The enemy was truly laughing in the face of death, which was something that Ikeda appreciated. Ikeda was not much for laughter, but neither would he blink an eye when faced with death.

Was the enemy sniper enjoying this game? Ikeda felt slightly unsettled, wondering what sort of enemy he had run up against.

He supposed that he and the other sniper were forged from the same metal. That didn't mean Ikeda wouldn't kill him, given half a chance. He might respect the enemy, but he had no fondness or softness toward him. He hated the Americans all the same.

With renewed resolve, Ikeda got a new grip on his rifle and scanned the slope through his telescopic site. The jeering from the enemy had been foolish in that it had helped to reveal the other sniper's position, but the man was not so much of a fool to put himself in Ikeda's sights.

Maybe he could change that.

Ikeda shouted back, hoping to goad the enemy into showing himself: "We have women in Japan who are better shots than you. Are you listening, Deacon Cole?"

"I heard you loud and clear, Ikeda. I'd sure like to meet one of them girls," the American replied, the man's hard drawl floating across the no-man's-land. "I reckon I will, soon as I get to Japan. Won't be long now."

Ikeda gritted his teeth. The thought of Americans in Japan was almost too much to bear. *That is why we must defeat them here, on Leyte. Each day that we do not crush them brings them closer to Japan.*

"Do not rest too easy, Deacon Cole," Ikeda replied. "You will be dead by morning. If I don't shoot you, then one of our glorious fighters will kill you tonight."

"You can try," came the reply. The American did not sound particularly concerned. "Sneakin' around is the only chance you cowards have to win."

Ikeda couldn't bring himself to respond. He would not give his enemy the satisfaction of an answer, but he wondered if the response was part of the plan to intimidate him. It was part of the game, after all. Marksman against marksman.

"What's the matter, Ikeda? Cat got your tongue?"

"I do not want to play games," Ikeda said. "Why waste my breath?"

"I've been watching you since I got up here on this hill. I know all I need to know. I know you can't shoot worth a damn."

Ikeda's anger flared up, and his breath grew rough, but he clenched his teeth and said nothing. He would not be baited into this childish game. He had resolved to do whatever it would take to bring down the other sniper, even if it meant enduring insults.

Again, Ikeda forced himself to tamp down the anger. It was just what the enemy wanted—to make him lose his composure, but that was not going to happen.

He scanned the ground opposite him through the scope. The no-man's-land was parched by the sun and torn by artillery shells, but there was no clear target.

The enemy occupied the other side of the no-man's-land, set up in trenches dug by the Japanese themselves. They hid behind sandbags and earthworks, their heads poking out to take shots at the Japanese.

Just for good measure, Ikeda fired a shot in the direction that he thought the voice had come from.

"You missed," came the reply. There was a cold laugh. "Aim a little to the left next time."

"Put your head up and see what happens next," Ikeda shouted.

Something moved across from him. A hat flashed into view. Ikeda recognized the flat-brimmed hat that he remembered the enemy sniper wearing during the raid. Instantly his sights lined up on the hat and his finger touched the trigger.

In reply a rifle shot cracked past his head, so close that he felt it disturb the very air around him. He flinched and sank deeper into his hiding place. Another shot ricocheted off the rock at the opening of his shooting spot.

Too late he realized that the hat must have been on a stick. The oldest trick in the world, and he had fallen for it, revealing his hiding place in the process.

He heard the oddly grating, drawling voice. "Damn, not bad, Ikeda. You done shot a hole in my hat. Too bad for you that it ain't on my head."

Ikeda didn't bother to reply but chewed his lip and decided to wait for dark. Now that the American sniper knew where he was hidden, it would be too risky to try to move while it was still daylight.

Shadows were already gathering at the base of the hill, almost like an incoming tide. Only the summit remained bathed in the last light of the sun, touched by the gold and red of a Pacific sunset.

A revving engine overhead caught his attention. The evening sunlight caught the wings of a lone American fighter plane that came in low and strafed the summit, moving at such an incredible speed that the antiaircraft batteries only managed to raise puffs of smoke in its wake. The plane swiftly flew out to sea, back toward the aircraft carrier that had launched it.

Ikeda sighed. Where was the Imperial fleet that had been promised to crush the Americans? If the battle was not to be won on the ocean, then it must be won here on land, starting on this hill.

So far he had not been able to shoot the American sniper. Perhaps he would go down the hill tonight and stick a knife into the American after all. That would certainly be satisfying—even better than a bullet.

CHAPTER FOURTEEN

THE STANDOFF between the Japanese and the GIs continued as the shadows on the hill deepened. One side wanted that ground; the other side refused to give it up. If the Americans were determined to take the hill, then the Japanese were just as determined not to give up one more inch of ground. No place but war was ownership of real estate settled with bullets, blood, and bayonets.

As so often happened in the tropics, the island twilight lingered and seemed to go on forever. The soft light began turning gray, hinting at the darkness to come but still tinged with color from the tropical sunset. It might have been a magnificent display if anyone had taken notice of it. The Gis had other thoughts on their minds, though, worried about the night to come.

The shadows of the soldiers jutted out of the trench from time to time, keeping an eye on the enemy, rifle muzzles gleaming dully in the fading light. Looking more closely, many of the soldiers' faces were etched in a rictus of fear, their eyes narrowed and mouths set in grim, stiff lines.

"Damn but I hate the nighttime here," Philly said. "We're still in this damn trench, which is the last place I want to be once it gets dark.

The Japs are right across from us. You'd think we would have kicked those bastards off the hill by now."

"What's your rush?" Deke wanted to know. He kept his eyes on the enemy position, rifle cupped against his shoulder, hoping for a flicker of movement to give one of the Japs away.

"I hate sitting around," Philly responded. "Back home I'd rather walk than wait for the bus."

It was the army way to go slow and steady, grinding down the enemy like a millstone, unlike the hard-charging marines.

The sun was setting, and the sky became the color of pink coral. Sheets of dark clouds hanging low on the horizon added deep reds and purples to the already stunning array of colors. It was yet another beautiful tropical evening. Grudgingly, Deke had to admit that the sunsets were spectacular in these parts. He wouldn't have said that the colors were any better than the mountain sunsets he knew so well. Still, they were beautiful in their own way.

Deke didn't spend much time admiring the glow of sunset. He and the rest of Patrol Easy knew the stalemate couldn't last for long, and the setting sun served only as a reminder that night and all its dangers were coming on fast.

All the while the Japanese gun battery at the summit kept up its steady fire, wreaking who knew how much havoc on the American forces on the beach below. Still, the Japanese artillery was a yapping pup compared to the big dogs of the American fleet. Those big guns had kept silent, however, for fear of dropping a shell on the heads of their own troops on the hill.

The air stank of gunpowder, and the sickly sweet odor of the dead began growing in the tropical heat.

The gun battery, meanwhile, had been knocking out American artillery on the beach and harassing the landing craft that were closer in, within range. Though the enemy was deadly accurate, they had been unable to halt the American advance, which brought in continuous waves of supplies to the beach area.

Through it all, the Japanese riflemen and machine gunners hidden in their defensive placements on the hilltop continued to keep up a steady fire, as if mocking the Gis.

"You wouldn't be wrong about nighttime," Deke said, agreeing with Philly's earlier comment. "The Japs will be on us like skeeters on a bare ass at the swimming hole, that's for sure. Philly, you got ammo?"

Philly snorted. "I carried as much as I could up here. Then again, I wish I had more."

Deke nodded. Most veterans took as much ammo as they could carry, even slinging bandoliers across their chests and backs like some kind of Mexican bandit from the days of Pancho Villa. Nonetheless, when the fighting got hot, they still managed to run low on ammunition. And resupply was out of the question on this hilltop.

"Yoshio, what about you?"

"I have plenty," Yoshio replied.

"I reckon that just means you ain't shooting enough," Deke said. "Give me and Philly some of your ammo. Grenades, too, if you got 'em."

Yoshio did just that. "Do you think you will need that much ammunition?"

"Once it gets full dark, the Japs will try to get behind us," Deke said. "They've got their damn trenches all over this hill. They probably wanted us to get into this trench in the first place, so they'd know right where we are."

"You mean it's a trap?" Yoshio asked.

"I don't know for sure, but I'd keep both eyes open. I hope you ate your carrots."

Yoshio smiled. "You know it."

Since the early days of the war, it had become a matter of common knowledge that eating a lot of carrots improved your night vision. The truth was that the story about carrots was pure fiction, having been made up by the military to cover the fact that Allied pilots could "see" at night because they possessed superior radar, not because they ate their vegetables.

Neither carrots nor radar would have done the men on Hill 522 much good. When darkness did come, it was swift and complete as a curtain being pulled across some old lady's parlor window.

The Japanese were notorious for their nighttime attacks, whereas the Americans felt content to stay put until daylight. Much of it came down to a difference in training and tactics.

The Japanese favored the cover of darkness. You couldn't blame them, because the darkness gave them an edge over what was usually the superior firepower of the Americans. Also, fighter planes didn't fly at night, which meant that any Japanese forces would not be attacked from the air. That was probably less of a factor on the hill. They were so close to the Japanese lines that the pilots were afraid of hitting their own guys.

"So now what?" Yoshio asked.

"We just wait," Deke said. "Let the Japs come to us—and they will, all right. Aren't you glad that you went and insulted that Japanese sniper? He probably can't wait to come over here once it's nice and dark and make good on his promises."

Yoshio looked a little pale in the dwindling light, and who could blame him? War seemed like an impersonal thing—until it wasn't.

In the dark of night, the password went around. The word was *lollygag*, which tended to be popular. It didn't need to be secret, because the password was all about pronunciation. Popular wisdom was that the Japanese could not properly say the letter L. Any password that the troops used had more L sounds in it than a porcupine had quills. *Lollipop. Delicious. Umbrella.* Those words were good as a barb-wire fence against infiltrators.

They had been placed roughly in groups of three along the trench, with the idea that each three-man team could act as its own unit in defending the trench. Spreading each man out along the defensive line might have been just as effective, but from a psychological standpoint, there seemed to be safety in numbers. An army of three felt a whole lot better in the dark than an army of one.

Deke kept his hands on the rifle, peering out into the woolly blanket of darkness. From time to time, he put his eye to the scope, which managed to gather just a little extra light, but he saw no sign of the enemy. He was fighting blind.

He kept his ears open, listening for the sound of stealthy footsteps, the scratch of a belly crawling over dirt, or the telltale knock of a Japanese grenade being armed against a rock or helmet.

The quiet was broken by the sound of a voice whispering, "Lollygag."

"Come on in," Deke whispered back.

A moment later Lieutenant Steele eased himself into the trench beside them. They couldn't see him well, but even in the darkness, the eye patch that Deke had made for him on Guam out of a piece of old boot formed an even blacker hole in the outline of Steele's pale, haggard face. It was like a gaping bullet hole, or maybe a glimpse into the dark part of the lieutenant's soul—the eye patch wasn't something you wanted to stare at for long. "How you boys holding up?" he asked.

"We're doing all right, Honcho. We're a little low on ammo."

"Then you'd better make each shot count," Steele said. "You're snipers, after all. That's all the ammo we've got for now. Nobody is going to resupply us before tomorrow morning. I don't need to tell you boys that we can expect some trouble tonight. The Japs don't want us here, and they are going to do everything they can to push us out of this trench. It's quiet for now, so you had better eat something while you've got the chance."

"You got it, Honcho," Deke replied quietly. The lieutenant hadn't told them anything that they didn't already know about what they could expect in the hours ahead.

"I put all the men in this sector into three-man teams. Your team is the right flank, so keep that in mind. I'd imagine that the Japs will try to get into this trench and roll up the whole line, so be ready. On your left, you've got Rodeo, Alphabet, and Egan. Egan's dog will be sniffing for the first whiff of the Japanese, so if he starts to bark, get ready."

"What about you, Honcho? Better join up with us," Deke said. "You can't take on the Japs all by yourself."

"I've got all the company I need right here," Steele said, hefting the twelve-gauge. "I'll be all right. When one of you gets killed, I'll fill in."

"That's awful nice of you, Honcho."

"You think I'm kidding? I wish I were. This is the best chance the Japs have got. They'll hit us hard tonight. They know that in the morning our planes will be back, and maybe we'll get more men to kick the hell out of them."

"If the Japs want to wait for morning, that's fine by me," Philly said.

Steele shook his head. "No such luck, Philly. You know the Japs. They'll be on us, whether we're ready for them or not. Deke, I know you won't let the Japs get past you."

"We'll be ready, Honcho," Deke said, feeling a sudden swelling of fondness for the lieutenant. He was a good man. Deke was also worried about him. Lieutenants and captains had a bad habit of getting killed.

"I know you will, son. Good luck," he said, then moved off toward the next group. Faintly, they could hear him utter the password once more.

"If there are any Japs listening, they probably know our password by now," Philly said.

"Yeah, but they won't be able to say it."

"If I hear anybody mangle that password, I'm going to shoot first and ask questions later," Philly said. "You hear me, kid? Better do the same."

"Got it," Yoshio said.

The lieutenant had ordered them to eat, so that was just what they did now, dipping into their K rations. Deke spooned cold stew into his mouth, barely tasting it, slowly chewing the mushy chunks of carrots and potatoes and stringy beef, then washing them down with a drink of his metallic-tasting canteen water.

It wasn't home cooking, that was for damn sure, but he didn't mind. Food was food. Some men griped all the time about the rations, but not Deke. He had gone to bed hungry enough times as a boy, growing up in the Depression-era mountains on a hardscrabble farm, not to complain about a full belly—even if it was army food out of a can. Besides, there were a whole lot of men on both sides who wouldn't ever be eating again.

Not for the first time, Philly seemed to be reading Deke's mind, which was a little unnerving. When two guys shared a foxhole long enough, you could expect that to start to happen.

"You know what I would miss the most if I buy it tonight on this hill?" Philly volunteered. Like Deke and Yoshio, he was working his way through a can of rations. "I'd miss good food. A cheesesteak and a cold beer, for starters. Spaghetti and meatballs and red wine. Also, I'd miss women. Well, maybe not women exactly, because they can be a pain in the ass, but I'd sure as hell miss a piece of ass. God, would I miss that. What about you?"

Deke snorted. He had never spoken it out loud, but he had dwelled on this very question before. Most soldiers agreed that it was better if a bullet just flipped your switch, like the lights going out. You'd never know what hit you.

But if death wasn't instant, then what did a man think about in the seconds after a bullet hit him and he lay dying? What were his final thoughts—if he even got the chance to have any?

Deke knew he wouldn't be thinking about food or women. "I guess I'd miss seeing Sadie one last time," he said, then added, "I'd miss the mountains. Just a cool fall morning, sun just touching the treetops, walking alone in the hills."

He had expected Philly to make fun of him for that, but to his surprise, the other man said quietly, "That sounds kind of nice. Yoshio, what about you?"

"I'd miss my family."

Nobody could argue with that. Deke finished his cold stew and tossed the empty can into the dirt at the bottom of the trench. "I got a better idea. Let's none of us get killed tonight."

Philly muttered a curse. "I sure wish these Nip bastards would go ahead and get this over with. They sure like to drag it out. It's dark, just how they like it. Why the hell don't they attack?"

"That's on purpose," Deke said. "I reckon they're toying with us, making us scared of what comes next."

"Yeah, well, screw that," Philly said. "Bring it on."

Deke felt the same way, although he would've been happier if it had been daylight. His skills with the rifle weren't much good when he couldn't see what he was shooting at. He felt for his bowie knife that had been custom made for him by Hollis Bailey, a bladesmith from back home. The grip in his hand was antler from a mountain buck, which was in itself reassuring.

Hollis had made it his mission to send fighting knives to each and every local boy he could think of who was in the war. Deke's army-issue knife had been sturdy enough, but the bowie knife was something special, something wicked. With its drop-point blade and razor-sharp edge, the steel almost looked *hungry*. There was no other way to describe it.

He unsheathed the knife and stuck it in the wall of the trench within easy reach. He didn't want to be fumbling around for it when the Japs came calling. After a while, Philly nodded off, and from his silence, Yoshio indicated that he was either sleeping or brooding on what was to come. It was a sign of their exhaustion that they could sleep at all.

Deke left them both alone and scanned the darkness, listening as best he could. The war was already beginning to take a toll on his hearing. They would be a generation of deaf old men—if they lived that long. A few minutes of combat—the deafening cacophony of rifle shots, mortars, and artillery—did more damage to your ears than a lifetime of hunting. At this point Deke had lived through far more than a few minutes of combat. It had left him with a condition that the army doctors called *tinnitus*.

If he tuned out that constant ringing in his ears, then he could still hear well enough. He gripped his rifle and waited.

It was well after midnight when he heard the skittering sound of a boot heel slipping on loose gravel. The sound was not followed by the password, which meant only one thing. This was all the warning that they were going to get.

"Wake up," he whispered, his hard tone jolting Philly and Yoshio out of their slumber. Both soldiers were instantly awake, weapons at the ready. "We've got company."

CHAPTER FIFTEEN

SECONDS AFTER DEKE'S WARNING, the Japanese attack arrived with furious force. Enemy soldiers launched themselves at the Americans in the trench, live grenades held in each hand. They leaped down before anyone could stop them, blowing themselves and any nearby GIs to kingdom come.

The suicidal fervor of the Japanese made the attack that much more terrifying—how did you fight back against soldiers who were already so eager to die?

Flares shot overhead, illuminating the scene with a ghostly light. Deke spotted a Japanese soldier running at them and fired. The soldier had been hanging on to a couple of grenades, which detonated with earsplitting blasts. Bits of rock and dirt rained down on their section of trench. Something warm and wet that Deke didn't want to think about glopped across his face.

"Watch it!" Philly shouted.

Deke whirled, too late to stop a Japanese officer who leaped into the trench to their left, flailing all around him with a sword in one hand and a pistol in the other. In the light from the flares, they could see that the officer's face was contorted in rage, a perfect picture of battle madness. The small Japanese pistol barely made more than a cracking sound, but it was deadly enough to drop a couple of men.

Deke, Philly, and Yoshio fired almost simultaneously, the shots striking the officer and knocking him down. Deke worked the bolt and put another round into the man for good measure. Even so, he half expected the Japanese officer to leap to his feet and attack them all over again.

This was the weapon that shook the American soldiers more than a Nambu machine gun or a dive-bombing Zero—the sheer fanaticism of the Japanese attacks. The enemy came out of the darkness like the Japanese *yōkai* demons of folklore, something inhuman, screaming in a language they couldn't understand. Holding live grenades, or wielding swords, the enemy had clearly come to die at close range. In doing so, they would take as many GIs with them as they could.

This mindset was something the Americans simply could not understand. Sure, there were times when a heroic soldier might make a last stand, selling his life dearly, knowing that he wouldn't survive. For the Japanese, suicidal attacks seemed to be a military strategy. Every enemy soldier they killed was making his last stand on this hill. It was hard to fathom.

"Aaaeiie!" a soldier screamed, running at the trench with a fixed bayonet.

Deke pulled the trigger and dropped him. At his elbow, Yoshio fired at a soldier who had belly crawled to within grenade-throwing range of the trench.

The soldier rolled behind a rock just as Yoshio fired, causing him to miss. He worked the bolt, but the rifle was empty. There wasn't time to reload.

"Deke!" Yoshio shouted.

"Got him," Deke replied, nailing the soldier just as he sprang up to hurl his grenades. The soldier slumped down, followed seconds later by the twin blasts of his grenades at a safe distance from the trench.

The Japanese kept coming. Yet another soldier materialized and dove for the trench as if the darkness had spit him out like a watermelon seed. He landed right between Deke and Yoshio. Neither man even had the space in which to raise his weapon. Fortunately, neither did the enemy soldier, but that wasn't his plan. He wasn't armed with hand grenades or a rifle. Instead, he was carrying a long Japanese knife known as a *tantō*. He slashed at Deke, who twisted away, the blade hissing through the air where his face had been a split second before.

Clutching the rifle in his left hand, Deke grabbed for the bowie knife that he had stuck in the wall of the trench. His hand closed around the bone handle, and he pulled it free. Again, he had to dodge away as the Japanese soldier swung the *tantō* at him. As the momentum of the enemy soldier's swing carried his arm away, Deke jabbed with the knife. The razor-sharp blade sank into the soldier's belly. Deke shoved it the rest of the way in and buried the knife to the hilt.

At that moment, Yoshio hit the Japanese soldier over the head with his rifle barrel. Deke yanked the knife free, and the enemy soldier sank to his knees, several inches of mountain-forged steel having carved a hole in his belly. Yoshio hit the enemy soldier on the head again, and he finally went down.

No more soldiers rushed at them out of the darkness. It had been a desperate fight, lasting no more than a few minutes, but it had felt like an eternity. Deke found himself gasping for breath. *That Jap was crazy as a mad dog.* He stuck the knife back in the wall of the trench and got both hands on the rifle again, ready for whatever came next.

Up and down the trench, similar scenes were playing out. Sometimes the GIs got the Japanese before they threw their grenades into the trench; sometimes they didn't. It was a brutal game of luck and timing, with life or death being the stakes. Finally the Japanese seemed to exhaust themselves. Those attackers who had survived slipped back into the enemy defenses to lick their wounds and regroup.

"That's it, that's it. Cease fire! We got them all!" Lieutenant Steele shouted. Up and down the trench, other officers and sergeants called out the same orders. Those shouts were soon followed by others.

"Medic!" someone called desperately. "Oh, for the love of God, where's the doc? Hurry it up!"

Deke kept his eyes trained on the darkness, but asked, "Philly? Yoshio? You fellas all right?"

"Yes," Yoshio said quietly.

"I dunno," Philly replied after a moment's hesitation. "It's too soon to tell. Ask me in the morning."

Deke knew just what he meant. There would likely be more attacks by the Japanese, each one increasingly desperate. It was going to be a long night.

* * *

WITH THE COMING OF NIGHT, Ikeda and his snipers welcomed a chance to join the attacks taking place against the American position. They had been killing from a distance, but this would be an opportunity to make the fight up close and personal. *The stalemate must end,* he thought. *The Americans must be pushed off this hill.*

A young officer organized the attack, leading a group of about fifty men against the enemy. All around the hill, similar attacks were being organized, but this seemed to be the largest group. Ikeda saw that the strategy was to overwhelm the Americans by attacking from several points at once.

And then what? Before darkness descended, he had seen the numbers of troops still arriving on the beach. If they pushed these soldiers off the hill, the Americans would only send more.

Due to attrition, the junior officers seemed to be getting younger and younger. The young officer was armed with a sword and a pistol. He appeared almost gleeful, as if he could not wait to die for the Emperor and for Japan. Ikeda was not much older than the lieutenant, but he couldn't help thinking, *You young fool.*

"It is easy enough to die," Ikeda muttered. "Let's try killing a few of the enemy first."

"Sir?" asked one of his *sogekihei* snipers who crouched nearby.

"Never mind."

Many of the Japanese soldiers had forgone their rifles or carbines and had laden themselves with hand grenades to maximize the damage against the enemy. The strategy was to get in among the Americans and kill as many as possible with the grenades. Several soldiers expressed their eagerness to die in the process. Others simply accepted their fate grimly and silently. They might not want to die, but they had little choice.

"Hang back and let the men with the grenades do their work," Ikeda quietly told his handful of men. He did not want to be overheard by the fanatical young lieutenant, who might think of them as cowards. But Ikeda did not see the point of dying needlessly. If all the soldiers were killed, there would be no one left to fight. *A broken knife does not cut.* "Use your rifles to pick off any enemy soldiers that you see; then we will withdraw. We will live to fight another day."

As expected, the lieutenant drew his sword and led the attack. In the darkness, Ikeda could see the glint of the officer's blade going down the hill. The group moved slowly at first, as quietly as possible. They picked up speed as they crossed the final few yards in front of the American position. It was hard to make out anything in the darkness, and the attackers spread out and became disorganized. Were they even going in the right direction? Once again, Ikeda caught a glimpse of the sword bobbing up and down as the officer ran.

"Follow me," he whispered, and led his squad that way.

At first it seemed as if the Japanese might fall upon the unsuspecting Americans in total surprise. However, something gave them away—perhaps the scuff of a boot on a rock, or the metallic clink of a string of grenades as the Japanese ran.

The Americans opened fire into the darkness, one of their machine guns blazing in the night. Rapid muzzle flashes from rifles followed, the Americans having the advantage of the rapid-firing M1 rifles and their BAR weapons. A flare was launched, bathing the scene in ghostly shades of white. The hillside that had been cloaked in darkness was now revealed, including the running figures of Japanese soldiers.

"Get down!" Ikeda ordered his men. There was no hope of reaching the trench without being cut down. "Fire! Choose your targets!"

He got to one knee, put his rifle to his shoulder, and fired at one of the enemy machine gunners illuminated by the muzzle flashes. The gun fell silent.

Ikeda had made sure to be in the attack that hit the American position roughly where the enemy sniper was located. But in the confusion, it was impossible to tell whom he was shooting at.

He saw their lieutenant, screaming a battle cry now, slashing with his sword as he leaped down into the trench. There were two quick muzzle flashes, and the lieutenant went down.

All along the line came the sound of explosions as the attackers set off their grenades. Even from this distance, he felt the concussion in his bones. He soon heard the screams of the wounded and the Americans shouting for medics.

Medics made good targets. When he spotted one of the medics with his white armband in the flashes of light, he shot him.

The attack had been savage. There was no doubt about that. But the Americans had clearly been expecting it, and their overwhelming firepower soon brought it to an end. There was no one left to order a retreat and no one to follow such an order, anyhow. Of the assault force, Ikeda and his men were the only ones who returned. *This was no way to win a war,* Ikeda thought.

During the night, orders came to withdraw into the deep caves and tunnels that honeycombed the hillside.

"The Americans will have to dig us out!" an officer said gleefully. It sounded like Major Noguchi. "They will never take this hill!"

Perhaps it was a sound strategy, perhaps not. The hillside definitely offered deep defenses. However, Ikeda had no desire to fight from underground, trapped like a rat. Perhaps that strategy suited Major Noguchi, who had dressed for his own funeral today, but Ikeda had other plans.

Before first light, when the American planes would begin to fly again, Ikeda led his men into the jungle.

* * *

IN THE MORNING, Deke and the others were surprised to find that the enemy positions across from them were mostly vacant. There were a few potshots to harass them, but not the withering fire that they had experienced yesterday. Most of the Japanese defenders appeared to have vanished.

"What I'd like to know is, where did all the Japs go?" Philly wondered.

Deke nodded at the slope above, littered with bodies in brown uniforms. "That's where they went," Deke said. "Look at 'em all."

Daylight had revealed the numbers of Japanese troops that had attacked during the night, only to be mowed down by the sheer volume of fire that had come from the US position. Most of the Japanese spread across the hillside were dead, but not all. A few of the men moved, badly wounded, crawling to who knew where. Shots rang out from the US position, putting the wounded out of their misery. Yoshio winced.

"So many dead. They have gone to meet their ancestors," Yoshio said quietly.

Philly snorted. "Yeah? Well, good luck to them. I'm in no hurry to meet my ancestors, that's for damn sure. I'll bet my granddad is up there right now, getting drunk all day with Saint Peter. And I don't want to spend eternity with my uncle Fred, who told corny jokes all the time."

"Perhaps the Japanese have a different view," Yoshio said.

"If you say so. Like I said, I'm in no hurry to meet up with any of my ancestors. As for the family I've got that's still living, seeing them at Christmas and Easter is enough—never mind eternity. How about you, Deke?"

Deke thought about his father and mother, his grandparents, old neighbors he had known. Good people. Ben Hemphill dead on the beach in Guam. Just another kid who was never meant to be a soldier. He shook his head. "You know what, Philly? Sometimes you talk too much. You don't know when the hell to shut up."

Philly could see that he had touched a nerve. "All right, don't get sore," he said quickly.

With daylight, the order came to push up the hill. Nothing was easy about it. Although the number of dead enemy soldiers seemed to indicate that the defenders had been wiped out, there were many troops still facing them, but not in the numbers that had confronted them before.

The Japanese had hidden rifle pits and tunnel entrances everywhere, popping out to fire on the soldiers. Frustrated GIs soon began tossing grenades into any hole they could find. Satchel charges were used to seal up the larger tunnel entrances.

Nearby, a knot of soldiers was engaged in pouring gasoline down what appeared to be an air vent into an underground passage. They took a step back and tossed a lit match at the vent. Instantly flames raced underground.

It was hard to know whether the Japanese had an escape route elsewhere on the hill, or if they were trapped inside for good. Nobody gave a damn that they were burying men alive, or if they did realize it, they tried not to think too much about it.

After all, it was hard to have much sympathy for the Japanese. The butcher's bill had been heavy. More than twenty men had died on the hill, with twice as many wounded. Most of those had been lost in the vicious nighttime attacks by the Japanese.

Patrol Easy had been lucky, but that luck hadn't extended to the unit that they had accompanied here. Many of the dead had been replacements, and their war had been all too short. Back home, telegrams would soon be going out to shatter the lives of the fathers and mothers, or wives and children, of the soldiers who wouldn't be coming back from Hill 522.

"You remember what the Filipinos call this place?" Yoshio asked. "Guinhangdan Hill."

"Guinhangdan," Deke drawled, stumbling over the pronunciation. "The name might be hard to say, but nobody is gonna forget that place anytime soon."

As they pushed up the hill, there was little respite for the weary GIs. No one had gotten any sleep for a couple of days now, other than grabbing a few minutes here and there. They had been living off cold rations and tepid canteen water—and there was precious little of that as the heat of the day began building again.

Through the haze and smoke, they could see the accumulation of US troops on the beach, everything from makeshift tents to groups of tanks and trucks were now ashore. The beach was looking more and more like a parking lot.

Another welcome sight were the formations of planes overhead, on the prowl for any Japanese resistance. These were all navy flyboys. It had been a long time since anyone had seen a Japanese plane—most had long since been blown out of the sky.

By midafternoon, the last push for the summit came. Men stormed toward the battery in the cave, their rifles loaded and at the ready. By now the attackers had it down to a science. They hurled in grenades and charges, ducked and covered, and the earth shook with the force of the explosions. It took just a few minutes to finally wipe out the battery. At long last, the Japanese artillery on the hilltop was silenced. The surviving enemy soldiers had been buried alive underground. Except for a few stray Japanese soldiers, Hill 522 was now in American hands.

The soldiers spent the remainder of the day mopping up or wandering among the many Japanese dead, collecting weapons and other souvenirs. Not everyone wanted to participate in that, thinking it wasn't right somehow—or maybe they just had an aversion to being around so many dead bodies starting to decompose in the heat. The smell grew more unpleasant as the sun rose higher. Swarms of flies appeared and settled over the bodies. When it came time to eat, the GIs desperately shooed flies off their food, knowing full well that those same flies had been resting on the body of a dead Japanese just a short time before.

Worst of all were the ants, which scurried across the faces of the dead in large numbers, making scavenging forays into ears and nostrils. The sight made more than one soldier shudder, thinking that if he'd been a little less lucky, that would be him out there covered in ants.

Even Philly contented himself with retrieving the sword from the Japanese officer they had killed the night before, and he didn't venture into the killing field to search for more souvenirs.

"Why, Philly, I reckoned you'd be busy emptying the pockets of those dead Japs."

"Just more to carry," he said by way of an excuse.

No orders came to bury the dead.

"Let 'em rot," said an officer. "Do you think that the Japs would have bothered to bury your stinking carcass if it had been the other way around?"

Nobody could argue with the officer's perspective, but it still didn't sit right with a lot of the men.

For the rest of their time on the hill, the men of the battalion looked for caves and tunnels that might be housing Japanese troops. They also killed a number of rats and snakes.

The men who had fought so hard for the hill were exhausted, their uniforms soaked with sweat and blood that was not their own. But they had won.

"I'll be damned," Deke muttered, looking around at the carnage. "I was halfway thinking that we wouldn't be here today."

"I hope you're not disappointed," Philly said. Like a lot of soldiers, he had embraced a black sense of humor. "Besides, the day is young. There's still plenty of time for us to get killed."

CHAPTER SIXTEEN

WHILE THE OTHER Japanese troops awaited their fate deep underground on Hill 522, Ikeda and his band of *sogekihei* snipers melted into the jungle at the base of the hill.

"*Isogashī!* Hurry!" he ordered them. "We must be swift and silent as smoke. *Isogashī! Isogashī!*"

Ikeda kept a nervous eye on the skies. Though tattered by artillery fire, the forest canopy provided enough cover to hide them from the watchful eyes of enemy planes overhead. Meanwhile, they had managed to slip away without being spotted by the attacking force, which was now intent on going after the Japanese in their underground bunkers, like a pack of terriers after fleeing rats. Ikeda winced at that mental image.

Some might have seen leaving the hill to the Americans as retreating, but not Ikeda. He planned to fight another day.

While dying for the Emperor was honorable, Ikeda saw no honor in dying like a cowering rat, deep underground, without taking at least some of the enemy with him. Deciding that his men needed a reminder of that fact, he called for a halt. Looking one by one into the faces of his small band, he said to them, "Each of you may die only after you have killed at least ten of the enemy. Then you may die with honor. Is that clear?"

"Hai!" they responded as if with one voice.

Morosawa offered a grim smile. Clearly he agreed with Ikeda's strategy.

Ikeda gave a nod of satisfaction and moved on.

He had no real plan of action or any destination. He knew only that the fighting in the vicinity was far from over, and they would lend a hand where they could.

They soon found that they were not alone in their intentions. Ikeda and his men joined a company of stubborn Japanese defenders who were making their way toward Palo, located at the base of the hill, eager for any chance to strike back at the Americans. The commanding officer accepted them readily, glad to have more men.

Until now, Palo had largely been left out of the defensive equation as having little strategic importance, but that changed as the Japanese became aware that American troops were using the bridge in Palo to carry supplies from the beach across the Bangon River to the interior of Leyte.

Japanese defenders had wired the bridge to be blown up, but the contingent tasked with destroying the bridge had been killed in a fire-fight with lead elements of the US invasion before they were able to carry out their mission. Palo had become a vital target for the Japanese, if only to deny the Americans use of the bridge.

"Hurry up!" said the Japanese officer in command of the unit that Ikeda and his men had joined, urging them toward the outskirts of town. "We must be in position by nightfall."

"Hai!" Ikeda replied as he and the other troops began pouring along the road toward town.

The Japanese troops were not the only ones using the road. Throngs of refugees were fleeing the town, which had been a hapless victim of the earlier naval bombardment. With their homes destroyed, and fearful of more shelling, groups of civilians were heading into what they hoped was the relative safety of the countryside. They would return once the shelling stopped for good. They were sure that the Japanese had fled the area, but they were soon proved wrong.

"Out of the way!" Ikeda shouted, shoving a Filipino family off the road. The father kept his gaze downcast meekly, even as the soldiers pushed his wife and children into the roadside brush. He did not dare to raise a hand or utter a word of complaint.

There was a good reason for that. The few men who had defended their families from the Japanese now lay dead at the roadside. Many of the refugees were now widows or even orphans.

From the look in Ikeda's eyes, it was clear that any protest on the father's part would have brought instant death to the villager and his family. If the father recognized Ikeda from his frequent visits to search for guerrillas in Palo, the man gave no indication of it.

Watching what was taking place, the man's young son seethed with anger. He hated to see his proud father forced to act like a coward, although he understood why. He followed his father's example and kept his mouth shut, hoping that the Japanese troops would pass over them like a rogue wave and be gone.

If only he had been older, he thought, he would have joined the guerrillas who were fighting for their freedom from the Japanese. He saw his younger sister, scratched and bleeding, pick herself up from a patch of thorns alongside the road. For a moment the boy glared defiantly at Ikeda, but lucky for him, the Japanese sniper did not notice.

Although it was daylight and US aircraft kept a close eye on any enemy ground forces, the fact that the Japanese had mixed with the refugees gave them a certain measure of protection. The US planes flying overhead would not fire on the Filipinos, even when they knew a few Japanese must also be using the road. The refugees provided the Japanese troops with perfect cover as they advanced toward the town.

So far they had not encountered any American troops on the road. The Japanese took it as a good sign that the Americans had not pushed this deep into Leyte. The fight for Hill 522 and other strongholds had bogged them down, keeping American forces close to the beach. Some of the Japanese soldiers took it as a sign that they might still be able to push the Americans back into the sea.

Ikeda smiled as a sudden thought came to him. "Stop!" he shouted at the Filipino family moving in the other direction. "What is your hurry? Where are you going?"

The father of the family could only stare mutely because he did not understand a word of Japanese.

"You are coming with us," Ikeda said. He turned to his men. "Do not allow any more refugees to escape. Turn them around. They are going back to Palo with us."

It didn't matter that the fleeing townsfolk could not understand Ikeda. The gesturing by the Japanese, along with the bayonets and rifle muzzles pointed at them, needed no translation. The soldiers forced the refugees to head back in the direction of Palo, prodding them at gunpoint.

If the townspeople had no idea what Ikeda and the other Japanese were planning, they would soon find out.

* * *

FOR THE UNFORTUNATE people of Palo, the long-awaited liberation from Japanese occupation had turned into a nightmare of war and destruction, starting with the shelling by the US fleet. The shells that rained down on their town had been intended for Hill 522 and other Japanese defensive positions, but some had fallen short and struck the town, wrecking houses and businesses. Some of the townspeople had been killed. The Filipinos had been caught between the proverbial rock and a hard place.

The town itself had a long history that had mostly been peaceful until the arrival of the Japanese. Even the Spanish-American War had resulted in a quiet transition to the American era that had lasted for four decades.

In other places, especially closer to Manila, the initial American occupation after the 1898 Treaty of Paris had not been peaceful. Some Filipino leaders fought for independence. More than four thousand US troops had died during the conflict against Filipino freedom fighters just after the turn of the century. The vast majority of those US casualties had been from tropical diseases rather than combat.

However, the insurrection had lost steam by 1906, in large part because of military defeats suffered by the insurrectionists and the fact that the US kept a light touch in governing their new territory. The

Philippines had autonomy and self-rule—as long as they stayed friendly to the United States government. The guerrillas lost any popular support.

Long before that the Spanish had colonized the islands in the fifteen hundreds. This town had been one of the first where Spanish Jesuits had celebrated Mass in the Philippines, making it among the oldest Spanish outposts.

The years of Spanish influence gave the town architecture a vaguely European air. The buildings were modest but stately, many covered in stucco and accented with colorful wooden shutters. A few green palms or coconut trees growing along the streets added a tropical flair to the old-world charm.

The town was laid out around a central square, with the river forming the western boundary. Several businesses and residences lined the road leading to the bridge across the winding, muddy Bangon River, which flowed into San Pablo Bay.

In more ways than one, the church was the center of the town's life. Whether it was by design or not, Palo Cathedral remained the tallest building in town, presiding over Palo with its sheer physical presence. Its original stones dated to 1598. As awful as this day was, the centuries-old stones of the cathedral served as a reminder that these events were merely a flyspeck in the flow of time.

The Japanese had no appreciation of the old Spanish culture or Western religion, especially when something as powerful in the lives of Filipinos as the church could challenge their own control. In fact, they viewed the traditions of their occupied country with contempt.

One of the cathedral's current priests, Father Francisco, had taken to the hills and jungles alongside the courageous Filipino guerrillas battling the Japanese. Persecuted as he was by the Japanese, the priest had no choice but to leave. It had been only a matter of time before the Japanese either imprisoned him—or worse.

Knowing of this connection to the guerrillas, the Japanese occupiers had shown little sympathy for the citizens of Palo.

To make matters worse for the town, the Japanese military could do anything it wished with impunity. As the highest power in the land, the Japanese army had no one to answer to but themselves. The town's civilian government had been disbanded or replaced with obsequious local men willing to do the bidding of the Japanese. Local military commanders understood that General Yamashita, the ultimate power on Leyte, had far more concerns than the treatment of the locals.

Consequently, Ikeda had been a familiar sight in the town, and a feared one as well, going door to door in search of guerrilla fighters, his band of soldiers acting like thugs. He hadn't held out much hope of finding any weapons or ammunition, much less an actual guerrilla fighter hiding in one of the houses. His real purpose had been to punish the townspeople for helping the guerrillas.

The way that Ikeda saw it, he had lost more than his fair share of men who had made the mistake of venturing too far into the forests occupied by the Filipino freedom fighters. Small bands of Japanese troops were easy pickings for the guerrillas. Why shouldn't the townspeople pay a price for their support of the guerrillas?

The arrival of American forces meant long-awaited liberation from under the Japanese bootheel. But not quite yet.

Liberation was not going to be as easy as the Filipinos might have hoped. As it turned out, Ikeda and the Japanese had one final cruelty and injustice to visit upon the town and its people.

At the moment the Americans were focused on taking strategic positions such as Hill 522. Although they were using the bridge across the Bangon, US forces had shown little interest in the town. When the Americans did get around to occupying Palo, the Japanese planned a surprise for them.

Having rounded up the fleeing townspeople, the Japanese drove them back into the streets at bayonet point, herding them like cattle.

Most of the Filipinos were women and children, old men or boys. The old men were frail, and the boys were very young. Any male sturdy enough to work had long since been drafted by the Japanese to dig rifle pits and carry logs or baskets of earth during the frenzied effort to build defenses before the arrival of US forces. Of course, many young men had given the Japanese the slip to join the guerrilla forces rallying around Father Francisco.

In the frenzied streets, some of the women chattered in frightened voices. Small children cried. They were all totally at the mercy of the Japanese soldiers.

"Be quiet!" Ikeda shouted at the cowed villagers who now crowded the street. An officer stood nearby. Although he was in charge, he gave Ikeda a nod of approval. "I must have silence!"

They could hear the sounds of battle growing nearby, the deadly clatter of machine guns and the thump of mortars. Any civilian could be forgiven for finding these sounds terrifying. Staring at the enemy's rifles and bayonets, the townspeople had no choice but to comply with Ikeda's demands. They fell silent.

"You have been chosen for a great honor," Ikeda said. He gazed around at the frightened townspeople in order to let his words sink in. The handful of Filipinos who understood Japanese translated for the others. "You will lead the fight against the Americans."

The confused townspeople looked at one another in bewilderment, not sure what the Japanese officer was talking about. They had no weapons, and more than that, they wanted to welcome the Americans, not fight them.

But from the looks of things, they wouldn't be given any say. Whatever the Japanese had planned for them, they would have no choice but to obey.

* * *

ON HILL 522, the bulk of the fighting was over, but the real killing was only about to begin.

A few Japanese soldiers popped up now and then to fire a few shots, or even to deliver a mortar shell, but meaningful resistance was over. The GIs had come to the part of the job that focused on smoking out the enemy wherever they could. Egan's war dog, Thor, was kept occupied going around to the tunnel entrances and the cave mouths, sniffing out the enemy. His frantic barking echoed across the hillside.

When word arrived that Patrol Easy would be joining the force moving to occupy the town of Palo, it was welcome news. They'd had enough of this place.

"Fine by me," said Philly, watching as a detail moved cautiously from one hole and pillbox to another, casting in grenades or satchel charges. The details had developed a deadly efficiency as they wiped out any Japanese defenders who might still be hiding on the hill. The ground shook with the detonations.

As the largest charges exploded, they sent a roar up the tunnels and out into the air. It sounded like a Hellcat engine in a dive, a giant buzzsaw and a volcano all rolled into one. He couldn't think of a worse fate than being trapped underground and awaiting certain death. Deke shuddered, some part of him sympathetic to the Japanese on the receiving end of these efforts. He supposed that he hated the Japs as much as any soldier. But this extermination didn't sit right with him.

Even worse was watching drums of gasoline or diesel oil being poured into the deeper holes. With theatrical nonchalance, an officer or sergeant would take a couple of puffs from a cigarette, then toss it down the hole. The message seemed to be that he gave as much thought to killing the Japanese in the hole as he gave to tossing away a cigarette butt.

What followed was not an explosion but a suffocating whoosh of fire. Angry orange flames soon rolled out and licked at the tropical air. The acrid smoke from the petroleum flames soon mixed with the disgusting odor of burned flesh and singed hair that wafted out from below. No matter how many times a soldier smelled that, there was no getting used to such a nauseating smell.

"This makes me sick," Deke muttered. "Sick to my soul, that's what. Burning folks alive. How the hell can a man do that to another man?"

The hollow look in Philly's eyes showed his agreement. "There's no answer to that, country boy."

"War is one thing, kill or be killed and all that, but this is something else," Deke went on. "This has got to be a sin. It ain't right."

"Tell it to Hirohito," Philly said, his voice suddenly taut with anger. He wasn't mad at Deke, but at the situation. "It's his damn fault, not our fellas. Hell, it's not even the fault of the Nips we're roasting alive down there. Well, not *all* their fault. Hirohito is the one that started this whole mess. He's the one that's done this to them."

Deke supposed that what Philly was saying had a lot of truth to it, but right now, Hirohito was nowhere to be seen. What he did see were lots of GIs eager to pour gasoline into the tunnel entrances.

As the day progressed, the pace of the annihilation increased. At first, one of the officers had gotten Yoshio to go around and shout for the Japanese to surrender. Dutifully he yelled into hole after hole, but there weren't any takers before the gasoline and grenades were poured in. After a while, no offer of quarter was given.

"Save your breath," the officer told Yoshio.

Not eager to join in the mopping-up operation, Deke and the other snipers found themselves cooling their heels. It was uncertain when they would be ordered down to Palo. Here on the hill, the Japanese artillery and mortars had been firing for hours. Not anymore.

The first thing Deke noticed when the barrage stopped was how quiet it had become. There was still plenty of artillery in the distance, but the sudden silence was eerie on the hill, like when the band stopped playing at a barn dance.

From time to time in the newfound quiet, they could hear strange singing underground as the Japanese soldiers awaited their fate. Maybe Deke was only imagining it, but he thought that he could hear that singing give way to the screams of the dying Japanese.

But the way most of the soldiers saw it, there was a job to do, however gruesome it might be. At least that was the story they told themselves. Any Japanese left alive were bound to reappear and cause more trouble. There was no question of making this a clean fight. This was no longer a battle but had become a slaughter, a killing operation. Deke reckoned that it was no different from eradicating gophers back home on the farm.

The enemy below had dedicated themselves to nothing less than the destruction of the United States and its allies. They had killed more than a few GIs here on the hill, and now they would pay the price. The GIs were exacting their revenge. Deke didn't like it, but he understood. He just wasn't proud of it.

It was all why the orders to get to Palo were welcome. When a line of infantrymen began descending the hill, Deke and Philly fell in once Honcho gave them the signal. The trip down the steep hill was only marginally easier than coming up had been, due mainly to the fact that

gravity was now on their side. But there was a lot of slipping and cursing, with no clear trail to follow. The troops found themselves plunged
back into jungle surroundings.

"I swear that if I find a banana leaf big enough I'm just gonna get
on it and slide down," Philly said after he had fallen yet again.

"You just ain't graceful like me," Deke said. Some of his good
humor had returned now that the smell of burning flesh from the
underground fires was fading.

Deke was indeed the only one who had seemed to keep his feet.
But while the others were busy falling down and picking themselves
up, he also kept an uneasy eye on their surroundings, rifle at the ready.
Not every Japanese had been sealed inside Hill 522. Due to the heavy
jungle growth, the terrain was perfect for an ambush.

Coming down off the hill and reaching the outskirts of town, the
jungle faded away. They walked through small plots containing rows of
vegetables—what they would have called kitchen gardens back home.
It served as a reminder that, for the Filipinos, this was not some
distant battleground. This was their home.

Feeling exhausted, the GIs managed to place one foot in front of
another, glad to be putting the hill behind them. Yoshio had been busy
trying to talk with a wounded Japanese soldier who had expired
without saying more beyond telling his wife that he loved her. He
hurried to catch up, but he hadn't gotten word that they were headed
into more action.

"Are we returning to the beach?" he asked eagerly.

"No, we're being pulled off Hill 522 to occupy Palo," Philly said.
"Assuming the Japanese aren't already there, in which case we'll have
another fight on our hands."

"More fighting? It seems like the army won't be satisfied until we
are dead," Yoshio remarked.

Philly smirked. "You catch on fast, you know that?"

Deke tried to reassure him. "It'll be different this time, kid.
Honcho says we'll have tanks with us. They'll bust through any Japs as
easy as pie."

"That doesn't sound so bad."

"You know what, kid?" Philly continued. "Maybe you ought to go first, ask any Japs in town if they want to surrender. If you ask polite enough, maybe they'll put down their guns and they won't fight."

"All right, stuff a sock in it, Philly," said Honcho, gathering the squad. "Listen up, fellas. We're going to hang back and watch for snipers while the rest of these guys go in ahead of us. Nobody knows how many Japs are in this town, if any, so keep awake. We've got armor to lead the way, so we're going to let the tanks go in first and do the heavy lifting."

Nothing cheered infantrymen so much as the sight of their own tanks leading the way. The tanks were not invincible, but they could take a lot more of what was thrown at them than a humble GI could. Even the bullets from the dreaded Nambu machine guns bounced right off. They could also dish out a lot of punishment.

"There they go," Philly said, sounding almost gleeful.

The two tanks rolled toward the town. Both tank commanders had their hatches open, to help them navigate the street ahead. The street was cobblestoned, and the tracks clacked down the street, sometimes cracking stones as they went.

Reassured by the presence of the tanks, most of the GIs figured that taking Palo was going to be a piece of cake.

CHAPTER SEVENTEEN

Once they had reached the town, Ikeda turned to his men and whispered harshly, "Follow me!"

They ran to the doorway of a commercial building and pounded up the stairs. A corner of the building was missing, damaged by a bomb, looking like a big bite had been taken out of it. Ikeda positioned his men along the open windows overlooking the street and square below.

From his perch above the narrow street, Ikeda looked down with satisfaction. He and his men had a commanding view of the street. They also had a front-row seat to the scene that was unfolding below.

The bulk of the refugees had been forced ahead of the Japanese, creating a human buffer. The Americans would be reluctant to fire on civilians—Japanese forces had no such qualms. He was sure that the Americans would be taken by surprise. Meanwhile, the horde of civilians would provide good cover, enabling the Japanese troops to get quite close before opening fire.

It was the perfect ruse. The trap had been set.

From their position up here, Ikeda and his men would wreak havoc on the unsuspecting Americans.

"Sir!" Morosawa shouted.

Ikeda looked in that direction and saw with satisfaction that the soldier was pointing at a small force of Americans advancing through the street, directly toward the mass of civilians flowing toward them. There were two tanks leading the way, but all that firepower would be useless against what was about to happen.

Ikeda put his rifle to his shoulder and waited for the Americans to come into range.

* * *

Looking around, Deke noted that Palo really was a proper town with masonry buildings and a handful of two- and even three-story structures. The buildings made him a little uneasy because he preferred being surrounded by fields or forests. He had yet to fight in anything resembling a town.

At the moment, the town also seemed to be deserted. There wasn't even so much as a dog in sight, which was a little unusual, because the lean little village dogs were usually found in abundance. The dogs seemed to be smart enough to have cleared out. The only dog in sight was Thor, straining against his leash as if to say, *Let me at 'em!*

Soldiers followed on the heels of the tanks.

"Hey, where are the Japs?" somebody shouted.

"Shut the hell up!" yelled a sergeant.

But the man had simply said what was on everybody's mind.

"Looks like the Japs didn't have time to put out the welcome mat," Philly said.

"If what you mean by welcome mat is shooting at us, don't be disappointed just yet," Deke said. "Might be that we're walking right into a trap."

"What trap is that?"

"Maybe they're waiting for us to come in closer."

"It could be that they turned tail and ran at the sight of those tanks."

"They're probably inside those buildings," Deke said. "I'll bet they've got snipers on the top floors. They're probably gonna shoot down on the troops from inside the buildings. That's what I'd do if I was a Jap."

"Which you're not."

"Thank the good Lord for that."

The quiet did not last for long. Rodeo, the squad's radio operator, got a message and passed the word in a whisper. "The boys in the tanks see movement up ahead."

"What the hell are they waiting for? Then tell them to start shooting!" Honcho exclaimed.

There was no need for Rodeo to relay the orders. The tankers knew what to do. As if on cue, the tanks opened fire with their machine guns. Moments later, what appeared to be the enemy came into view, flowing like a tide down the street toward the advancing US forces. The tanks' machine guns mowed down the advancing enemy in rows, their bodies quickly piling up.

But something wasn't right. So far there wasn't any return fire. It soon became apparent that the street wasn't filled with enemy soldiers, but with women, children, and old men.

"Hold your fire!" Honcho shouted. "Rodeo, get on the horn and tell those tanks to stop shooting, for God's sake. They're killing kids and old ladies!"

The advancing Americans took their fingers off their triggers and stared, aghast at what they beheld. Many of the helpless civilians now lay dead or dying, their blood flowing along the cobblestones.

But there were wolves among the sheep.

A boy broke away from the mass of people still in the street, running toward the Americans. It was the same boy who had been forced earlier to watch his father cower before the Japanese. He held his head high, pumping his arms, running flat out on skinny legs for all that he was worth.

"What the hell?" somebody shouted.

"Don't shoot, for Chrissake. It's just a dumb kid."

As the Americans lowered their weapons, Honcho stepped forward to meet the boy. Nearly breathless from his sprint, the boy reached the lieutenant and spoke the only word of English he knew. "Japanese!" he shouted, then pointed frantically behind him. "Japanese!"

Realization dawned on Honcho. He shoved the boy behind him, out of the line of fire. "Get ready! Japs! Here they come!"

Hiding among the terrified civilians had been several Japanese soldiers using the Filipinos as cover. They opened fire indiscriminately, having no compunctions about their bullets taking out a few more civilians.

The Americans struggled to react. To shoot back meant killing and wounding more civilians. Up ahead, the tanks' machine guns had fallen silent.

A few of the GIs felt sufficiently confident about their marksmanship to shoot back, Deke among them. He picked out a Japanese soldier with a fixed bayonet and dropped him.

"Aim for the Japs," Honcho urged. His own twelve-gauge lacked the finesse to do any good, but that didn't stop him from grabbing a pair of binoculars and calling out targets to his sniper squad.

Undeterred, the Japanese raked the tanks with fire and unleashed their weapons at the advancing infantry. Many of the GIs held their fire, unsure of whom they should shoot at. The Japanese shot several soldiers while they tried to figure out what was going on.

In the confusion, the Japanese quickly got the upper hand. Patrol Easy held steady, but some of the GIs nearby started to melt away in the confusion in the streets.

"Hold your positions!" Honcho shouted in frustration.

* * *

FROM THEIR VANTAGE point on the second floor, Ikeda and his snipers picked off several GIs. Ikeda put his crosshairs on one of the tank commanders and pulled the trigger, watching with satisfaction as the man's lifeless body slid back into the hatch.

But the tank wasn't full of fools. One of the crew must have seen where the shooting was coming from and took command of the situation. Slowly and deliberately, the muzzle of the tank's gun swiveled in their direction.

"Down!" he cried, rolling away from the open window.

In the next instant, he was thrown back, ears ringing, dust clogging his mouth and eyes. On his hands and knees, dragging his rifle, he managed to reach the stairs. With a final glimpse behind him, he could see that many of his men were dead. He spotted Morosawa's shattered body in the rubble, the man's blood mixing with the dust.

Ikeda headed for the stairs before the tank could fire again. Even he had to admit that a rifle was no match for a tank.

Leaping down several steps at a time, he led the few men he had left down the stairs and into the safety of the alley just before another tank round blew the building to pieces.

* * *

"PICK YOUR TARGETS!" Honcho shouted, mainly for the benefit of the GIs within hearing range. He had managed to rally enough of the soldiers to put up a fight against the Japanese.

Deke and the rest of Patrol Easy already knew what to do. Deke swung his rifle from one Japanese soldier to the next, dropping them where they stood. More and more GIs opened fire, their magnificent M1 rifles spitting out bullets as fast as they could pull their triggers. They might not be snipers, but at this range they did just fine singling out enemy soldiers.

Fortunately the Japanese stealth attack started to fall apart as the Filipino civilians scattered. They ran for whatever shelter they could find, darting down alleys and into doorways, many of them screaming. Soon only the Japanese remained, caught out in the open.

The tanks opened fire once again with their machine guns, cutting the enemy to pieces.

Despite the clever, vengeful Japanese attack in which they had used civilians as camouflage, Palo was now in American hands.

CHAPTER EIGHTEEN

ABOARD USS *NASHVILLE*, preparations were underway for another landing operation—much smaller but no less momentous than the storming of the beaches. This would be the landing that carried General MacArthur back to the shores of the Philippines.

Captured with movie cameras, it would become one of the most iconic moments of the war. MacArthur's political enemies and even some cynical Americans would scoff at the film images as a publicity stunt. Others would find the scene inspirational, proof of American promises kept and a hard-won moment of victory in what had been a costly war.

But at that moment, the film cameras had yet to roll, and Captain Jim Oatmire was more worried about getting the chin strap of his helmet adjusted properly.

"Dammit," he finally said in exasperation after trying for the umpteenth time to get the strap the right length to hold the helmet in place. Looking around, he could see that many of the other soldiers and officers simply let their straps dangle.

"Relax, Oatmire," said Major Lundholm, who had watched in amusement as the staff officer fidgeted with his gear. "If the Japs decide to shoot you, that helmet won't do you much good. And if you fall in the drink, the last thing you want is that steel washbowl dragging you under."

"Yes, sir," Oatmire said, gritting his teeth.

"You're the one who said he couldn't wait to hit the beach," Lundholm pointed out. He spoke with the smug assurance of a man who was staying put on this mighty Brooklyn-class cruiser, safe from any Japanese snipers. "Your wish is my command."

Not for the first time, Oatmire regretted ever lamenting that he wanted to see some action. Most headquarters staff were happy enough keeping their heads down and counting their blessings that they weren't out there with the rest of the troops, dodging bullets and swatting mosquitoes. *I had to go and open my big mouth.* Major Lundholm had promised that he would get a chance to see a combat zone up close and personal. That had been back in Brisbane, when the planning for the invasion of the Philippines was still taking place.

The planning had become a reality when the US invasion fleet finally steamed toward Leyte with General MacArthur and his staff aboard. Not long after the voyage began, the major had informed Oatmire that he'd be going ashore on A-Day. Oatmire hadn't been able to sleep for several nights, thinking that he would be going ashore with a combat unit.

Like any man, he'd had to face his fears. Chief among them had been the very real threat of death on the beach. Second, Oatmire had wondered how he would hold up. Would he act like a man, or would he be a coward? It was easy to be brave before the bullets started flying. To his surprise, Oatmire had eventually realized that he feared being a coward more than he feared dying.

But early that morning, just when he'd been ready to scrabble down the rope netting into one of the landing craft carrying the first wave of troops ashore, Oatmire had been pulled aside and told, "Not yet, Oatmire."

Oatmire had been mystified at first, but then he realized it was all part of a cruel joke on Major Lundholm's part. What the major hadn't told Oatmire was that he *wasn't* going to be part of the beach landing but would be part of the team going ashore with the general. It was just like Lundholm to let Oatmire stew over thinking that he would be baring his teeth into a storm of Japanese lead rather than the pop of flashbulbs. All those sleepless nights had been for nothing.

Hours later, he was fiddling with his chin strap. He didn't even have a rifle or a sidearm. Instead, he had been given a briefcase full of documents to carry ashore. The briefcase was damn heavy. The primary beach landings might be over, but the paperwork was just beginning, Oatmire thought ruefully. Then again, if it came down to it, he supposed that the briefcase would do a pretty good job of stopping a bullet.

He glanced over at Major Lundholm and thought, *You son of a bitch*. What he'd like more than anything was to whip off his heavy steel helmet and beat Lundholm to death with it. Considering that he was younger and bigger than Lundholm, he had no doubts that he'd be successful. However, he didn't want to spend the rest of his days in Fort Leavenworth. Lundholm just wasn't worth it.

Deep down he had to admit that he'd experienced a sense of relief when he'd been held back from getting into that landing craft. He felt guilty about that. Worst of all, he was never going to be able to answer that question he had wrestled with for the past three nights, tossing and turning in the sweaty sheets of his bunk aboard USS *Nashville*. Was he a coward or was he a real soldier? Oatmire now feared that he'd never find out.

Nearly two and a half years had passed since MacArthur's defeat at the hands of the Japanese during their surprise invasion of the US-controlled islands. Some still blamed MacArthur for the defeat, but the US forces had simply been overwhelmed from the air and from the sea.

His famous vow had been made at that time: "I shall return."

On this day, that was just what the general was doing.

However, he was not making the trip alone. This was a symbolic landing.

Despite the seemingly spontaneous air that would be captured for newsreel, nothing about the landing had been left to chance. The general's staff had made certain that there were plenty of film cameras on hand to capture the moment, both on the landing craft taking the general and his party to shore and on the beach itself. Perhaps more than any other general, MacArthur understood that the people of a democracy didn't just need to hear the news of victory—they needed to see it on movie screens back home.

Along with the craft carrying MacArthur, there was another boat filled with newspaper and magazine writers. They had been hand-picked because they had written articles that were favorable to the general. On deck, he had taken a few minutes to joke with the men and even pose for a group photograph. Long before he had been the commanding general, MacArthur had been a press officer. He understood how to work with reporters—he even liked them.

On the surface, these men seemed to be more cogs in the wheel of MacArthur's well-oiled publicity machine, even if some of their bylines were semifamous. But in all fairness, the truth was that folks back home didn't want to read any negative news about the war. They'd had enough bad news from places like Guadalcanal. They wanted to read about ordinary heroes and larger-than-life generals and admirals. The journalists were happy enough to give them just that.

In the small vessel bobbing alongside the ship, the official group assembled. The VIPs included Sergio Osmeña, president in exile of the democratic government of the Philippines.

Wearing a pith helmet and an army uniform despite his civilian role, Osmeña had acquired a rifle and appeared ready to use it on any Japanese. Oatmire had to admit that the wiry politician looked as though he could hold his own if it came down to a fight. Also along for the landing was General Sutherland, who was MacArthur's chief of staff.

Front and center was General MacArthur, wearing his Philippine Army field marshal's cap, a pipe stuck between his teeth. He wore a sharply pressed uniform and well-shined shoes—no combat gear for him. A pair of aviator sunglasses made his face appear stony and unreadable.

Oatmire got aboard last, tumbling the last few feet when a wave slapped the boat away from the netting, causing him to miscalculate the final drop. He landed heavily, hugging the briefcase to keep it from splashing into the Pacific. It was a less-than-glamorous arrival, prompting MacArthur to remark to the military cameraman, "Be sure to cut out that last bit."

"Yes, sir."

Then the boat was moving away, cutting through the blue waters of the Pacific. They had ten miles to go before reaching shore, but the hills of Leyte soon came into sight—along with the columns of smoke from burning fires.

The boat did not race to shore with any urgency. The experienced helmsman seemed to be taking his time, finding a path through the waves that didn't kick up so much spray that his high-ranking cargo got soaked through before the photo op. During the trip, MacArthur chatted with Sutherland and Osmeña, but Oatmire couldn't hear what they were saying over the sea breeze.

The breeze wasn't enough to mask the sound of artillery, which grew louder as they approached the beach. Now and then the chattering sound of a Nambu machine gun carried out over the water. It was a reminder that the fight for the Philippines remained in full swing. The passengers in the landing craft seemed nonchalant about the danger, but the truth was that they were headed into a war zone. Oatmire touched his helmet and gulped.

The beach itself looked as busy as Times Square—if Times Square had been bustling with landing craft, tanks struggling through the sand, and hordes of soldiers moving in every direction. Planes roared over it all, sometimes no more than a hundred feet above the sand. As a backdrop, they could see more smoke and hear the steady thump of artillery and mortars.

Closer to shore, the water was filled with vessels of all shapes and sizes, so that the helmsman had to steer carefully through the competing wakes. He had a designated landing spot in mind.

Captain Gaetano Faillace, the general's staff photographer, had gone ahead of the landing party to capture the moment. Oatmire could see him on shore, a solitary figure armed with a camera.

Despite the experienced hand at the helm, the vessel encountered trouble when it ran aground on a sandbar. The pilot worked it free, but getting closer to shore was problematic in the confusion. Seeing the situation, one of the general's staff on shore approached the beachmaster, whose job it was to manage all this chaos, about clearing a path for the general's vessel.

But sometimes even a general became not much more than another headache for the beachmaster trying to ride herd on the incoming vessels laden with troops and supplies.

The man yanked a soggy cigar from his mouth. He had already dropped it in the salt water more than once, and it was sandy to boot, but he didn't have time to notice. "They're only fifty yards out. Tell *His Majesty* to walk from there!" he shouted.

The response relayed to the general's craft was more diplomatic. Minutes later, the landing ramp splashed down, and General MacArthur waded ashore, head jutting forward, shoulders set, pipe stuck jauntily between his teeth, appearing as determined as a bull. He looked nothing short of magnificent.

Shutters clicked and film cameras rolled. The iconic photograph came from the lens of Captain Faillace. The moment had been captured, even down to Oatmire at the fringes of the scene, struggling ashore with a briefcase clutched in his arms.

In a larger sense, it was a perfect study in contrasts as the conquering American general came ashore in full view while the Japanese commander remained well hidden.

There hadn't been any welcoming ceremony, but with so many troops on the beach, large numbers of soldiers had been witness to the momentous landing. A kind of excitement spread across the beach. The big boss had arrived. Decades later, they would be telling their grandchildren about this one.

MacArthur wasted no time making a personal inspection of the beachhead. But the general wasn't there to bark orders. He was there to learn. More than one captain or major was surprised to find himself answering questions asked by the general, who nodded with satisfaction and the parting words, "Well done. Carry on."

However, the general did have a specific reason for being at the beach. He waved Oatmire over, and the briefcase was opened. The briefcase contained documents that included the speech the general planned to give once ashore.

Almost immediately after completing his impromptu inspection of the beachhead, MacArthur issued a directive announcing that the Japanese would be held accountable for any war crimes against civilians or US prisoners of war. After what the troops he had left behind had suffered at the hands of the Japanese, notably during the Bataan Death March, MacArthur was more than bitter about their treatment. Liberating any current POWs was high on his list of priorities. He also feared that, in desperation or retaliation for setbacks in the field, the enemy might begin killing prisoners. MacArthur had put them on notice that there would be severe consequences.

Two hours after landing on Red Beach, he was standing before a radio microphone, relaying his famous message of liberation:

"To the People of the Philippines, I have returned. By the grace of Almighty God our forces stand again on Philippine soil—soil consecrated in the blood of our two peoples. We have come, dedicated and committed, to the task of destroying every vestige of enemy control over your daily lives, and of restoring, upon a foundation of indestructible strength, the liberties of your people.

"As the lines of battle roll forward to bring you within the zone of operations, rise and strike. Strike at every favorable opportunity. For your homes and hearths, strike! For future generations of your sons and daughters, strike! In the name of your sacred dead, strike! Let no heart be faint. Let every arm be steeled. The guidance of divine God points the way."

Standing nearby, Oatmire listened to the words and found himself flooded with emotion. Say what you wanted about General MacArthur and his famous ego, but he had put that aside today. The general's words had invoked basic American principles. His statement made it clear that the United States stood in stark contrast to the crushing regime of the Japanese.

Freedom. Democracy. It was what every man, woman, and child on this island was fighting for against Japanese forces. The goal was liberation of an entire nation. Considering that there were seventeen million

Filipinos—more than twice the population of California at that time—this was no small achievement.

Maybe Captain Oatmire hadn't stormed ashore into a hail of lead, but all the same he found himself proud to be on this beach, part of something much larger than himself.

CHAPTER NINETEEN

THE FIGHT for Hill 522 and then for the town of Palo had left the men of Patrol Easy worn out and exhausted. Sleep and hot grub were fondly remembered without any real hope of experiencing them anytime soon, kind of like a kiss from a nurse at the USO dance back in Hawaii.

As they knew all too well, there was no rest for the weary, not when there was a war on. The army had pushed inland, but pockets of stiff Japanese resistance remained. They did not control the peninsula. They had taken Palo, but the port city of Ormoc—and its important nearby airfield—remained in enemy control on the far side of Leyte. Until they had taken Ormoc, US forces couldn't claim to be in control of Leyte.

Nobody was going to forget Red Beach anytime soon, but Ormoc was the next square of the chessboard that was the Pacific campaign.

"Sounds like somebody else got the short end of the stick for a change," Philly remarked, listening to the not-so-distant hammering of machine-gun bursts, punctuated by rifle fire.

"Poor bastards are catching hell," Deke agreed. "Just as long as it ain't us this time around, that's fine by me."

"Amen to that," Philly said.

As the men dug into their rations, Lieutenant Steele came around. He wore a fresh bandage around his upper left arm, a souvenir of the fight on Hill 522. The bandage was none too clean, a little frayed around the edges, as if it had been torn from the tail of a shirt, and stained with blood.

"You ought to have someone look at that, Honcho," Deke said.

"In a minute. I've got something to say to you all first."

Lieutenant Steele carried his shotgun slung over one shoulder, the wood showing a fresh scar where he had used the stock to parry a Japanese sword during the fight in that godawful trench. The lieutenant looked a little beat up, but to be fair, Deke supposed they all did.

Steele's one good eye fell upon the soldiers, taking them all in, one by one. If he liked what he saw, his expressionless face didn't show it. Even though they'd been together since Guam, Steele remained something of an enigma. He didn't talk much about his life before the war, or about Guadalcanal. On the other hand, he didn't ask the men in his patrol much about their own civilian lives.

The lieutenant's aloof nature didn't mean that he didn't care—just the opposite. You could tell from his tone of voice that when he called a soldier "son," there was a fondness there—he just didn't always show it. Steele had learned the hard way that an officer always had to keep his distance. How else could he give orders that put his men in the way of an enemy bullet? Outwardly Steele gave the impression that he had one interest, and one interest only, and that was killing Japs.

Deke would have followed the man anywhere.

"I'll bet the Japs didn't think we'd take this part of Leyte so fast, did they?" Deke wondered.

"Who knows?" Lieutenant Steele replied. "The enemy is still full of surprises, and the Japs are far from beaten. We're just lucky that we have planes, and tanks, and naval artillery. The Japs don't have much of that left. We're winning this war because we can replace what we lose and they can't. We're pushing them back everywhere right now, so that's something. But you know the Japs. They don't give up. They don't surrender—not many of them, anyway."

"Fine by me. You know what they say—the only good Jap is a dead

Jap," Philly said. He glanced in Yoshio's direction. "Present company excepted."

"I am not Japanese," Yoshio pointed out for the umpteenth time. "I am an American, just like you."

"If you say so."

"All right, knock it off, Philly," the lieutenant interrupted. "The reason that I wanted to talk to you boys is that I've just gotten word from battalion that we're moving out again."

"Of course we are," Philly grumped.

"They need us to hit Ormoc on the other side of the peninsula," the lieutenant said. "There's two ways to get there. One way is by boat, sailing right down the Surigao Strait and around the tip of the peninsula, then up the Canigao Channel—dodging Japanese planes and whatever is left of the Japanese Navy the whole way."

"Hell, Honcho, after what we've been through, that sounds like a pleasure cruise."

"If you say so, Philly. It won't be so pleasant once we get there, believe me," the lieutenant said. "I hear there's a wide-open beach that we can land on, plenty of time for the Japs to give us hell while crossing it. They'll be expecting us."

Nobody had much to say about that. They had now landed on at least two beaches while under fire, and those landings hadn't been a picnic. The thought of doing that a third time was almost too much to contemplate.

Even Philly, loudmouth that he was, was left shaking his head quietly, words having failed him.

Steele wasn't finished. "Three of you lucky bastards won't be going with us. The thing is, we're going to split up." When the men started to protest, the lieutenant raised his hands to quiet them. "This wasn't my idea. It came from on high, so there you have it. Deke, Philly, and Yoshio, you won't be taking our little pleasure cruise."

"Please tell me we're being sent home for a war bond tour," Philly said.

"No such luck," Honcho said. "Remember how I said there were two ways to get to Ormoc? We'll be coming at the Japs from two directions to keep them confused. The boat is one way. The other way is directly across the peninsula. Twenty miles of jungle, mountains, and Japs. It's going to be Charlie Company's job to cut across the peninsula. Battalion wants some scout-snipers to go with them on account of the jungle terrain, so I picked you three."

"Why us?"

"Because it's my belief that you three have the best chance of making it to the other side alive—not to mention that you're the best chance for Charlie Company too. From what I hear, a lot of them are green troops, so they need a few veterans like you to show them the ropes." Lieutenant Steele sighed. For the first time, he seemed to allow himself to display a flicker of the emotion that he had been holding back. A look of sadness crossed his face, but that look was quickly replaced by a wry smile. "Good luck, boys. You're going to need it. You know what? We're all going to need it. I suppose I'll see you again in Ormoc—or in hell."

* * *

As it turned out, Charlie Company was moving out in a hurry. It was going to take a lot longer to reach Ormoc by traversing the interior of Leyte than it would to get there by ship. Deke, Philly, and Yoshio barely had time to digest the news and say their goodbyes to Rodeo, Alphabet, and Egan—and to give Thor's ears a scratch—before they had to hurry up and report to their new captain. Honcho had informed them that they were looking for Captain Merrick. They found him bent over a map with a lieutenant and a couple of sergeants. Deke didn't know how much use a map would be—all they had to do was follow the direction that the sun took each day until they hit the ocean on the other side.

Of course, nobody dared to salute him. There might not be any Japanese snipers in the immediate vicinity, but it was a bad habit to get into.

"You must be my scouts," the captain said, looking away from the map. He had his helmet off, and from his youthful face and lack of gray hair, it was plain that he was a lot younger than Lieutenant Steele. Not for the first time, Deke wondered who the lieutenant had upset so thoroughly that he couldn't seem to get promoted. "I hear that at least one of you is the best shot in the army—the army on Leyte, at least. I'm pretty sure that's you."

The captain was looking at Deke, who drawled: "If you say so."

"Well, you're the mean-looking one." Captain Merrick squinted in surprise at Yoshio, then took a step back in a double take. "You a Jap?"

"I speak Japanese, but I am an American," Yoshio said calmly.

"Hell, that's what I meant," Merrick said after a moment's hesitation. He appeared a bit flustered by the sight of a Nisei, but he recovered quickly. "We're all Americans here. Our orders are to capture a few Japs and interrogate them, but you know how that goes. Not many prisoners. The Japs don't like to give up, and our boys tend to shoot the ones who do. They've lost too many of their buddies at this point. Anyhow, glad to have you, son. Glad to have all three of you. When we head out, the three of you will take point. I need somebody up front who knows what the hell they're doing. I'll have a handful of veterans at the rear of the column to deal with any Japs who try to shoot us in the back. We know they're good at that."

Deke nodded, and the captain turned back to the map, indicating that they were dismissed.

"He doesn't seem so bad," Philly remarked as they walked away. "On the sly, I asked a couple of the guys in his company what he's like, and they said he's a solid officer."

Deke nodded. That had also been his impression of the captain during their brief introduction. Captain Merrick appeared competent enough, with that no-nonsense exterior so common to officers with combat experience. He seemed like a good man, and Deke hoped that he'd last more than a few days. The war was hell on young officers, lost at an alarming rate. Too often they were targeted by Japanese snipers. Other times they died leading from the front. The only men that the army seemed to lose more of were the medics.

Before they headed out, there were preparations to make, made easier because they had already said their farewells to Lieutenant Steele and the rest of Patrol Easy. Lieutenant Steele had given Deke his orders and wished him luck.

"Do you think we'll ever see them again?" Philly wondered. He appeared to be experiencing a rare moment of introspection. Philly's usual conversation didn't vary much beyond the categories of broads, beer, and bratwurst—make that food in general—unless he was complaining about something.

"I don't rightly know, Philly," Deke answered honestly. "It's a big war. We're all just itty-bitty leaves, caught up in the whirlwind."

"Well now, listen to you." Philly pitched his voice up a notch and mimicked Deke's country drawl. Nearby, Yoshio cracked a smile at Philly's attempt to sound like anything but a blue-collar working stiff from the row house neighborhoods of Philadelphia. "You're a regular hillbilly philosopher, ain't you?"

"Stuff it, Philly."

The other man gave a short laugh that somehow ended in a sigh. "I hate to say it, but a part of me already misses those bastards."

"If we want to see them again, we'll have to live through the next few days," Deke pointed out. "They'll have to do the same. It ain't easy with a war on."

"I guess you're right. As for us, we'll have to be like the Three Musketeers. All for one, and one for all."

From what Deke knew of the Three Musketeers, they had managed to fight for one another despite their differences. Here they were, a farm boy, a city boy—and Yoshio, who was hard to typify. He knew that Yoshio had also grown up on a small farm, but with his thoughtful air, he was more like a schoolteacher.

Deke thought back to the double take that Captain Merrick had done upon seeing Yoshio. The sight of a Japanese face in a US uniform tended to do that. "Yoshio, don't you ever get tired of people wondering which side you're on?"

"Not really," he said. "You see, I have never wondered myself, which makes it an easy question to answer."

"Amen to that," Deke said. "Now let's see if we can find some extra ammo. Something tells me that there's gonna be plenty to shoot at in this jungle."

Deke wanted to travel light. If they had to hump it through the hilly jungle terrain, then he wanted to carry the essentials. That meant his rifle, spare ammo, cleaning kit, bowie knife, canteen, rations, first-aid kit, flashlight, poncho, and blanket. Along with a few extras like a spoon and matches, everything he needed fit into a small haversack. He made certain that nothing rattled or clanked. An unwanted noise at the wrong time could bring attention from the enemy.

He shook his head, watching some of the greener troops prepare for the jungle trek. Some brought too much. Deke figured this was less of a concern because when their packs got too heavy, they would figure out what to discard along the way. Those who didn't bring enough would find themselves shivering in the frequent rain—even the jungle could get cool on a wet night.

To Deke's surprise, he spotted the soldier with the eyeglasses whom he had rescued from the sinking landing craft. The soldier recognized him as well and gave Deke a nod. Deke was glad to see that his efforts had paid off in that the young green bean had made it this far. Whether he'd come out alive on the other side of the peninsula remained to be seen. Ruefully, Deke realized that went for himself too. This wasn't going to be an easy mission.

The only man who managed to carry less than Deke was the Filipino guide who had been assigned to them. The man carried a rifle and a big-ass bolo knife slung across his back. That seemed to be the extent of his gear. Other than a small bag of rice that was stuffed into a game-bag-like cloth sack that hung from one of the man's shoulders, he didn't even carry any rations that Deke could see. Maybe he expected the Americans to feed him?

Hope you like beef stew, Deke thought.

Like many of the guerrillas, his uniform, such as it was, had been pieced together out of battered civilian clothes and military castoffs. He wore stained chino pants that had been torn off below the knee like a pirate's breeches, and an army shirt that had seen better days. The Filipino didn't even wear any shoes. That was too much for Deke. He'd gone barefoot on the farm plenty of times in the summer as a boy, but his feet weren't nearly as leathery as the guide's. Then again, those bare feet enabled the man to move so silently it was as if he floated over the ground.

Up close, the man even smelled like the jungle, a wild, damp, earthy odor—with a bit of campfire smoke and sweat mixed in—that clung to the Filipino like a second skin.

The Filipino guide's name turned out to be Danilo. Deke learned later that it was a Tagalog version of Daniel. Danilo would be joining them at the head of the column. He was a couple of inches shorter than Deke, lean and muscular as a panther, with dark, watchful eyes. One thing for sure, Danilo was a tough customer. He looked Deke up and down, assessing him, then gave him a satisfied nod.

"Do you know Padre Francisco?" Deke asked him.

Surprisingly, the hard set of Danilo's mouth widened into a smile. *"Padre Francisco? Si."*

Briefly, Deke tried to explain about the raid and how Father Francisco had helped them, but he gave up when he saw the blank expression on Danilo's face as he struggled to understand English.

Still, the guide nodded as if he'd gotten the gist of what Deke had said. *"Compañeros!* Kill many Japs!" He grinned again and gave Deke's shoulder a friendly slap and added in Tagalog, *"Mga kaibigan!"*

Deke nodded back. He reckoned that he and Danilo would get along just fine. They seemed to have Father Francisco in common, and, more importantly, they both agreed about killing Japs. Deke tried to repeat the Tagalog phrase, mangled it, and settled for saying, *"Compañeros."*

No time was wasted getting the column moving. Some liked to joke that the military's motto was "Hurry up and wait." Maybe that was true under normal conditions, but not today. Although it was already afternoon, the company moved out. Deke would have preferred to get started in the morning. However, he understood the need for urgency. They had many miles of jungle to cross before this expedition was over, and each hour of daylight mattered.

There would be no point of even trying to go anywhere once night arrived. Deke knew from experience that the jungle dark was so thick that you really couldn't see your hand in front of your face. The one exception was on bright, moonlit nights, when the jungle came alive with sounds and night creatures. Even then, moving along the narrow jungle trails after dark was hazardous enough without the Japanese to also worry about.

It was Danilo who led the troops down the trail, followed by Deke, then Philly and Yoshio close on his heels. Nearer to the village, the trail started out wide—it was essentially a dirt road leading into the forest. A few small homesteads had been carved out of the trees, but most seemed deserted, their inhabitants having fled to avoid getting caught in the middle of any fighting.

They were greeted by barking dogs and scratching chickens. A few of the soldiers broke ranks long enough to grab a chicken or two, wring its neck, and stuff it into their haversacks. Fresh chicken beat the hell out of canned rations. Deke could tell by Danilo's scowl that he didn't approve. For all they knew, these might be his friends' chickens that would be roasting over Charlie Company's fires tonight.

After a couple of miles, the road narrowed to a trail and the forest closed in. They arrived at a fork in the trail. There were no signs or markers of any kind, just trails leading in two directions. Danilo considered and then took the left fork. More time passed, and they came to another fork. After a moment of deliberation, Danilo took the right-hand turn.

Deke wasn't encouraged by Danilo's slight hesitation. *I hope he knows where he's going,* he thought.

Deke realized that they had put an awful lot of trust in this Filipino. Who had picked him out as their guide, anyhow? He wasn't worried about Danilo betraying them to the Japanese. Aside from a few obsequious public officials who had hoped to align their fortunes with the occupiers, the Filipinos seemed to universally hate the Japanese. However, it didn't mean that they all made excellent jungle guides, even if Danilo looked the part. But it was too late to go back and find a new guide. At this point, they no longer had any choice but to follow the man. Deke just hoped they had the right man for the job.

The jungle was thick, the air hot and humid to the point of feeling like a wet blanket. The breeze that helped dispel the tropical heat closer to the sea had disappeared.

Deke wiped sweat off his face with his sleeve. There was so much dirt ground into his uniform at this point that it was hard to say if there was even any cloth left, but it seemed to do the job. He wiped off several bugs in the process—the air was thick with gnats and mosquitoes.

The last thing he needed was sweat in his eyes to foul up his aim. They didn't expect any trouble from the Japanese yet, but Deke figured that you could never tell what those sneaky bastards were up to next.

Danilo glanced back at them from time to time, nodding as he urged them forward, scowling at the sluggish pace, but Deke and the others were forced to move slowly, picking their way along the trail, which had dense undergrowth lining the sides and clutching at them.

It didn't help that each calling bird or rustle of an animal in the underbrush set Deke's nerves on edge. He was worried about the enemy ambushing them, but so far the jungle was empty.

Where the hell were the Japs?

CHAPTER TWENTY

DEKE FOLLOWED DANILO, maintaining an interval. He could almost feel the tension in the Filipino's wiry shoulders, so he knew Danilo was alert and watchful. Again, Deke didn't think there were any Japanese around, but maybe Danilo knew something they didn't. He had been fighting the Japanese for much longer.

The trail was well worn underfoot, and it was clear that a large number of men had passed this way recently. The boot prints were not American. Deke realized that would have been the Japanese column, retreating deeper into the jungle.

From time to time, a tree limb or vine would block the path—it seemed to be the jungle's not-so-subtle attempt to reclaim the trail or warn them off. Whenever that happened, Danilo's huge bolo machete would be in his hand in a flash, lopping away the intruding brush. Much as Deke loved his bowie knife, it didn't have the heft to chop away vines and branches in one swift blow. No wonder so many of the Filipino guerrillas carried bolo machetes. They were the right tool for the job, all right.

Captain Merrick came up, his uniform striped with dark sweat stains. Like most of the men in the company, he carried an M1 rifle. His uniform and helmet bore no insignia—he didn't need it because all the men in his unit knew who he was. It would have been hard to pick him out as an officer at all, except for the confident way that he held himself, as though he had a ramrod for a spine, even moving down this jungle trail.

"What was your name again?" he asked Deke.

"Private Cole. Most just call me Deke."

Merrick nodded. "Listen up, Deke. We need to pick up the pace," he said. "We're never going to get across the peninsula at this rate. Tell this Filipino gentleman to hurry it up."

"I don't think he understands much English."

"Figure it out. Poke him in the rump with a bayonet if you have to. That's kind of a universal message."

Captain Merrick fell back along the trail, checking on the men as he went.

Fortunately Deke didn't need to poke Danilo with a bayonet. The guide seemed to have understood the urgency in Captain Merrick's tone of voice; either that, or he understood more English than he let on. He glanced back at Deke with a questioning look.

"You heard the man," Deke said. "Hurry it up. Rapido."

Danilo picked up the pace. Danilo didn't seem happy about moving faster along the jungle trail, and neither did Deke. He understood the captain's sense of urgency, but some things were better off not being rushed.

It had been growing darker and darker under the trees, and now it started to rain, which was a frequent occurrence on Leyte. An hour later the sun would be out again.

The rain fell gently at first, creating a soothing patter of raindrops on the leaves. Soon the rain fell more heavily, turning each broad leaf into a miniature waterfall that sluiced water onto the heads of the troops. Inside a helmet, the falling water hitting the steel echoed annoyingly. More rain dripped down the backs of their necks and ran under the collars of their field shirts.

A few soldiers stopped to put on their ponchos, but by then they were already wet. He caught a glimpse of the four-eyed soldier struggling to get his poncho over his haversack, holding up the line to the point that a sergeant shouted at him. The clumsy kid managed to get so tangled up that another soldier had to fix his poncho for him. Deke shook his head, wondering what the army expected them to do against the Japs with soldiers like that. It didn't help that as they waited in the rain, the column of troops looked less like soldiers and more like miserable drowned rats.

Deke didn't like the rain one bit because it muffled any sound and disguised any movement. All that he could see ahead were wet leaves and sheets of falling rain. There could be an entire Japanese battalion waiting in ambush around the next bend in the trail.

The jungle presented its challenges, so different from the mountain forests back home. Whenever he had been able to slip away from farm chores, Deke had spent hours wandering the woods and overgrown fields of farms abandoned during the Great Depression, the land slowly reverting to a state as wild as it had been when the first settlers arrived before the Revolutionary War.

It took surprisingly little time for trees to begin growing in the fields, for fences to rot away, for sheds to crumble. The landscape was all too eager to become wilderness again. For some reason, these scenes of lonely ruin appealed to him. He had gone out rambling in all sorts of weather and in different seasons, trekking through snow, summer thunderstorms, the chill winds of late autumn under bruised skies.

More often than not, he'd had a rifle or shotgun in hand in case he came across any game for the stewpot. It was just how his ancestors had lived and survived in those mountains, and Deke was formed from the same clay.

While other men like Philly griped and complained about the Philippine forest, Deke managed to appreciate it. The thick canopy created a green roof under which they moved in shadow, even during the daytime, and the walls of vegetation pressing against the edges of the trail created a sense of isolation that he enjoyed. Even the heat and humidity were something he could embrace when he thought back to all the times he had shivered his way through the farm chores on a winter's morning.

The thousand shades of green and brown, broken up with bright flashes of color from flowers or jungle birds, were hard not to appreciate. Other men kept their eyes focused on the mud and dirt of the trail, but Deke's eyes roved the surrounding landscape, ever alert. Maybe he was only imagining it, but the jungle seemed to be watching them in turn as the column of soldiers passed by.

There was so much to see, from a bird with brilliant plumage taking shelter from the rain to massive vines, each the thickness of a man's arm, that hung from the canopy like tendrils. If it hadn't been for the threat of the Japanese, he would even enjoy walking through a place such as this, rain and all.

The Japanese, he reminded himself. *We're going to fight the Japanese. The Japs are going to be more than happy to fight us.*

He kept repeating the thought, trying to make sense of it, trying to fathom what that meant here in this dense jungle cover. It seemed a fool's errand, in a way. Why hadn't they simply gone by ship around the peninsula with the bulk of the troops? But some general had decided to keep the Japs guessing, or maybe to keep the pressure on them, so here they were.

Captain Merrick called a halt. "Ten minutes, boys. Get a load off if you want. Just make sure you don't sit on any snakes or set off any booby traps."

Some men flopped down on the dank, rotting leaves immediately, while others took their time, investigating first. It was hard to say what worried them more—the captain's mention of snakes or booby traps. The ones who had simply dumped themselves into the mat of rotting leaves were probably too tired to care, one way or another.

In the middle of the jungle trail, Danilo squatted on his haunches the way the Filipinos did. It didn't look comfortable to Deke, but it did keep your ass out of the mud.

Deke didn't rest but moved along the line, taking the measure of the men. He passed the soldier that he had pulled out of the wreck. He couldn't help but shake his head at the sight of the soldier's chubby frame. Baby fat. The kid couldn't have been more than eighteen. He was poking around in the weeds with a stick, making sure the coast was clear before he sat down. Deke wanted to tell him that whatever critters might be in the bushes were the least of his worries.

That kid was no soldier. What was he doing here? Why was Deke here? Why was any of this happening?

All because the Japanese had decided to bomb Pearl Harbor, that was why. December 7, 1941. His cousin Jasper had been one of the casualties that day, along with thousands of other sailors. Oddly enough, the coming of the war had liberated Deke from the sawmill. *Give me the jungle any day.*

Deke looked into the chubby soldier's face. It was expressionless, blank. A lamb headed to slaughter. He wasn't afraid. He sat there on the rotting leaves, rifle practically tossed on the ground, waiting for whatever would happen next.

"What's your name again?" Deke asked.

"Dickie Shelby," he said in a squeaky voice.

"Didn't you have glasses before?"

"I broke them when a branch slapped me across the face."

"Uh-huh. Can you see anything without your glasses?"

"It's a little blurry," Dickie admitted.

"Keep your rifle out of the mud," Deke said. "You might be needing it soon. Just make sure you're close enough to tell it's a Jap you're shooting at."

A man nearby didn't seem to like the fact that Deke was handing out advice that bordered on orders. He asked harshly, "What are you, our new sergeant?"

"Shut up," Deke growled.

The man seemed like he was about to say more, but he got a glimpse of Deke's cold eyes and clammed up.

Deke moved on. He found Merrick a little farther down the line. The captain gave him a nod of acknowledgment, waiting to hear what he had to say. "Got something on your mind, Deke?"

"I don't like this," he told the captain. "We could be walking right into an ambush in this rain. Let me and Danilo go on ahead and make sure the trail is clear."

"Who the hell is Danilo? You mean that Filipino?"

Deke nodded. "I can tell that he knows this ground."

"All right," Merrick agreed. "Send word back if you come across something."

"Don't worry," Deke said. "I reckon you'll hear me shooting."

He returned to the front of the column and told his plan to Philly and Yoshio. They would stay with the main column. He rousted Danilo off his haunches, and they left the column behind. He felt better without the distraction of the rain-soaked column following immediately after. With just him and Danilo, it would be a lot easier to sense any enemy activity ahead.

The trail began to climb, then kept going up and up. The trail was steep and slippery in places, with roots trying to trip him. Clearly they had reached some of the mountains they had glimpsed earlier in the distance. That was progress for you. The jungle kept getting thicker and thicker, the heavy leaves seeming to absorb more of the light so that they were moving through shadow.

The air remained hot and humid, almost stifling down here where there wasn't any breeze. The rain had stopped, but there was still so much moisture dripping from the trees that it was hard to tell.

The bare ground of the trail was wet and slippery, but if you stepped off the trail for a moment, the layer of damp, dead leaves felt as though you were walking on a soggy sponge.

Up ahead, a vine thick as his arm hung down from an overhanging tree branch. The vine moved, which was odd, considering there was no breeze. Taking a second look, he realized that it was not a vine at all, but a large snake. He gulped, keeping an eye on the snake as it slithered along the branch and out of sight, taking its time. The sight of snakes back home didn't much bother him, but he felt a shiver run down his spine. *That ain't a garter snake.*

The place was also lousy with mosquitoes. They buzzed in Deke's ears, landed on his sweaty neck, flew into his nostrils. Deke was soon covered in bites. Some sort of centipede dropped from overhead and landed on Deke's arm, then quickly legged it toward the back of his bare hand. Before he could flick it away, he felt a sting, and within minutes a marble-size welt grew on the back of his hand. It hurt like fire, but he ignored the pain, keeping his attention focused on the trail ahead. He reckoned that a Japanese bayonet through his guts would hurt a whole lot worse.

Everything in this place seemed to be out to get them, never mind the Japs. He recalled how Father Francisco had shared a story about how an expedition of Spanish conquistadors had entered the deep jungle during their exploration of Leyte and were never seen again. The priest had shared the story with a certain amount of pride, as if the jungle had settled some kind of score against the Spaniards. At the time, Deke had taken it as an old wives' tale that those tough bastards with their swords and armor had simply been swallowed up by the jungle. Now he wasn't so sure.

For whatever reason, the pesky critters didn't seem to bother Danilo. Maybe he was just used to them. He didn't swat at mosquitoes or so much as give the snake a second look.

Fortunately, Danilo hadn't led them astray yet. Even Deke, for all his woodsy skill, wasn't sure that he could have found their way back, considering that none of the trails were marked. The various forks and crossings got confusing. Their orders were to forge ahead. Either from instinct or experience, Danilo was finding the way forward.

It was hard to say how far they had come. A few miles, maybe? Surrounded by forest, the lack of any visible landmarks made it hard to judge. Somewhere behind the clouds, the sun began to go down. Deke was sure that when darkness came, it would come quickly. He looked around a little uneasily at the dense trees on either side of the trail. Already he couldn't see more than fifty feet before the trees receded into the jungle gloom.

When they reached a wide place in the trail, Danilo signaled a halt. Deke nodded in silent agreement. It was getting dark, and there was no point in continuing. It would be too easy to simply wander off the trail. Deke pitied anyone who happened to.

He went back and found Captain Merrick, who agreed to a halt.

"Do you want us to dig in?" a sergeant asked, studying the ground beneath his feet doubtfully.

Merrick looked at the ground, thick with tangled roots. "Tell the men to do what they can," he said. It went against every bone in the captain's body not to at least try to dig in. "I don't know how they'll get through this mess. Let's make sure we have guards posted at either end of the trail. If there's trouble, that's where it's going to come from."

Orders were given and the guards were posted. Some men managed to scoop out a shallow hole that was soon filled with rainwater, mud, and all sorts of creepy crawlies.

Deke saw that he'd been right—night fell swiftly. There was no tropical afterglow as there was near the beach areas. It was like being inside a cave.

Before it was completely dark, Danilo produced a string hammock from his bag, along with mosquito netting that he draped over his face. In minutes he was asleep in relative comfort.

The soldiers weren't nearly so lucky. After their C rations, nobody slept, or not well. The men not on guard duty managed to snatch some sleep, dozing off as they sat upright, clutching their rifles. A few of the men rigged shelter halves in the branches in an attempt to stay dry. Others had a better idea and used the canvas to cover the soggy ground.

Deke sat beside Philly and Yoshio, the three of them huddled under ponchos. Although the rain had stopped, the trees still dripped, and the night was cooler than expected.

"I can't decide if it's wetter on the inside or the outside of this poncho," Deke said.

"It's a toss-up," Philly agreed. "I do know one thing, which is that it's darker than the inside of a cow out here."

Yoshio spoke up. "Philly, how do you know what the inside of a cow looks like?"

"Stick with me, kid, and you might learn something yet."

Deke strained to see much beyond their little huddle. He could hear the other men—coughing, muttering in low tones, the sound of a canteen cap being screwed back on—but he couldn't see them. "There's an old country saying about passing the night—in other words, getting through the dark hours. This is gonna be a night to be passed."

Deke decided he was all right with that—not that he had any real choice. Beside him, Philly and then Yoshio dozed, but Deke stayed awake, listening.

Once the rain had stopped, the nighttime jungle came awake. He heard singing insects louder than an orchestra, night birds, screech owls. At some point he heard a low growl in the distance and the sort of animal scream that came only from something being torn by claws and teeth. Hunters and prey. You've got to be one or the other in this world.

The jungle noises unsettled the men nearby, who gave voice to their complaints, or even pointed their rifles into the forest.

Deke didn't mind the noise. If the creatures that lived here were going about their business, it meant that there weren't any Japs on the prowl. If the jungle fell silent, that was when they'd have to worry.

Minute by minute, hour by hour, the night passed.

As for tomorrow, it was anyone's guess what the dawn would bring.

CHAPTER TWENTY-ONE

THE SUN CAME out in the morning, instantly transforming the wet air to steam. On the trail, the jungle that had seemed so mysterious and even threatening at night was lit by dappled sunlight that streamed down through the trees and fronds of vegetation. Mist rose up and caught the glow of the morning sun. Droplets of moisture trapped in the myriad of spider webs sparkled like jewels.

Deke found himself thinking that he might not mind returning to this place someday when peace returned. What a different experience it would be to explore the Philippine mountain slopes without the threat of Japanese attack. Seen by the morning light, the jungle held a million wonders.

But their reality was that they were in the heart of war. If he forgot that for an instant, it could be disastrous not just for himself, but for the entire unit he was scouting for.

Besides, there was not much time to contemplate their surroundings. Within minutes of the sun's appearance, Captain Merrick had them up and moving.

"Frazier, where the hell are you? I want you and your BAR gun up front," he said. "It's been too quiet, and I don't like it. If anything moves on the trail ahead of us, I want you to turn the trees into toothpicks."

"You got it," Frazier replied.

Most BAR gunners were big men, considering that they had to haul the heavy BAR weapon along with ammunition, and it turned out that Private Frazier was no exception. Well over six feet tall and broad shouldered, he handled the sixteen-pound weapon with ease. The Browning Automatic Rifle used a twenty-round magazine that added to its weight.

The BAR gunner joined Philly and Yoshio near the front of the column.

"Try not to shoot my buddy in the ass with that thing," Philly said.

Private Frazier snorted. "Your buddy, the sniper? He looks mean."

"You have no idea."

"Listen, if I start shooting, chances are your buddy will have walked into a Japanese ambush. He and that Filipino will already be dead."

Philly just shook his head because he couldn't argue with that.

Deke and Danilo once again led the way, with a gap between them and the rest of the column.

"Buenos días," Danilo said, nodding at Deke after the Filipino had bundled away his hammock and mosquito netting.

That son of a bitch actually looks well rested, Deke thought.

They headed out once more, Deke registering the tiredness of his body that only amplified the weight of the heavy, damp uniform and boots.

Today's weather was already shaping up to be much different. By midday they had climbed higher, and the jungle thinned out, replaced by tall stands of kunai grass—jungle grass in the soldiers' parlance. Some of the clumps stood more than six feet high—*perfect ambush cover,* Deke thought ruefully. He noticed that Danilo moved forward more cautiously.

The trail followed a ridge through the high country. The strange thing was that it didn't appear to have rained at all at this higher elevation, or if it had, the sun and heat had evaporated any trace of moisture. Grass crackled underfoot. The trees had retreated, leaving no shade other than a few scrubby bushes. It was less humid at these higher elevations—just plain hot as the sun beat down.

The morning trek passed uneventfully. Just before noon, Captain Merrick called a brief halt. Nobody was very hungry, not with the heat, but they welcomed the chance to get off their feet. However, the lack of shade meant that the halt left the men baking in the sun. In the middle of the day, there was little shade offered by the scrub trees. It wasn't much of a relief. The column moved on after twenty minutes.

Water was becoming a problem. With the rain yesterday, none of the soldiers had thought to refill their canteens. This high up, they didn't pass any springs or streams. As the sun baked the soldiers, canteens were emptied by the thirsty GIs. Soldiers began to beg water off buddies who still had something in their canteens.

Deke shook his canteen, realizing that he was starting to run dry. He wanted to kick himself, thinking of all the rain that had fallen yesterday during their hike through the thickest portion of the jungle. Why the hell hadn't he bothered to refill his canteen then?

There was just a swallow or two of warm water left swishing around in the bottom of his canteen. *Damn it all. Maybe Philly has got some water.* As for Danilo, the man must have been part camel because Deke hadn't seen him take a drink yet.

Sweat in his eyes, Deke was distracted by thoughts of water, rather than giving the surroundings his full attention. They had reached a high open plateau without a lick of cover on it aside from the kunai grass and scattered boulders. This terrain was as different as could be from the thick forest they had passed through yesterday.

He listened to the sounds around him. The birds and insects were silent, and it was eerily quiet. Never a good sign. Far in front of the column, Deke and Danilo exchanged worried glances.

There was higher ground off to their left, a ridge that overlooked the plateau. The plateau itself dropped away into a series of steep, brush-covered ravines that would provide perfect cover for a sniper. It was just where Deke himself would have been hiding, had the tables been turned.

Then the anxious silence was shattered by the crack of an enemy sniper's rifle. From the trail behind him, Deke heard the pained cry of a wounded soldier.

"Japs!" somebody shouted, and the soldiers scrambled for cover.

One of the soldiers was on his knees, both hands grasping his bloody belly as if trying to hold in his guts. The Japanese sniper had shot him through his stomach. *Gut shot.* It was just where you would shoot a man if you wanted him to die slowly and painfully. Deke believed that it went against some kind of code to shoot a man on purpose that way, enemy or not. The enemy had deliberately left the soldier with a lingering, painful wound.

Deke felt sick. He looked away and tried to block out the sounds of the dying soldier's cries. Along with a sense of horror, Deke felt himself getting angry. Damn those Japs.

Another bullet whip-cracked past Deke's head, and he hit the dirt. To his surprise, Danilo was already there. Damn but the Filipino was quick. Another bullet cut the air where Deke had been standing an instant before.

Other soldiers weren't so quick or so lucky. Several men fell as the quick *pop, pop, pop* of the smaller-caliber Japanese rifles came from the ridge above and from the cover of the ravines below. They were being shot at from all directions. The fortunate casualties dropped in their tracks, killed instantly by well-placed shots. The less-fortunate ones fell wounded, their bright blood staining the brown, tinder-dry kunai grass with sprays and droplets of crimson.

"Medic!" someone shouted. "Doc!"

The medics ran to do their job, but they were targeted by the enemy snipers. As Deke watched, one medic spun around like a top, struck in the shoulder by a sniper.

The small-caliber Japanese rifles did not always kill instantaneously, requiring more precise aim because they didn't pack the wallop of a US .30-06 round. Then again, Deke was convinced that the Japanese weren't always shooting to kill—the man wounded in the belly being a case in point.

One of the more pernicious strategies he had witnessed was for the Japanese to wound a man out in the open. It went against every fiber of a soldier's being to leave his buddy like that. However, when he left cover to help the wounded man, a Japanese sniper would pick him off.

"Stay under cover!" Merrick shouted. "Don't let the Japs lure you out."

Soldiers cursed as they abandoned trying to retrieve their wounded buddies. The ones who disobeyed and tried to help were soon lifeless corpses sprawled in the jungle grass, hit by bullets coming at them from several directions at once.

More orders were given to dig in. Some soldiers returned fire, while others wielded shovels, trying to scratch out foxholes in the rocky soil of the plateau.

Deke looked around for Danilo and finally spotted him behind a boulder, rifle to his shoulder. The Filipino had the right idea. It was time to pick off some Japs.

From the cover of a cluster of boulders, Deke looked up to see the ridge from which the Japanese snipers were firing. Bad as it was, he realized that it could have been worse. The ridge lay between them and the Japanese roadblock. If the Japanese had placed mortars up there, the GIs would've been dead meat. As it was, they'd already taken a few casualties, and now they were pinned down here.

Like the others, Deke found himself trapped by the enemy fire. They were all sitting ducks up here on the ridge. His only option was to move down into the ravine and try to work his way back up the mountain to the right, where the Japanese had to be coming from. He rolled over to get a better look at the landscape surrounding them.

The terrain set the perfect stage for an ambush, which was so cleverly disguised that they never saw any sign of the Japanese. They had walked right into the Japanese trap. The ground was so good for an ambush that Deke found himself envious. If the tables had been turned, he realized that it was just the ground that he himself would have chosen to stage a sniper attack.

All through yesterday's trek, then today, they had seen no sign of the enemy except for occasional footprints. Now it was apparent that the Japanese had pushed deep into the heart of the peninsula to make their stand against the Americans.

It was hard to say just how many Japanese there were, but he didn't think that Merrick's company was outnumbered. They were just being outsmarted and outgunned.

Deke's mind worked furiously as he tried to figure a way out of the trap. The options were few. He decided that Captain Merrick's best bet for saving his company was to get off the ridge and into the cover provided by the ravines. But with most of the company pinned down, that wasn't an option.

Philly came running through the kunai grass, Yoshio on his heels. A bullet kicked up dirt at Philly's feet.

"Get down, you dang fool," Deke said, reaching up and pulling Philly down into the long grass. Yoshio dove into the grass headfirst as bullets snapped the air around him.

"Hey, Deke!" Philly shouted in his ear, even though he wasn't more than a foot away. "You got any ideas?"

"Yeah, go to the beach and bring back some mortars to blow these bastards to hell. If we had a flamethrower, or those mortars, we could maybe root them out of there."

"OK, if I do that, it will take me a couple of days to get there and back. How about a better idea?"

"Start shooting Japs," Deke said. "How does that sound?"

"I would if I could, but I can't see any Nips. They've got good cover."

"Yep, there is that," Deke agreed, even as he began using the scope to scan for targets. "Good thing for us that they don't have any mortars, or we wouldn't even be here. As it stands now, they're gonna have to kill us slowly."

He hadn't seen any sign of mortars. Maybe the Japs were saving them as a surprise, letting the GIs get their hopes up. In an effort to travel light and fast, the Americans hadn't brought any mortars with them into the jungle. Those would have been useful. Maybe the Japs had found it just as difficult to carry supplies using the jungle trail. Good thing—the ambush could have been much worse.

What the Japanese did have was a Nambu machine gun set up on the high ground. The steady and rapid *peck, peck, peck* of the machine gun targeted any movement on the plateau.

Captain Merrick had decided that he'd had enough of that. Off to his right, Deke heard Merrick shouting for the BAR gunner. "Frazier, get your ass in gear and hose down that Japanese machine gun!"

Private Frazier didn't need to be told twice. Against all odds, he wasn't shot down when he leaped up to get better control of the BAR, making himself a target in the process. Aiming the BAR in the direction of the hilltop that the Japanese were firing down from, he unleashed a long burst. Clods of dirt and bits of shrubs whirled up as he walked the burst along the enemy position. The shooting from that sector fell quiet. Frazier dropped back under cover behind a boulder before the Japanese could take him out. He slammed in another magazine.

"I'll be damned," Philly said. "That was impressive."

"Waste of ammo," Deke grumped. "I'll bet he didn't even hit anything."

The team of snipers went to work, fighting back the only way they could. Yoshio was using binoculars to glass the ravines, calling out targets as he did so.

"Two o'clock, behind that big bush," Yoshio said.

Deke put his sights there and fired. The grunt of satisfaction that came from Yoshio indicated that Deke had hit his target.

Deke worked the bolt. "Next," he said.

"Do you see that ravine on our right? Halfway up, I saw a glint. Something caught the sunlight. Might be a rifle scope."

Deke peered through the scope but didn't see any targets. "You sure?"

He heard Yoshio suck in a breath. At first he feared that Yoshio had been hit. But then Yoshio said, "I don't believe it."

"What?"

"You know that sniper from Hill 522? Ikeda. If I didn't know better, I'd say that's him."

Deke swung the rifle in that direction and was rewarded with a glimpse of a Japanese soldier wearing a field cap with a havelock, or "sun cape." He seemed to be issuing orders to other soldiers, who were unseen. Something about the determined set of the shoulders looked familiar. Otherwise the man was unremarkable, just another Japanese soldier. But in his gut Deke knew it was the same man.

That was when he saw the rifle in the enemy soldier's hands. It was an Arisaka with a telescopic sight.

Instantly Deke put his crosshairs on the Japanese sniper. But it was as if the man had read his mind. No sooner had he begun to pull the trigger than the man took cover, disappearing from sight. The man knew better than to stay out in the open too long. Deke's brain had already set his finger into motion, and the rifle fired into empty space.

"Yeah, that's him all right," he said.

"Where did he go?" Yoshio asked. "I don't see him."

As it turned out, Deke's attempt to shoot Ikeda hadn't gone unnoticed. A bullet struck the rock behind which Deke was hiding. Then another, glancing right off the top of the rock. Too damn close.

"He figured out where we're at," Deke said. "Keep your head down."

Peering through the scope, Deke had a good idea of where Ikeda was hidden. There were a couple of big rocks up on the ridge. The cleft between them created a perfect shooting spot. *That's just where I'd be,* Deke thought.

He put his crosshairs on the rock, fired, and raised a puff of dust.

In return, a bullet smacked into his own rock. *That's him, all right.*

The enemy sniper shouted something. Deke was too far away to hear it clearly amid the shooting, but he was fairly certain that it was a taunt. "Hey, Charlie!"

I am sick and tired of these Japs. He worked the bolt and took aim through the scope, waiting for his chance.

CHAPTER TWENTY-TWO

AFTER THE AMBUSH WAS SET, Ikeda studied the details with satisfaction. It was almost a textbook position—troops on the high ground and hidden in the ravines surrounding the plateau. The trail through the jungle ravine was now a death trap.

They knew that they were being pursued by US forces. While it was true that they could have turned and attacked at almost any point, the narrow jungle trail meant that they could only have attacked the enemy head-on. Waiting until the enemy reached this more open terrain meant that they could ambush the entire column at once, with devastating results.

The US troops soon walked right into the trap that had been set for them. With so many targets, Ikeda was having a field day.

He aimed and fired, aimed and fired, dropping soldiers with virtually every shot.

It wasn't until he had made the mistake of exposing himself to pass orders to his snipers that the enemy had nearly picked him off with a lucky shot.

Or maybe not that lucky. Perhaps it had been skill.

"What have we here?" Ikeda muttered to himself. Safe behind cover, he saw where that accurate shot had come from. Behind a rock, he spotted an American sniper who had a rifle with a telescopic sight and the telltale hat with one side pinned up. This must be the same sniper he had tangled with before.

Ikeda smiled. Things had just become more interesting.

The American sniper had ducked back down behind a rock. Aiming carefully, Ikeda sent a bullet that raised a puff of stone chips and dust off that rock.

"Hey, Charlie!" he shouted in heavily accented English. "I kill you now, Charlie!"

* * *

AFTER THE INITIAL fury of the attack, the fight settled into an intense and prolonged gun battle. Anything that moved on either side became a target. Given that the troops on both sides were firing from behind cover, the GIs began to rediscover some of their marksmanship skills, taking their time to make each shot count.

"Got one!" whooped a soldier.

But the Japanese marksmen were also taking their toll. Now and then a soldier suddenly sagged. More often than not, those were fatal head shots. Nobody bothered to call for a medic in those cases.

All the medics were down anyhow.

Nobody said it out loud yet, but there was the nagging concern about running out of ammo. Far as they were from the beachhead, there wouldn't be any resupply.

"Make them keep their heads down, boys," Merrick shouted from time to time. Without saying it aloud, he seemed to address the ammo issue. "We'll fight 'em with bayonets if we have to."

Things were bad. The Japanese had the advantage of higher ground, along with the cover of the ravines. Fortunately the US troops had managed to scrape foxholes into the soil or were taking advantage of whatever cover they could find. The problem was that the enemy nearly had them encircled, firing at them from three sides. In response, the Americans had formed a roughly U-shaped position.

Deke told Yoshio to turn his binoculars in the other direction, directly down into the ravine behind them, to keep an eye out and make sure the Japanese did not try to encircle them. The GIs were already spread so thin that he didn't want to think about what would happen if the Japanese hit them from the rear.

"I reckon I've just about had enough of this," Deke muttered. He racked his brain for something, anything, that he could do to help get them all off this godforsaken ridge. They couldn't stay in the open.

But it was easier said than done, with the Japanese snipers pinning them down. Right now their best hope was to wait for dark to make their move.

Deke wasn't the only one thinking that way. The soldiers were spread out but close enough to be within shouting distance of one another.

"Merrick says to sit tight until dark," Private Frazier called out to them in his gravelly voice from his own hiding spot fifty feet away. He was now trying to conserve the BAR ammo by firing in short bursts wherever he saw enemy movement. "We'll make a move then. Pass it on."

Deke looked to his left. There wasn't anyone to pass it on to. Like it or not, he, Philly, Yoshio, and their new best friend, Danilo, were the left flank of Charlie Company.

Beyond the four of them was nothing but the jungle ravine and Japanese.

"Don't that beat all," he muttered.

If the Japanese decided to rush them in any numbers, the fight might be over in a hurry.

* * *

IT WAS BRUTALLY HOT, and the sun beat down on the soldiers' helmets. Deke could feel the sweat running down the back of his neck, the rivulets streaming under his shirt collar. His uniform felt perpetually soaked. He tried to keep his mind focused on the task at hand, but instead, his thoughts wandered. He imagined haying time at home, the heat of the day, and how wonderful a drink of cool, sweet water dipped out of a spring had been.

You couldn't drink the jungle water safely without dissolving halazone tablets in it. Men had quenched their thirst with the untreated water, and they'd gotten sick as dogs. The water back home was right out of a mountain spring, filtered through clean granite, pure as the snow and mountain rain it had come from.

He'd been so hot on those July afternoons working on the farm that there had been times when he had lain on his belly like a dog beside the spring, sucking up water. Couldn't get enough.

He was just as thirsty now, but there was no cool spring nearby to slake his thirst. The adrenaline from the gun battle, along with the acrid gun smoke that hung in the air, had reduced his mouth to feeling dry as old straw—and tasting about the same.

He raised his canteen, shaking the last drop or two into his parched mouth. The warm drops of water didn't do much good, maybe even made his thirst worse somehow, so he put a pebble into his mouth and sucked on it—an old trick that his father had taught him when they were putting up hay on July days so hot and dry that the field was like an oven. The pebble alleviated his thirst somewhat.

"You got any water left?" Philly asked hopefully, having seen Deke raise his canteen.

"That was it, fella. I just drank the last two drops."

"Yeah, same here. Just think how wet we were hiking through that jungle yesterday. What I wouldn't give for a little of that rain now."

"Suck on a pebble. It helps."

"What kind of a bumpkin do I look like?" Philly griped. "Suck on a pebble, my ass." But after a minute, he gave Deke a sidelong glance, then popped a pebble into his mouth and didn't complain about it.

He and Philly weren't the only thirsty ones. Just about everyone had an empty canteen, and there was no hope of going off to find a water source to refill them—not with the Japs keeping them pinned down. Some men plucked the sharp-edged kunai grass and chewed it, hoping to suck a little green juice from it, but the grass was so dry that it offered little relief.

One GI had spotted a coconut that had fallen from a solitary tree on the ridge. The coconut sat on the ground in plain view, tempting someone to crack it open for the sweet milk inside. In his desperation for something to drink, the soldier had started to crawl toward it. A Japanese sniper quickly picked him off.

Deke shook his head at the thought of a man's life tossed away in hopes of a few swallows of coconut milk, but that was what thirst did.

Off to the right, Deke heard a metallic clatter coming at them. Automatically Deke swung his rifle in that direction.

"Don't shoot!"

To his surprise, he saw Dickie Shelby crawling toward their position on all fours, his back and shoulders crisscrossed with webbed belts and empty canteens. It was the clatter of the canteens that had gotten Deke's attention.

"Dickie, what the hell do you think you're doing?"

"I'm going for water."

"Like hell you are. You're drawing fire, that's what you're doing!"

As Deke said it, another shot ripped the air inches from their heads. Laden down like a pack mule, Dickie made an irresistible target. He didn't so much as flinch when another bullet passed close by. The young soldier's fear seemed to have melted away, even if his baby fat remained.

"Give me your canteen."

"Look here now. Don't get killed on my account."

"C'mon, give it here."

Deke handed it over, if for no other reason than to get Dickie out of the line of fire.

"I'm pretty sure there's a stream down at the bottom of that ravine," Dickie said, nodding in the direction of the ravine directly behind them. "I have to try to find one, at least."

"It's your funeral," Philly said. "Are you sure you want to do this?"

Dickie didn't answer but jumped up and ran for the cover of the ravine at their rear. He zigged and zagged as he ran, the clanking canteens swinging every which way, making him a ludicrous sight. He looked like a cluster of khaki-colored grapes with legs. By some miracle, their new water boy wasn't killed right away. Perhaps the Japanese were laughing so hard that they couldn't get off a good shot.

"We'll never see him alive again," Philly announced.

"I don't know about that," Deke said. "Sometimes fortune favors a fool."

"I guess you'd know, huh?"

"Keep it up and you won't have to worry about the Japs."

Philly snorted at that, but he kept his mouth shut.

As the afternoon heat intensified, the promise of water only added to the torment. It might have been better if there hadn't been any hope of water at all. At one point they heard rifle shots coming from that direction—the sharp crack of an Arisaka. Deke figured that was that—Dickie's luck had run out, and some Japanese sniper had gotten him for sure.

Less than an hour later, they heard shouting from that direction. Dickie came into view, calling, "Cover me!"

The soldiers on the ridge obliged by pouring fire at the Japanese position. Still, bullets plucked the air near Dickie, or churned up the dry dirt at his feet.

"Magnificent," Captain Merrick muttered, shaking his head. "I don't think I can put him in for a medal for fetching water, but damned if he doesn't deserve a gold-plated canteen."

"He's a regular Gunga Din," someone said.

Against all odds, Dickie had run the gauntlet of Japanese fire, found a water source, and returned. Deke had seen more than a few amazing sights so far in this war, and this had to be one of them. He was witnessing an act of sheer bravery.

Dickie threw himself down next to Deke, positively sloshing. A bullet had struck one of the canteens, punching a hole in it, and Philly grabbed it up and let the precious water flow into his mouth before any more could spill on the parched ground.

"You should treat the water first with halazone," Yoshio warned, but Philly was beyond caring about that.

Deke fired off a couple of quick shots in the direction of the Japanese who had been shooting at Dickie.

"Here's a canteen," Dickie said. "I'm not exactly sure it's the one you gave me."

"Don't matter. Hell, I'd drink out of Hirohito's canteen at this point."

Before Deke could say more, Dickie was up and running again at a crouch. He threw himself down once more next to Private Frazier, the BAR gunner, who was the soldier nearest to the snipers' position. He left a canteen for Frazier, who covered Dickie's dash for the next position by letting loose a long blast from his BAR.

"I do love that thing," Philly said in admiration, after he had taken a long gulp of water. "It's the sound of revenge."

Dickie ran on, dodging bullets like he must have the luckiest rabbit's foot in the world in his pocket.

The question was, How long could that luck last?

CHAPTER TWENTY-THREE

FROM HIS SNIPER'S nest in the rocks, Ikeda watched the water bearer running across the ridge, laden with canteens. He decided that the soldier was either very brave—or very foolish.

The soldier also seemed to live a charmed life. Despite drawing fire from so many of Ikeda's comrades, the American soldier had managed to dodge their bullets.

But he had not yet tried to dodge a bullet from Ikeda.

Intrigued, Ikeda tracked the soldier through his scope. Shot after shot was aimed in the water bearer's direction, kicking up dirt around his feet. Ikeda spotted a bullet clip one of the canteens, which spit out water in a long stream, like a miniature fountain. Fortunately for the Japanese, they had plenty of water. They had filled their canteens earlier, probably from the same stream that the American had discovered at the foot of the ravine.

He saw the water bearer leap down beside the rocks where he was sure the American sniper was hidden. *So he is thirsty too.* Ikeda took pleasure in knowing that his enemy was experiencing some discomfort.

He watched intently, hoping that the American sniper might raise his head to take a drink, offering Ikeda a momentary target, but the man kept his head down. Most of the Charlies were anonymous targets

—medics, officers, everyday soldiers—all to be targeted. But this sniper was something different. He was like Ikeda himself—a skilled marksman. This made him not only a worthy opponent but a dangerous enemy to be eliminated.

Shooting the enemy sniper would be like claiming a prize. Also, Ikeda could not forget the fact that this same sniper had played a role in the raid that had destroyed the powerful battery on Hill 522. Had that battery still been in place, it would have obliterated the invasion fleet.

Suddenly, through the scope, Ikeda saw the water bearer leap up and run. Covering him, one of the American soldiers sprayed the ravine with an automatic weapon. His comrades dove for cover. Ikeda did not flinch, knowing that the bullets were not aimed directly at him.

Instead, he kept his eye to the telescopic sight, focusing on the running man. Hitting a moving target was never easy, but fortunately for Ikeda, he had plenty of practice from picking off the lazy Filipino workers on Hill 522. They had seemed to move quickly only when they were being shot at.

He swung the rifle in a gentle motion that kept pace with the water bearer, keeping the crosshairs a little ahead of him. It wasn't anything that Ikeda could have explained. He was operating on pure instinct.

And then he squeezed the trigger.

The soldier tumbled, went down, struggled to rise again. His legs kicked feebly, lacking the strength to get him to his feet.

Ikeda grunted with satisfaction. He had hoped that the bullet would not kill the water bearer outright. With any luck, other soldiers would run to help him.

Ikeda pressed his eye to the rifle sight, waiting for more targets.

* * *

IT SEEMED as if every soldier had been watching Dickie Shelby, rooting for him as he dodged the Japanese fire. Not only was the water welcome, but Dickie's ability to dodge bullets made it seem like he was thumbing his nose at the Japs.

But Dickie's luck finally ran out. He fell in a heap, water from a holed canteen running out into the dry dirt and mixing with his blood.

"The bastards got him!" Philly cried out.

Deke had been watching the rocks opposite him. He was certain that the fateful shot had come from there—just where the Japanese sniper Ikeda was hiding. Deke couldn't see anything to shoot back at except rocks and more rocks. That Jap lurked in there like a spider, waiting to pounce on whoever entered his sniper's web.

He glanced over at Dickie and saw that he was still moving, struggling to get up. "Stay down, you dang fool!"

Of course Dickie couldn't hear him. He struggled to get to his hands and knees but couldn't seem to get any traction.

Another soldier broke cover and ran to help. Just as he reached Dickie's side, a shot rang out from the pile of rocks where Deke believed Ikeda was hidden. The soldier fell.

Philly had also seen what was happening. He swore. "Dammit, he's luring them in."

"Cover me," Deke said. He crouched, preparing to dash across the open ground.

Yoshio touched his arm. "Wait. I have a better idea."

Without bothering to explain, Yoshio started shouting in Japanese at the top of his lungs. The fire from the Japanese position suddenly slackened.

"What the hell did you shout at them?"

"I ordered them to hold their fire. It will confuse them, but it won't last for long. Go!"

Deke didn't wait for Yoshio to say it twice. He sprinted across the open ground faster than a fox after a rabbit. A couple of bullets buzzed around him like angry bees, but Yoshio's ruse had bought him some time.

He grabbed the back of Dickie's collar and dragged him behind a boulder. It took some effort—the kid was a lot heavier than he looked. No sooner had they taken shelter than a solitary, well-placed bullet struck the boulder, scattering rock fragments in its wake.

Deke checked Dickie's wound and saw that it wasn't good. He had a hole in his side that was sucking air, pink froth showing on his lips.

Lungshot. Wasn't much that he could do for this kid. It was only a matter of time.

Deke propped him up and gave him a drink of water. Dickie's eyes had been closed, but now they fluttered open.

"You're gonna be all right," Deke lied. "That was some chance you took, going to get that water. What the hell did you go and do that for?"

"I wanted to show that I could do something," he said, flecks of blood showing at the corners of his mouth. "I wanted to show that I was a good soldier. If I get killed, it won't matter."

"We all matter, kid. Every last one of us. Don't forget that."

"The thing is, you don't seem scared like the rest of us." As shock set in, the kid was babbling like a drunk. He grimaced in pain. "You saved me off that boat. You led us through the jungle. I guess I was just tired of being scared all the time. I guess I wanted to be more like you."

"Never mind about me." He gave the young man's shoulder a squeeze. "You're a dang fool, you know. But I've never seen anything like what you did. You're a better man than I am, Dickie Shelby."

"A sniper got me," Dickie said. "I saw a glimpse of him, back in those rocks. I saw him taking aim at me."

Ikeda, Deke thought. "You let me worry about that sniper. You just hang there."

"He's a good shot. He nailed me while I was running. You've got to get him. I've seen you shoot. You're the only one who can get him." Dickie winced in pain, his breath shallower. He reached out and grabbed Deke's arm with surprising strength. "Make sure the captain puts it in the letter to my parents what I did. Let them know I died doing something useful."

"Save your breath, kid. You can write them yourself."

Deke couldn't be sure that Dickie had even heard those last few words. The young soldier's eyes had glazed over, and he had stopped breathing. Deke shook him roughly by the shoulder, but there wasn't any response.

Just like that, he was gone. Dickie wasn't the first soldier that Deke had seen die right in front of him, and he probably wouldn't be the last. It didn't make it any easier.

The Japanese had started shooting again, having wised up to Yoshio's tricks. They were shouting back at him, probably with insults. Despite the fusillade of bullets and curses, a soldier managed to sprint across to the boulder where Deke was sheltering. He slid behind it like a baseball player crashing toward home plate.

"He bought it?" the soldier asked.

"Yeah, he bought it," Deke replied.

"Dammit." The soldier whipped off his helmet and swiped a grimy sleeve across his sweaty face.

"Listen, take these canteens and bring 'em around to anybody who needs a drink. That kid brought the water this far, so the least we can do is make sure everybody gets it."

Deke thought about Dickie Shelby, whose body now lay in the hot sun. He put the dead soldier's helmet across his face to keep the flies off. It was a hell of a thing. That young man would never go home, never marry or have a kid. It was all over for him, the end of the story just when it was getting started. All across the Pacific, too many young American lives had been snuffed out too soon by the Japanese.

He didn't think that he hated the Japs, but he was starting to wonder. These deaths, this war—it was all their fault.

Deke supposed that this was how the war was won, so many brave young men doing small deeds that added up the way that buttons filled a button jar. But Dickie's death weighed heavily on him. That was strange, considering that he had barely even known the kid. But Deke had saved him from drowning off the beach, only to see him gunned down by the Japanese sniper. In some strange way, he had felt responsible for him.

Maybe, just maybe, if Deke had gotten that sniper, then Dickie might still be alive. Dickie had held up his end of the bargain by fetching that water, but Deke felt like he and his rifle had let him down.

Dickie's incredible courage—or perhaps foolhardiness—in finding water enabled the GIs to hold out the rest of the afternoon, even as the Japanese poured fire at them from a superior position. While

Deke's marksmanship helped keep the Japanese in check, along with occasional bursts from the BAR, it was ultimately a few canteens full of jungle water that had saved the day.

The way some told it, especially those who had not confronted the enemy except in headlines and newsreels, killing Japs was as easy as firing one shot and watching them all fall over and die as easily as knocking down ten pins at a bowling alley. But that wasn't how it worked at all. Not by a long shot. The Japanese were tough customers.

In part, the Japanese had gotten their reputation for dying so easily due to their banzai attacks. Though terrifying for the defending troops, the banzai attacks were almost always futile. What many who weren't there didn't understand was that the charges were a form of mass suicide—desperate Japanese forces had no intention of surrendering, so why not take a few of the enemy with them?

Not for the first time, Deke reckoned that the Japanese mind was a difficult thing to wrap your head around. *They sure as hell don't think like us.*

Finally, the shadows stretched longer, and the light started to fade to the point where Deke could easily see the muzzle flashes of the enemy soldiers hidden among the rocks. One by one, he picked them off, keeping his head down. A few shots pinged off the rock in front of him. If he could see them, then they could see him as well. No sense giving the Japs any more of a target than necessary.

In the rocks across from him, there was no sign of Ikeda, who remained elusive.

Show yourself for just one second and see what happens.

He stared at the seemingly vacant vine-covered ravine, and the shadowy ravine stared back like the soul of the jungle itself.

CHAPTER TWENTY-FOUR

ONCE DARKNESS BEGAN to flow in like the tide, Captain Merrick started giving orders to move out. If they stayed put on the ridge, there was no doubt that the Japanese would begin a series of night attacks to annihilate the Americans.

"We have to get moving," Merrick said, delivering his orders in hushed tones. "We need to get the hell off this ridge and back into the cover of the jungle before it gets completely dark, or those Japs are going to be on us like flies on you know what."

Nobody could argue with that. They all knew it was true. However, escaping from the Japanese trap was easier said than done.

They slipped off the ridge in small groups, using the narrow trail to go back in the direction that they had come from hours before. Retreating didn't feel right, not when their mission was to get across the peninsula and link up with the rest of the division converging on Ormoc, but at the moment they had little choice. This was a matter of survival.

Everybody was worried about the Japanese slipping in behind them in the gathering darkness. Deke, Philly, Danilo, and Yoshio were the last men on the ridge, firing a few shots to trick the Japanese into thinking that the Americans were hanging on to that position. Finally, they joined the others crowded onto the jungle trail.

Once again, it was a lousy place to spend the night. The vegetation grew right up against the trail so that there was no place to really stretch out. Most men hunched themselves into a sitting position, so exhausted that they still managed to drift off. The only consolation was that the dense undergrowth made it unlikely that the Japanese could come at them from any direction except head-on. Nonetheless, fear of the Japanese had loomed large in their minds since the defeat that they had been handed in the ambush. Was there nothing that the Japanese weren't capable of doing?

With that in mind, Captain Merrick posted the BAR gunner at the head of the column.

"If those Japs come at us, light them up," Merrick said.

"I hope they do," Private Frazier replied. "I wouldn't mind cutting some of those Nips in half."

"That's the spirit," Merrick said. "Keep talking that way, and don't you worry, you'll get your chance soon enough—we have to get across that ridge and on our way in the morning, no matter what. We can't let those Japs hold us up."

Deke sat on the ground near the others, rifle between his knees. Normally he would have set about cleaning the weapon, especially considering the number of rounds that he had put through the barrel today. He had given a good accounting of himself as a sniper, but they hadn't managed to push the Japanese out of their stronghold in the ravine. The fight had also left Deke and the rest of the company perilously low on ammunition. They had scavenged what they could from the dead, but the truth was that they had only enough ammo for one more good fight.

He really ought to clean that rifle. However, as evening set in, he lacked even that much ambition. He was bone tired, worn out from the jungle trek and the grueling heat that they had faced all day.

He felt utterly defeated, outsmarted by the enemy sniper. He was sure that Ikeda had helped engineer the ambush that had taken the company by surprise. He had very nearly gotten the drop on Deke. Worst of all, Deke felt the loss of Dickie Shelby keenly. The young soldier had gambled with his life to bring them water during the worst of the tropical heat. He had managed to bring them the full canteens that sustained them through the fight, but at the cost of his life. What had Deke done? He shook his head, disgusted with himself.

"You ought to eat something," Philly said quietly. It was as if he had read Deke's mood. He handed him an open can of beef stew. It seemed to be the only thing there was to eat anymore. "Here, take it."

Deke took the can, spooned in the cold stew without tasting it. "Much obliged," he muttered.

"Don't worry about it, I've got plenty more. Let's just say that if I run out of bullets and grenades, I can throw cans of stew at the Nips. God help them if they try to eat it. I'm sure the stuff could kill you if you haven't built up a tolerance for it."

Under the canopy of the forest, the dank air hung still, laden with the fecund smell of rotting vegetation. Insects buzzed in soldiers' ears, got into their eyes and nostrils. Small creatures—some maybe not so small—rustled in the leaves and set their nerves on edge. From time to time, they felt something scuttle across their hands or the backs of their necks. Most of the men were too tired to care about that anymore. It was going to be a long, uncomfortable night.

To compound their misery, there was concern that the Japanese would be paying them a visit. They always favored night attacks. They would know just where to find the Americans, who would have no choice but to shelter for the night along the narrow jungle trail. It would likely be another sleepless night for the GIs.

Philly had also given a can of stew to Danilo, who looked at it suspiciously but produced a small knife that he used to scoop out a mouthful. Deke had never seen anyone eat stew before with a knife, but the consistency of stew straight from the can was just thick enough to make it possible. Danilo's knife was soon scraping the insides of the can to get every last drop. Deke wasn't sure if the Filipino was starving or if he seemed to think that the stew was the best thing he'd ever eaten. The scraping carried deep into the vegetation on either side of them, but Danilo appeared unconcerned. When he was finally finished, he tossed the can away and stood up.

"*Venga conmigo,*" he said, looking down at Deke. Just in case Deke wasn't sure what to make of that, Danilo waved at him in the universal gesture for "come with me."

Deke stood, not sure what the Filipino had in mind. He had slung his rifle over his shoulder and taken out his bolo blade. He swung it deftly once, twice, and parted the brush beside the trail to reveal an even narrower track—some kind of animal path. Deke hadn't noticed it before—and no wonder, as the path disappeared quickly into the gathering gloom. Not for the first time, Deke found himself impressed by Danilo's jungle craft. He chided himself for not paying better attention to his surroundings. Maybe he'd been too tired and just plain busy feeling sorry for himself.

Danilo ducked and moved into the forest.

Deke grinned. He knew exactly what Danilo had in mind.

"You're not going with that crazy bastard, are you?" Philly asked. "That looks like a path for rabbits—if they even have those here—or maybe something even smaller. Chipmunks, maybe."

"I reckon I know what he's up to," Deke said. "Let's just say that I'm cookin' corn bread in my own house, and I know where the corn-meal's at."

Philly shook his head. "I sure wish I knew what the hell you were saying. Honestly, Deke, it's like you speak a foreign language some-times. One from the last century."

"Let's just say that me and Danilo are gonna give the Japs a taste of their own medicine."

He knew that Philly was right about one thing, which was that Deke was a farm boy, through and through. In 1940s America, there were still many soldiers who had grown up on farms. They knew a thing or two about hard work. They didn't complain about the rain or the heat. Having taken part in hog killing and other country rituals that you got used to when your meat didn't come wrapped up neatly from the butcher shop, the sight of blood didn't bother them. Farmers made better soldiers than city boys.

When Deke was growing up and heard others' stories, he realized that he hadn't had any similar experiences. No birthday parties. No baseball games. Growing up on the farm had been hardscrabble. He took a bitter pride in that.

All the softness had been wrung out of Deke a long time ago, like green wood that had been left to dry in the sun and wind.

He gave Philly a nod, wondering if he'd ever see him again, considering that Deke was about to head into a jungle crawling with Japs and who knew what else. Without another word, Deke ducked low and began to follow Danilo, who was already threatening to disappear, barely more than a specter in the gloom.

Despite his boast, the truth was that Deke didn't have any plan in mind, other than to follow this path. He supposed that was the only plan Danilo had in mind. Given the language barrier, they couldn't discuss it. Danilo led the way and Deke followed. From time to time, the Filipino paused long enough to hack through the thicker overhanging branches and vines with his bolo. Deke slung his own rifle and slashed at the vegetation with his bowie knife. It wasn't as long and heavy as the bolo, but its blade did more than a passable job cutting away the dense branches and vines.

It was almost as if they were carving a tunnel through the greenery. Fortunately, the animal trail was well worn, providing their only guide through the jungle. It was impossible to tell what direction they were heading in. Deke looked up through the interwoven branches to catch occasional glimpses of the night sky, trying to get his bearings. However, no stars glittered, and the moon wasn't visible. Was it cloudy? The sky was nothing more than a dark slate. Deke heard a distant rumble and flicker of light. Thunder or artillery? It was hard to know.

The Filipino's instincts had proved right after all. The trees began to thin out. Looming ahead in the darkness was the ridge where the Japanese had ambushed them. Deke felt rather than saw damp ground under his boots.

Danilo stopped, hunched over, and touched his finger to his lips. The gesture was hardly necessary. With the ravine nearby, the Japanese must be so close that they could have reached out and touched them.

Deke realized that they must have reached the water source that Dickie would have used to fill their canteens. A trickling stream ran down into the ravine, no wider than a man's stride. Over time, the jungle animals had pawed away the soil to create a pool, the black surface of the shallow water reflecting like onyx in the jungle night.

Again he heard a rumble and flicker of light that played across the surface of the jungle pool. This wasn't artillery but the thunder and lightning of an approaching storm. The rumbling and flickering light came faster and closer together.

As so often happens in the tropics, the weather was changing again. The storm seemed to be headed in their direction, and it sounded like the start of something serious. The jury was still out on whether a storm would help or hinder their reconnoitering. Deke found some reassurance in the fact that Danilo seemed to be ignoring the distant storm.

After a quick stop to fill their canteens, Danilo moved on. Deke had been content to let the Filipino take the lead. Soon enough, Danilo's plan became clear. He was looking for a route around the base of the ridge so that they could pick up the trail on the other side, potentially avoiding any surprises that the Japanese had in store for them.

Passing quietly through a landscape of kunai grass, stunted trees, and jumbled rocks, they moved around the base of the ridge toward where the trail entered the jungle on the other side. They had taken the long way around to avoid getting too close to the enemy lines.

So far the only sign of the Japanese that they had seen was the glow of a cigarette among the rocks in the ravine, no more than one hundred feet away, smoked by a careless enemy soldier—certainly against orders. An angry voice barked what sounded like a reprimand, and the cigarette went out.

If there was one, then there were probably many more enemy soldiers lying in wait nearby. Maybe it was just Deke's imagination, but he thought that he could smell the enemy on the night breeze stirred up by the approaching storm. The Japanese had a peculiar odor, an almost fishy smell. He hoped to hell that the Nips couldn't smell *him*. He supposed that he gave off an odor that was a mixture of canned beef stew and rank sweat.

Both he and Danilo were skilled outdoorsmen, able to move silently, not giving the Japanese any clue that they were there. It would have been impossible for all of Captain Merrick's company to cross this same ground without giving anything away. Even if they had eventually found a route around the base of the ridge, how in the world could they ever use it?

The wind was picking up, rushing between the trees and swishing through the tall grasses like something alive. Deke realized that the sound and fury of the approaching storm would provide him and Danilo with excellent cover.

They moved closer to the Japanese position and began to climb the ridge. In the harsh light provided by the flickering lightning, Deke could pick out a few enemy soldiers scattered throughout the ravine. It was clear that the Japanese were in position, ready and waiting for the Americans to cross the ridge once more at daylight. Their plan seemed to be that they would hit the Americans again once Captain Merrick's company attempted to keep moving. There was only one path through the jungle, and the Japanese were the roadblock.

Deke shook his head. Surely the Japanese knew that they were losing the battle for Leyte. Stopping Merrick's company wasn't going to win the fight. But the Japanese apparently planned to make them bleed for every step of the way. They were a determined enemy.

A plan began to take shape in Deke's mind. If Captain Merrick could get his company to this point, they could swarm up the side of the ridge and take the Japanese by surprise. Also, it wouldn't be necessary to cross the killing field that the enemy had clearly planned on the ridge. It would be even better if Deke could distract the enemy somehow by creating a diversion that would take their attention away from the company attempting to move around their flank.

Deke looked at Danilo. He had let the guide call the shots so far tonight, but the time had come for Deke to take charge. The Filipino's dark eyes were hard to read in the occasional lightning flickers. With just a handful of Spanish words between them, he knew it would be challenging, to say the least, to relay what he was thinking.

"All right, pardner, here's what we're gonna do," Deke drawled in his soft mountain accent. "You go on back and fetch Captain Merrick and the rest of the boys while I distract these Japs. By *distract*, I mean shoot a few of 'em."

Danilo stared hard at Deke, as if trying to comprehend.

Deke pointed at Danilo, then back in the direction from which they'd come. He spoke a single word, *"Soldados."* And then he pointed toward the ground at his feet.

Danilo's leathery face cracked into a grin. *"Sí,"* he said. Without another word, he melted into the night.

Now it was all up to Deke.

CHAPTER TWENTY-FIVE

HE CROUCHED ALONE in the darkness, all coiled energy and sinew, like some jungle beast. He held himself perfectly still and quiet. Noises from the jungle filled the night—the cry of a night bird, the singing of insects, wind strumming the branches, and the growing rumble of thunder as the storm approached.

Slowly the Japanese began to reveal their positions—a cough here, a muttered word there. He couldn't see the enemy soldiers, of course, but he had a sense of where they were spread out around the ravine. They had a strong position against any sort of attack that came along the spine of the ridge, but they would not be expecting an attack on the ravine.

Grasping the solid rifle in his hand, feeling the heft of wood and iron, Deke felt a kind of power flow into him. It was the power of the predator, the hunter. At this moment, the Japanese were nothing more than prey.

Some part of the bear that had almost killed Deke as a boy seemed to live on inside him. The bear had left him scarred for life, but something of the bear's power resided in him. *What doesn't kill you makes you stronger.* Sadie had told him that once, and he had taken her words to heart.

It wasn't something he could ever admit to anyone, but he enjoyed this sense of power. There was no greater thrill than seeing an enemy soldier in his crosshairs, pressing the trigger, and sending a bullet to bury itself into the man with that satisfying *thunk* of lead hitting home. The fight on the ridge, Dickie Shelby being shot down after fetching the canteens, and most of all his inability to get the Japanese sniper Ikeda in his crosshairs had leached away that feeling and left him feeling beaten. Then again, Dickie had been right when he had pointed out that there was nobody better at this than Deke.

The tide had turned. He was a hunter again. There was nothing on God's green earth that gave a man power like a rifle did.

And yet Deke wasn't foolhardy. He was just one man, and the Japanese were many. They had trained to fight at night. Even now they might be planning an attack on Captain Merrick's men sheltering on the jungle trail.

He touched the hilt of his bowie knife. If it came to it, he might have to rely on the blade if he encountered any Japanese before the rest of the company was in position. A single rifle shot would give him away.

What he needed was a trick, a ruse.

The wind was picking up. A few drops of rain touched his face under the brim of his jungle hat. The approaching storm might work in his favor, providing cover for his movements.

In the flicker from the lightning, a gnarled shrub took on the shape of a man. It gave Deke a start, but it also gave him an idea.

Growing up on the farm, they'd often had to contend with all sorts of critters intent on raiding their garden or crops. Birds, mostly. You couldn't be there to shoo them away all the time, so they relied on a scarecrow to do the job for them. Sadie had been especially good at making the scarecrows, using a stuffed grain sack for a face and tattered old pants and shirts filled with straw. In the Cole family, the last stop for worn-out clothes was a scarecrow in the garden. Deke had to admit that there were times when a scarecrow dressed in his old rags had looked downright lifelike and spooky, like a doppelgänger.

"If I didn't know better, I'd say that was you standin' around the garden," Sadie had remarked. She had grinned. "I've got to say, one of you is bad enough."

It was just what he needed now. Two versions of himself. One to distract the Japanese—and one to kill them.

Scrounging on the ground, he found just what he was looking for. A longer branch that he could post upright, and a shorter crosspiece. Using his boot laces, he quickly lashed the shorter branch crosswise to the upright post to form a cross-like shape.

He didn't have any spare tattered clothes, but he did have his uniform. He slipped off his trousers and shirt, then hung them on the scarecrow frame. Like many GIs in the jungle, he had long since given up on underwear and gone commando. Dressing the scarecrow meant that he had completely undressed himself.

He used his bowie knife to cut a few leafy branches to fill out his clothing. He tied one final stick to the arms, as though the scarecrow were grasping a rifle. Maybe it wasn't as good as one of Sadie's scarecrows, but it would get the job done.

Now it was beginning to rain in earnest as the storm blew in. Deke worked his way through the ravine, climbing the ridge, moving awkwardly on account of dragging along the scarecrow. He had slung the rifle and kept the big knife in one hand, hoping and praying that he didn't run into any Japanese.

Slowly he climbed the ridge. This same ground had been hot and dry during the daylight. Now his feet slipped as the thunderstorm poured buckets of rain on his head. The task was made doubly hard by the fact that his boots flopped on his feet, the laces having been used for the makeshift scarecrow.

As the storm struck, the surrounding brush and jungle beyond was transformed into a confusing patchwork of blowing leaves and shifting shadows. Deke reckoned that any Japanese soldier with good sense was keeping his head down—certainly not looking for the strange sight of a buck-naked GI carrying a scarecrow up the hill. Most of the Japanese would probably have turned tail and run at such a spectacle. Deke smiled at the thought.

He managed to reach the top of the ridge, slipping one last time and gashing his knee on a rock. He cursed, but it didn't do much good, considering that he had to be so quiet about it.

Still no Japs in sight. The jungle squall was making him muddy, wet, and miserable, but at least it was keeping the Japanese hunkered down.

He planted the scarecrow at the far end of the ridge, out in the open, near where the trail entered the jungle on the other side. It would be the last direction that the Japanese would expect an attack to come from—if they expected any attack at all from the American troops.

As a final touch, Deke stuck his broad-brimmed jungle hat on top of the stick. Then he ran at a crouch through the downpour, tropical rain warm on his bare shoulders, and slithered behind a big rock maybe twenty yards away.

He set his rifle across the rock and stretched out in a pool of jungle goop behind it, getting mud and decomposing leaves into places he didn't want to think about. Didn't matter. He pushed any thoughts of discomfort from his mind.

He put his eye to the scope and cupped the butt of the rifle to his shoulder. Once again he felt the power of the rifle flowing through him. The storm and his own physical discomfort melted away as his world shrank to the size of what he could see through the telescopic sight.

The scarecrow stood out on the ridge like some crazed sentinel, the dancing lightning appearing to give it motion. Even down here among the trees, the sharp crack of thunder was enough to give one pause. It would be one hell of a thing to get killed by a lightning bolt while on the verge of attacking the Japanese. Deke settled down to wait, but he didn't have to wait for long.

Shouts rang out through the noise of the storm as the Japanese spotted the scarecrow. Somebody opened fire, and Deke picked off the silhouette illuminated by the muzzle flash. His own rifle shot was drowned out by the confusion of the storm and the Japanese gunfire. He fired again. Worked the bolt. Fired again. And again.

But the Japanese weren't fooled for long. He couldn't understand the words, but he heard the tone of command that seemed to say, *Cease fire.*

On the ridge before Deke, a figure stepped forward. Deke thought that he recognized the set of the shoulders, but more than that, he spotted the telltale noncommissioned officer's hat with its long fabric havelock that came down and covered the man's neck. Lightning forked the sky, and in the blinding flash Deke saw the Arisaka rifle with its telescope sight in the man's hands. *Ikeda.*

He put his rifle sights right between Ikeda's shoulder blades.

Deke reckoned that it would have been more sporting to give the man a shout. Give him a chance to turn around and defend himself, or at least to know that he was about to die.

To hell with that.

Deke squeezed the trigger.

* * *

AT THE FIRST growls of the storm on the horizon, Ikeda had welcomed the opportunity to launch a raid against the Americans he knew were cowering in the jungle, probably along the path that led to the ridge.

The Americans had been beaten back from the ridge during daylight, and he was sure that they would try again at dawn. He and the other Japanese did not intend for them to sleep well, he thought with a rueful smile.

The storm arrived even faster than he had expected, wind gusting through the trees and forks of lightning in the sky. Some of his fellow soldiers cowered among the rocks, which he found amusing. Considering all that they had faced, a storm seemed to be the least of their worries.

Cutting through the growing noise of wind and thunder, he heard excited shouts and then gunshots from the other side of the ridge. What was going on? Were they under attack? It would have been a bold move by the Americans. Rifle at the ready, Ikeda hurried in that direction to investigate.

In a pulse of lightning, he saw a lone figure standing on the ridge. The figure wore an American uniform and stood defiantly, not moving even as the Japanese troops began firing at him.

What caught Ikeda's attention more than anything else was the hat that the lone soldier wore. It was a broad-brimmed bush hat with one side pinned up—exactly what the American sniper wore. He had faced this same sniper on the ridge today, and even during the Americans' raid on Guinhangdan Hill, when they had managed to knock out the massive battery guarding Leyte Gulf.

The other soldiers couldn't seem to hit the man, but Ikeda had no doubts about his own marksmanship. He put the rifle to his shoulder and looked through the telescopic sight. At this range he couldn't miss.

But the lightning faded and plunged the ridge into darkness. Ikeda cursed silently and waited, still as a statue himself.

Another bolt of lightning revealed the American sniper still standing there. Ikeda felt himself both surprised and outraged by the way the American seemed to scoff at them, as if sure that the Japanese were such poor shots.

Ikeda knew that he would not miss. As the flash of lightning lingered, he put his sights on the defiant figure and fired.

He worked the bolt of his Arisaka rifle, stamped with the chrysanthemum emblem of Emperor Hirohito. He had to wait a few moments for the next flash of lightning. To his amazement, the figure still stood on the ridge. Now a machine gun opened fire, hurling tracers at the figure, which still didn't move.

What? How?

Ikeda realized that the figure was a trick. It was nothing more than a *kakashi*. A scarecrow. Enraged, he started to run toward it to tear the thing down, then thought better of it with so many soldiers firing wildly at the ragged scarecrow.

The enemy must have erected the *kakashi* as a diversion. Where would the enemy sniper be? Behind them, that was where. Ikeda started to turn.

Too late.

He felt a hammer blow between his shoulder blades. He toppled forward into the mud and rainwater, unable to move, dimly aware that he had been shot, unable to breathe. As his vision faded, the last thing he saw was the scarecrow with the broad-brimmed hat looming over him.

Then Ikeda died.

* * *

DEKE HUNKERED down as the Japanese fired wildly, expending a lot of ammunition to shoot up the dark trees and clumps of kunai grass. Little did they know that there wasn't anybody out here but him.

But not for long. He was suddenly aware of movement behind him and swung his rifle in that direction, worried that the Japanese had somehow gotten behind him. A clump of grass parted to reveal Danilo's grinning face.

"Hola," he whispered.

Philly appeared, then Yoshio.

"I can't believe I'm actually happy to see you fellas," Deke said.

"We couldn't let you take on the whole Japanese army by yourself," Philly said. He looked Deke up and down as more lightning illuminated the ridge. "Holy hell, did the Japs steal your clothes? You're bareass naked."

"Still got my boots on," Deke pointed out.

There wasn't time to explain. Behind them came Captain Merrick's company, pushing up the ridge to attack the Japanese, who were in complete disarray on account of Deke's diversion. The storm added to their confusion.

The BAR added its own lightning to the night, the muzzle flashes reaching nearly two feet from the barrel. It was the Japanese who were now exposed on the ridge, and the Americans used the lightning flashes to target any Japanese that they could see. Those enemy soldiers who didn't die right away scattered into the night.

Once the shooting died down, Deke walked over to the scarecrow with Philly and Yoshio and retrieved his uniform. He held up his shirt and trousers, which were shot full of holes. "I reckon those Japs can shoot, after all."

"Look at it this way," Philly said. "You won't need to unbutton anything to take a leak."

Somehow his hat had come through unscathed. Some guys had a

lucky rabbit's foot or a Saint Christopher medal to keep them safe, but Deke was starting to think that maybe the hat was his lucky charm.

They found the Japanese sniper facedown in the mud left by the downpour. There was a coin-size bullet hole right between his shoulder blades.

The Arisaka sniper rifle lay nearby. Deke picked it up and presented it to Danilo. The Filipino guide looked through the telescopic sight, then nodded with satisfaction.

The ridge never had been Captain Merrick's real objective but only an obstacle to a clear route forward. As the thunder and lightning faded away, they dug in. Their accommodations were soggy, muddy, and buggy, but with the Japanese dispersed and less of a threat, each man got a few hours of sleep when he wasn't on watch.

The company was up and moving at first light, with Deke and Danilo leading the way. Out in the open, sunlight appeared quickly and dried their wet uniforms and gear. The morning sun added warmth and a touch of optimism. But all too soon they were back in the shaded depths of the jungle itself.

Even so, Deke felt relieved that there didn't seem to be any sign of the Japanese. They were surely still out there, licking their wounds, but they were apparently too disorganized to be a threat at the moment.

The jungle path was now open before them.

CHAPTER TWENTY-SIX

ON THE BEACH NEAR PALO, more supply vessels and men continued to pour in. The roar of aircraft overhead was constant, but this was no longer cause for concern. These were friendly aircraft. Not an enemy plane was to be seen.

By now, the firing from Japanese positions had been silenced. However, that didn't mean there weren't the usual challenges of tides and surf, reefs, wet sand that mired vehicles up to their axles, and the omnipresent tropical heat and rain.

The dense, humid air and unrelenting sun were enough to make soldiers wistful for the cool fall weather that would be arriving back home. It was October, after all, and the leaves would be changing colors everywhere from the hills of Virginia to the mountains of New Hampshire. There would be football games and cheerful orange pumpkins on front porches, apple butter making and cider pressing, not to mention the not-too-distant promise of Thanksgiving. Roast turkey. Stuffing and gravy. A fella could be forgiven for feeling a little homesick.

But there was no hint of autumn on the tropical beach. Most soldiers stripped off their shirts and got the best tans of their lives as they toiled in the Pacific sun, unloading endless crates of material that included food to feed the Filipinos who had suffered so much during the cruel Japanese occupation.

Along with the supplies came armies of clerks, who set up their typewriters under tarps and set to work keeping track of everything from crates to copies of orders written during the heat of combat. They also tallied the dead.

Losses of American troops were tallied into the thousands, and the campaign was not yet over. Japanese losses had been even heavier, reaching into the tens of thousands, but the clerks didn't concern themselves with that. Those numbers would be left up to the military historians to figure out.

Although the shooting on the beach had stopped except for the frequent infiltrators at night, the fight for Leyte was far from over. Even if American victory must have seemed inevitable to General Yamashita, whose career had been sidelined at times for his pragmatic views, surrender was not an option. After all, he was known as the "Tiger of Malaya" for his conquest of Malaya and Singapore during the early days of the war. General Yamashita was now a cornered tiger, making him a dangerous adversary.

Similar to other Pacific campaigns, it had become clear that no matter how many more troops landed on the beach, no matter how many more American planes filled the skies, there would be no capitulation. The Japanese would fight on, whether in large units or small groups, holding out until the bitter end in remote jungle caves and clearings.

On paper, at least, the Japanese remained in considerable strength on Leyte and the Philippines in general. The Japanese still possessed tens of thousands of soldiers, all with a fanatical determination to fight the enemy until their last breath.

However, the numbers belied the fact that the Japanese were in jeopardy because of their shattered supply lines. Japanese supply ships or flights would no longer be arriving on Leyte on a regular basis. The noose had been tightened around the Philippines. The ships and planes constantly lost by the Japanese could not be replaced. Not only that, but with the United States controlling the seas and skies, enemy supplies and reinforcements had a difficult time getting through.

It was true that the Japanese insisted on sending more men to Leyte, but only a few transports reached shore. The effort to reinforce Leyte made as much sense as smashing eggs against a brick wall in an attempt to make an omelet. The resulting loss of men as the Japanese troopships were sunk was senseless and even tragic—so many young lives wasted in the seas around the Philippines. However, the Japanese high command was unwavering in its efforts to resupply the Philippines.

There was a reason for this tremendous effort to retain the Philippines. It was an act of desperation. Although at a considerable distance from Japan, the Philippines was not quite on the doorstep to Japan, but it was certainly in the neighborhood. The soldiers on the ground couldn't see it, but on the big maps on General MacArthur's headquarters it was clear that whoever controlled the Philippines also controlled the main sea routes that supplied Japan with vital materials. Being a vast island made Japan itself more defensible, but it also made it vulnerable. The island nation simply did not produce all the resources that it needed, particularly oil to power its planes, ships, and war machine.

Finally, once the Japanese were ultimately defeated here, it meant yet another base of operations one step closer to the home islands of Japan. More bombers would soon be on the way to reduce Emperor Hirohito's proud cities to ashes.

The plans that MacArthur had made while studying the maps on his office walls were finally becoming reality.

He had returned as promised. However, the Japanese were not yet defeated.

* * *

ON A TROOPSHIP STEAMING TOWARD ORMOC, the other members of Patrol Easy kept an uneasy eye on the skies. Against all odds, the Japanese still managed to put a few aircraft into play from remote airfields, including the one at Ormoc.

"Planes!" someone shouted.

"Are they Japs or ours?"

Nervously, the soldiers on deck watched the squadron pass over-head without paying any attention to the ship below. They were exposed on the deck, helpless, unable to fight back. Sitting ducks. It wasn't a feeling anybody liked.

"Relax, boys, there's nothing we can do about it," Lieutenant Steele said. "We're in the hands of the United States Navy. From the looks of it, these sailors have had plenty of practice shooting Japs out of the sky."

It was true that the sailors were manning their antiaircraft guns with the confidence of men who had used the weapons before. They stared grimly into the blue tropical sky. The thought wasn't lost on more than a few men that it was too nice of a day, what with the blue sky and the sea breeze, to be fighting a war.

"It's all right. They're ours," Lieutenant Steele announced. He had only one good eye, but he could see out of it like an eagle. "You can go change your underwear now."

A collective sigh of relief could be felt across the deck when others also realized that these were US planes.

The approaching planes had gotten everyone's attention, all right, but the sailors stationed at the antiaircraft batteries began to visibly relax as the aircraft passed them by. The Japanese would have at least tried to strafe the transport ship.

The planes had come in from the sea, meaning that they were carrier aircraft. When the planes were completely past the ship, the buzz of their engines faded and the planes turned away, headed north toward the mass of the Philippines.

"I wonder where they're headed?" Alphabet asked, reaching into his pocket for a deck of cards now that the danger had passed.

"Probably to give the Japs hell somewhere," Rodeo said. "Go get 'em, boys!"

The soldiers went back to passing the time as best they could. Egan snoozed on the deck, using his war dog, Thor, as a pillow. Man and dog had been oblivious to the sight of the planes. Alphabet and Rodeo were playing cards with some other soldiers, betting a few dollars just to keep things interesting.

By chance they had once again found themselves on the same ship as Woodall's Scouts. Having seen action already on Leyte, they were no longer the clean-shaven braggarts that they had been. They had learned that it took more than wearing a fancy uniform and being a good shot to survive on the battlefield.

Steele couldn't take it easy like the men because the army wouldn't let him. Due to the shortage of officers—many of them lost on Guam or in the initial fighting on Leyte—Steele had been given command of somebody else's platoon. It wasn't his idea, because he could have done without the headache. The men were veterans, though, and kept their heads down. They could tell that their new lieutenant knew his business, and there wasn't any resentment toward him, as there might have been toward a "butter bar" replacement. The streaks of gray in his hair conveyed more than his rank. Steele may have been the oldest man on the ship, including the skipper.

He let the sergeants do the heavy lifting in terms of organizing the men on deck and keeping order. When the time came, Steele would lead them ashore with what remained of Patrol Easy.

He glanced at the navy boys still studying the skies. They seemed to know their business. Still, it wasn't easy putting your fate in someone else's hands. A soldier preferred to have both feet firmly on the ground—not the deck of a troop transport—with his rifle in his hands.

Grimly, Steele knew that they'd have that opportunity soon enough. The transport ship was taking them to the far shore of the Leyte Peninsula, where the Japanese still had a stronghold around the town of Ormoc and its airfield. There would be another beach landing ahead of them.

Meanwhile, Steele wondered about the fate of Deke, Philly, and Yoshio. They were probably hiking across the mountainous interior of the peninsula while Steele and the others took a "shortcut" by sea. He wasn't entirely sure who had gotten the better deal. Going along for the ride with the navy wasn't as easy as it looked. With any luck, he would see them again down the road and hear all about it.

* * *

FOR DEKE AND THE OTHERS, their victory at the ridge did not mean that their worries were over. Other Japanese units occupied the mountainous jungle interior. Captain Merrick's orders were simple in that regard. He was supposed to push across the peninsula and eliminate any Japanese troops that he came across.

The company was hung up now near a grove of dense trees, which gave cover to a squad of Japanese soldiers.

"Can't be more than a dozen of them," Philly said.

"If you say so," Deke replied, then spat into the rotting humus of the jungle floor—or tried to spit, anyway. His mouth was too dry to do anything but go through the motions. He didn't understand how the rest of him could be soaked through with sweat while his mouth stayed so dry.

Wistfully, he thought of Dickie Shelby's heroic canteen run. He could have used some of that water right about now. The men had taken to recounting that day until it had taken on the proportions of myth—and rightfully so. Deke still didn't think that he'd seen anyone so damn brave or foolish as that kid.

Deke had taken to carrying a pebble in his pocket because they weren't readily available on the jungle floor. He popped it into his mouth to relieve the dryness. Maybe it was his imagination, but he was beginning to think that the pebbles had some flavor—salt, a bright mineral essence, mixed with a bitter tang. It was the taste of Leyte.

He studied the jungle patch that they had to get around. The path went through a clearing, and this patch of dense trees was almost like an island—or maybe like a fort guarding a harbor.

"No more than a dozen," Philly repeated, like it was a weather forecast—a chance of showers for their picnic.

"Don't matter if it's a dozen or a hundred," Deke said. "They've got to go. We can't have them sneaking in behind us after we go by. Yoshio?"

Beside him, Yoshio nodded grimly. Not so long ago he might have called out in Japanese to see if the enemy hiding in the grove would surrender. Those days were over. There was only one language that the enemy understood. He held a grenade in his hand. The pin was already pulled, the charging handle gripped firmly. Yoshio popped up from cover and, with a grunt of effort, hurled the grenade deep into the trees.

"Good arm," Philly observed.

Then they all ducked.

There was a shattering explosion, followed by a scream or two. Then the shooting started. It was hard to say what the Japanese thought they were shooting at, because bullets flew in every direction.

An enemy soldier broke from the trees, trying to get away. Deke led him through the scope, then dropped him in his tracks. Danilo and Philly both got a couple more Japanese who made a run for it. One of the Japanese ran right at them, screaming bloody murder, gleaming bayonet like a spearpoint in front of him. Deke shot him.

"Damn, he got too close for comfort," Philly said.

"You think?" Deke asked.

"I could use a shave, but not like that."

Private Frazier had come up, and now that the Japanese had broken cover, he opened fire with the BAR. Bits of leaves and shredded bark filled the air as he let loose with a short burst. By the time he took his finger off the trigger, no more firing came from the Japanese position.

"Love that thing," Philly muttered.

Despite the impressive show of firepower, Deke still thought that the BAR was all smoke and no fire. Snipers didn't waste bullets.

"I reckon we got 'em all," he said, then straightened up from behind a low-growing tree with massive green leaves and a patterned trunk that reminded him of a pineapple skin.

Deke approached the grove where the Japanese had been hiding and poked the barrel of his rifle through the grass and fronds. He found none of the enemy left alive. Maybe the BAR hadn't been a waste of ammo after all.

"Come on through," he called back to Captain Merrick, who brought up the rest of the company a minute later.

"Good shooting," Merrick said. "Lots of dead Japs and none of us dead."

"Not so bad," Deke agreed.

"How many did we get?" Captain Merrick asked. "I ought to put it in the report."

"I think half a dozen, maybe eight."

"Make that nine," Merrick said, nodding at a Japanese soldier who suddenly broke cover and ran at them with a grenade.

"Got him," Deke said.

He raised his rifle and shot the Japanese soldier. Danilo fired at the same time, shooting from the hip. Hit twice, the Japanese soldier fell. The grenade rolled harmlessly from the dead soldier's grip because he hadn't had a chance to arm it with a quick knock on his helmet. Deke observed that it was something of a strategic failure on the part of the enemy soldier, considering that the Jap might have taken out at least some of them with that grenade. He wasn't going to complain about it.

Deke stepped around the dead soldier and continued along the trail, with Philly, Yoshio, and Danilo right behind him. "Keep your eyes open, fellas," he said. Deke was unable to resist a small smile as he added, "It's a jungle out there."

NOTE TO READERS

When I started working on *Jungle Sniper*, I thought that this would be the last novel set in the Philippines before Deke and Patrol Easy moved on to the next adventure. However, I soon found that I was mistaken. There was too much to squeeze into one story. I haven't even gotten into the fight for Ormoc or Manila, the liberation of POW camps, or the daring raid on Leyte by Japanese paratroopers. What about Father Francisco and his guerrilla fighters? Did I mention typhoons? To do these aspects of the Pacific campaign justice, Deke and Patrol Easy will be returning to the Philippines in the next book.

That said, there are plenty of adventures here. What I found to be a fascinating aspect of the Leyte invasion was the arrival of General Douglas MacArthur on Red Beach. Although the moment was highly orchestrated right down to arranging for photography and a film crew, the long-range planning and the efforts that made this moment possible should not be underestimated. MacArthur's "I have returned" speech remains inspiring today for encapsulating many of the ideals for which the WW2 generation fought.

As noted in other books, the language and slang used by the soldiers reflect their era, although we find these terms distasteful today. The Japanese people remain our close allies. The scene with Yoshio's mother and her teapot was inspired by *Farewell to Manzanar*, a memoir that recounts one Japanese American family's experience in the internment camps.

This story is just that—a story—and it falls short of the actual events endured by our parents, grandparents, great-grandparents, and uncles while fighting in the Pacific. Many of the events and even the small scenes described in *Jungle Sniper* have been adapted from the memoirs of these individual soldiers. I hope that this book helps their memory live on in some small way.

Finally, I want to thank the advance readers and "armchair generals" who gave advice and corrected some of my factual errors. Their help was deeply appreciated. Hopefully I won't keep them waiting too long for the next book.

—DH

ABOUT THE AUTHOR

David Healey lives in Maryland, where he worked as a journalist for more than twenty years. He is a member of International Thriller Writers and a contributing editor to *The Big Thrill* magazine. Join his newsletter list at:

www.davidhealeyauthor.com
or
www.facebook.com/david.healey.books